EPIPHANY MAN

D. B. PATTERSON

EPIPHANY MAN

D. B. PATTERSON

DBP Press 2016

ISBN-13: 978-0692640463

DBP Press c/o D.B. Patterson
P. O. Box 399 | Tarpon Springs, FL 34688

This novel is a work of creative fiction. Its story takes place in Tarpon Springs, Florida, but the portrayal of its geography, history, and people are exaggerations, generalizations, or outright fabrications. Resemblances to actual people or events are purely coincidental.

This book is Rated-PG-13 for adult language and themes; mild drug and alcohol use; descriptions of naked boy parts; mild violence and sensuality; and miracles of all shapes and sizes—reader discretion is advised.

Photograph by Toni Frissell
Weeki Wachee Springs, Florida (1947)
LC-DIG-ppmsca-10079

AUTHOR'S NOTE

When I first began my storytelling journey in earnest, I made a choice to focus my creative efforts into the exploration of three notions—Love, Forgiveness, and Redemption (not necessarily in that order). I attempted doing just that in my debut novel *Perdido River Bastard*. An ambitious undertaking whose result is a mixed bag. I'm pleased with the work, as a whole, but it is a challenging read—what with the improbable connections between myriad characters; a narrative that switches between past and present via flashbacks and stories; and a deliberately meandering plot with twists and turns. Then there's the banquet of naughty words served up by powerful elderly female characters. Well, in a modern Southern novel with BASTARD in its title, what do you expect?

Epiphany Man is a very different story than the one I tell in *PRB*. It isn't a sprawling multigenerational tale. The main protagonist undertakes a more personal journey, an existential one—his is a private communion between himself and God. The events, incidents, and character arcs take place solely in Tarpon Springs. Nestled along Florida's Gulf Coast, Tarpon is a coastal city rich in culture and history. I love this city. My wife grew up here. We've planted roots here, cultivated a life here. I'd never intentionally paint this place with ugly colors.

St. Nicholas Greek Orthodox Church really looks like the Hagia Sophia. Greek teenagers really dive into Spring Bayou for the Epiphany cross every January 6. And then there are the Sponge Docks, the Greek Village, Silverking Brewing, the Pinellas Trail, and Mr. Souvlaki—all real, all wonderful. I take delight in twisting reality, squeezing it like an orange to collect and distill its juice. But *Epiphany Man* is not a history—its Tarpon Springs is an amalgam of reality and fantasy.

I know I shouldn't feel the need to qualify how I create verisimilitude, but I must be clear: *Epiphany Man* is a work of fiction.

PLEASE keep that in mind as you read this trifle of a novel.

~ D. B. Patterson, January 6, 2016

For Doreen.

"Then Job arose, and rent his mantle, and shaved his head, and fell down upon the ground, and worshipped, And said, Naked came I out of my mother's womb, and naked shall I return thither: the Lord gave, and the Lord hath taken away; blessed be the name of the Lord."

Job 1: 20-21

At my best, I could be worse
Than I had been the day before;
Breaking hearts and losing lovers—
I was closing every door.
So, I guess I want to ask you
What the hell you want me for?

Brik Buckman, *Song of the Wonderworker*

SUMMER

They set sail for the emerald green islands in seas
Where the rocks and the trade winds are brothers.
There are mountains nearby and they reach to the sky,
Shearing clouds and warding off others.
Warm mists o'er the blue bring a mermaid or two
Up fathoms from the cold briny water.
Sailors in the nest may spy the beautiful breasts
And the tail of the Ocean God's daughter.
It happened one morning as daylight was dawning
On a ship that was already a-stirrin'.
A soft salty breeze put the crew to their knees
With a song that sent their senses a-blurrin'.
In the gray morning light, a young sailor caught sight
Of a beautiful mermaid a-swimmin'.
He then made a wish to be loved by a fish
That was better by far than most women.

—Brik Buckman, *Song of the Wonderworker*

JUNE

CHAPTER 01

The Countdown Begins

"I have had a dream, past the wit of man to say what dream it was."
~ William Shakespeare

It was the first day of summer, half an hour before sunrise, and Jonathan Nikolas Christakos was wide-awake. Three hours of sleep was all he managed. Headaches that began in February were stronger now—coming earlier, staying longer, *getting worse*. He gently massaged his temples, dreading the visit with his oncologist that afternoon. As if it would make any difference. He already knew what rough beast had slouched back inside his head to be reborn after a 20-year absence.

It's only brain cancer, not the Second Coming, Jon thought wryly.

Confirmation of that ugly truth was just pouring sea salt onto a re-opened old wound. There were other older wounds, of course. And they would make his life a much fresher hell were *they* to be reopened. Past injuries publicly put on parade would push him into the deep end of a Big Sleep faster than this secret tumor would—*without a treatment that works, you've got six months.*

Six months.

Or 26 weeks.

Or 182.5 days.

Or 262,000 minutes.

Not enough time to remedy a lifetime of transgressions. Not enough time to check off all the items of a Bucket List.

Not enough time to make peace with God—well, not without a host of angels and a pocketful of miracles.

Jon chuckled at the thought.

The Icon of Saint Nicholas had a better chance to start weeping again. Now THAT would be a sight to see. Bearing witness to a divine sign was a better activity than watching the drawn-out exit of Jonathan Christakos from the world. *God, feel free to throw an angel or miracle my way, just saying—Amen.*

The shapely warm lump under the covers beside him moaned. Jon smiled. Headache and worry were not the only reasons for last night's sleeplessness. Pale light peeking through the curtains revealed a mocha colored arm draped across his chest—the only visible part of her naked body. The long fingers resting in the dip of his sternum suddenly wiggled and grew still. Beneath the five pink tips bloomed tiny flesh bumps. Tingles rippled across his flesh.

Snip-snip. SNIP!

Jon traded the satisfied smile on his face for a worried look. And then for one of confusion. He craned his head toward the window to his right. Those sounds were starting up again.

Snip-snip. SNIP!

Had the grasshopper slaughter begun two weeks early? The annual swarm of leaf-gobblers usually arrived the second week of July.

SNIP! Snip-snip.

The sleeping woman beside him flipped onto her side, body facing the opposite direction.

With an unhappy grunt, Jon sat on the edge of the bed and put his head into his hands—*Lord, deliver me from Evelyn Kouskoutis.* His next-door neighbor had disturbed what remained of his peaceful morning. The curvature of her landscape was a natural amplifier that fed directly into his bedroom. The thin walls did nothing to buffer the metallic shearing sounds that assaulted his ears.

He blamed the delicate panes of glass in his high window, the hardwood floors, the vaulted ceiling—all made for the perfect echo chamber.

Snip-snip. "Kera-TAH!"

Jon listened to Evelyn defending her property, now swearing in Greek as she sliced ribbons out of the morning air. Epithets were to be expected, as hers was an unbelievably messy business.

He chuckled as he opened the window.

A cacophony of chewing and chittering filled the air with dry unholy music. Thrusting his head as far outside as he could manage without falling, he cupped a hand to his mouth and hissed, "It's six in the morning, Evie. I have a guest. We're trying to sleep!"

Evelyn looked up. Even from two stories below, the woman seemed to loom high above him. His vision of her was a bit blurry, but she was larger than life nonetheless. "Morning, *rey*—the grasshoppers are HUGE this year," she said, twisting and turning. "They're chewing my shrubs and bushes to bony twigs! Quit nagging me, *grioúla!*"

And with a raspberry, she made an obscene hand gesture that may or may not have been intentional. "Take your pills and go back to your *pórni*," she sang, adding, "Grandma."

"It can't be this bad," Jon said, rubbing his eyes for a clearer view. "It's too earl—*skatá!*"

Snip-snip. "Skou-PEE-dee!"

There was no denying it now. The woman who helped raised him was at the epicenter of a disaster. Dressed in a satin nightgown and fuzzy slippers, Evelyn stood her ground before her ivy-laced chimney. Fog rolled around her feet. In one hand, a glass stein of burgundy wine—in the other, a comically big pair of stainless steel sewing shears.

She was laughing maniacally.

Beneath her were scores of decapitated grasshopper carcasses, their spiky legs and wings still a-twitching. Several dozens of shiny walnut-sized heads, like sunset flecked alien helmets, lay strewn about in haphazard piles. Hundreds more of the living giants hung like nightmare ornaments in the trees.

Snip-snip. "Kerata!"

The spectacle was mythic. Like Manto Mavrogenous reborn, Evelyn

hoisted her mighty weapon high above her head and howled as she sev-
ered grasshoppers. She grinned triumphantly through aubergine lips. "I
called a lawn service to end this Egyptian plague—I wouldn't look in *your*
backyard if I were you," she said before screaming her battle cry.

Snip-snip. "SKOUPIDI!"

"How much wine have you had, Evie?"

"Oh, like YOU could do this sober," she replied with a flourish.
"Who's up there with you?"

"Nunya Damn's up here," Jon said, closing the window with a smile.
Of all his neighbors, Evelyn was his favorite—but then, she was the only
family he had, so there was that.

"You could've told her it was me," the lump in the bed crooned in
sexy Caribbean tones. "No, don't bother joining me. I have to get to my
hotel. My flight leaves Tampa at noon." The woman's head popped out
from under the comforter. Her lush brown hair parted like curtains, revealing her sleepy face. She smiled. "I did have a nice time though," she
said, switching off her accent. "Good thing I know where you live. Otherwise, I'd never get to see you."

Jon crawled under the sheets. "Write me a letter next time. Sure you
have to go now?"

"Oh, no—one night with you is enough," she said, grabbing her stock-
ings and heels. She put them on her clutch in the corner chair. "There are
plenty of women who'd love to be with you."

"If I knew I wasn't going to die in six months, I'd ask you to marry
me."

Felicity plucked her red dress from under her side of the bed. She
slipped it on and gently grabbed his chin. "You don't love me and I don't
love you—for the tenth time, no. I'd like you to zip me up—that's a good
white boy. Jonny-baby, star-crossed leopards such as ourselves can't
change our spots."

"I suppose not," he said, turning over. "Do I look sick? Be honest."

Felicity offered a gentle smile. "I already know what you look like
without clothes. You've lost some weight, a little muscle. Not too bad

though. You scared?"

"About dying? Not really," he said. "This ain't my first rodeo, you know. I have faith that Raj Patel will come through in the end. I get scared when I get dizzy or nauseous. When I panic or get lost in a mood swing. When the headaches get bad. When I blackout, as you saw last night."

Felicity put a hand on his chest. "You know what I wish for you?"

"What do you wish for me?"

"That you'd fall in love again—hard fall on your head kind of love. And I wish that she'd fall hard in love with you, all of you, including whatever time you have left on this earth."

"But I only love you, Felicity."

"You're a bad liar, and a fool, but I forgive you," she said, flipping on her accent again. "You couldn't handle a woman from the Caribbean anyway. A dog would be better for your heart and soul." She laughed as she shook her hair into shape. "Six months—you need better odds."

Snip-snip. "SKOUPIDI!"

"Six months is the consensus of four doctors," Jon said. "What I need is for the very dangerous, very experimental, and very risky surgery they've planned to work."

"Very expensive too, I'd imagine."

"I'm pretty famous around here, so a telethon could be in my future."

Almost everyone in Tarpon Springs knew Jon Christakos by name, if not by face. There were many reasons why he was so well known. Sleeping with a supermodel was the primary reason at the present moment. But his life had been packed with other whys and wherefores—his life was a shell game of hidden facts, lies, secrets, and urban legends. Difficult waters to pilot, let alone analyze. More often than not, the public spotlight made him feel like a looking-glass cousin of the Lindbergh Baby.

Here were the facts. Jon's mother had been a world-famous Weeki Wachee Mermaid. His father may or may not have been a Polish Mafioso. A week after he was born, his parents drowned. His mother's Aunt Bessie and Uncle Dmitri adopted him. And their next-door neighbors Evelyn and George Kous-koutis raised Jon alongside their newborn son Panos. Later, Jon inherited Bessie's historic house on the Golden Crescent as well as Dmitri's store at the Sponge Docks—drowned, the both of them, on the 20th anniversary of losing his parents.

A juicy tragic life had done much to keep Jon in the public eye ever since he came into the world—gossip surrounding him filled in the gaps, whether or not the information was true. Not that Felicity Noel cared about such things—she had her own fame to navigate.

"Barring your untimely death or either one of us falling in love with another somebody," she told him, "I'll see you in December."

Jon smiled. "Sounds like a plan. Bring a miracle."

"Bring your own damn miracle. I'd better see Evelyn before I go."

"There's a HAZMAT suit in my—hey, are you crying?"

Felicity stopped in the doorway. "If I am, it's not over you—bye, Jonny-baby."

Jon sat on the cold floor. He listened to her soft footfalls as she went down the stairs. The front door opened and closed. And when the house was silent again, he got up and shuffled down the hallway. After a shower, he shoved a toothbrush into his face and looked at his naked body in the full-length mirror behind the door.

He did not like what he saw there. He always considered himself above average looking. Stocky build and broad shoulders. Bowed legs that made him look shorter than he was. He moved closer to the mirror. Would he be able to see the disease in the sunken sockets of his eyes?

He pulled down each lid and grunted—*dammit, I can* feel *it eating me from the inside out.* Maybe it was the thinning hair on his head. Maybe the thick array of dark bristles carpeting his arms, legs, back, and chest. Or the baseball mitts-for-hands that made him more homunculus than man. Or the outlines of his ribs and unhealthy contours of his stomach—*Felicity will be the last woman who'll ever want to be in my bed.*

Jon snorted at the thought—celebrity was usually a trump card whenever his looks failed. But then again, that was before the cancer came back for an extended stay.

He dressed and rushed downstairs to the kitchen.

He shoved a roll of deli meat in his mouth. Poured himself a tall mug of Irish coffee (to settle the nerves, as Uncle Dmitri often said). He glanced at the orange letter burning a hole through his granite countertop. Another warning from the Historic Homeowners Society of Tarpon Springs. The HHS had been complaining that his "property and house were in disrepair, a violation demanding immediate remedy pursuant to Golden Crescent bylaws."

Jon rolled his eyes as he went outside—*bylaws don't govern me.*

It was hot already, at 7:15 in the morning. He noted his empty driveway with a sigh.

There was a neon green flyer stuffed in the heavy iron doorknocker. 'Brik Buckman: Handyman, Carpenter, Photographer, Musician, Dog Whisperer, Nanny, Landscape Tamer, Bartender, Exterior Designer, Pest Wrangler, Day Laborer, Everything Between.'

Clicking his tongue, Jon read the note scribbled on back.

'There's plenty of work between us—my treat. Buckman's talented, professional, fast, and nice to watch without his shirt. I gotta feeling you're going to need him around anyway, so after I hire him, YOU BE NICE TO HIM.'

"What's that supposed to mean?" Jon whispered. "I'll show her nice."

Snip-snip. "Skoupidi!"

He crumpled the flyer and tossed it—*I got plenty to worry about besides entertaining Hot Handyman for the menopausal widow next door.* Mug in hand, he headed across his patchy brown yard. Plucking tufts of weeds from between the pavers of his drive, he tossed them into the storm drain.

Jon turned to view his house from the curb.

Here were the facts. While his house was a collage of styles—Mediterranean, Queen Anne, Dog Trot, Bungalow—Evelyn's was a singular Colonial construction. The buildings occupied a swath of waterfront property that once belonged to one of the town's founding families. The Saffords sold the land to George Cheyney, who promptly moved their dwelling back from the bayou in order to build the houses now belonging to Eve-

lyn and himself. Tourists got the impression that the two homes were connected, like twin stars orbiting each other inside a nebula of magnolias
and elephant palms.

Jon often thought of his house as an architectural love poem to Tarpon Springs—an opinion not shared by many residents of the Golden
Crescent. "Bentley Safford, may you burn in hell," he hissed, the swig of
coffee burning his throat. He looked at his watch and frowned—*I'm late.*

Snip-snip. "Kerata!"

It was a perfect day to take the long way to work.

*

CHAPTER 02

The Sponge Docks

"There is rapture in the lonely shore, by the deep sea,
and music in its roar."
~ Lord Byron

The Greek Village was a collection of older neighborhoods settled by the first wave of immigrant sponge divers, ship builders, and boat captains in the early 1900s. Generations of these salt-of-the-sea folk made Tarpon Springs what it was. Strolling through winding tree-lined streets of the residences, Jon finally reached a wide parking lot. It belonged to the Sponge Factory, a purveyor of sponges and ocean-themed bric-a-brac, with signage that bragged, 'World's Largest Selection of Natural Sponges'.

Jon headed for Dodecanese Boulevard.

The road split the wharf into dockside and landside. Dockside had all the diving, fishing, and sightseeing boats, attractions, and restaurants. Like a Hollywood back lot, it had rocking boats, swaying palms, salty deckhands, arguing seagulls and pelicans, and barnacle-crusted men and women pitching their sightseeing tours.

Landside had most of the shops and boutiques.

Jon kept to this side. He stood on the curb and stared at the vacant building across the way.

Here were the facts. The old Pappas Riverside Grille building was the first thing that tourists saw when they came to the Sponge Docks. Three stories, multiple tiers with hanging block balconies, a veranda deck—roughly 50,000 square feet of space in its entirety. The building was the architectural lovechild of Frank Lloyd Wright and Bauhaus, with Greek accents and flair. It bestrode the northern lip of Dodecanese and the Anclote River like a squat Miami castle.

The building was for sale—and it deserved a real visionary with unlimited funds to renovate it.

Jon strolled down the marina. A warm wind rich with aromas of pastries, honey-dipped baklava, fried crab cakes, roasted coffees and nuts, fresh fish, and the heady decay of harvested sponges drying on clothes lines hooked above the decks of docked boats. Few people recognized him this morning. Locals mainly. Several shopkeepers waved to him as he ambled along the sidewalk.

Jon veered into Katina's Greek Market, a grotto of little shops and cafés, bubbling fountains, and whitewashed statues of dolphins and Greek gods playing in the water. On display in the center of the wide plaza was a 42-foot sponge diving boat, her azure cypress hull shellacked with thick varnish over canary yellow trim.

A wave of dizziness knocked him hard. He would throw up if he did not sit down—there, a nearby bench. His entire body seemed to tremble as he bent his knees and dropped. He closed his eyes. Focused on his breathing—*I need some pot to help me manage this,* he thought.

Yeah, but buy it from who?

"Excuse me. Are you Jon Christakos?"

Jon opened his eyes and nodded carefully. An older woman about 60 years old was standing in front of him. At her side was a sweet-faced younger man, about 20 or so, who fidgeted with his hands and fingers as the woman spoke. "My name is Lizzy, and this is my grandson Tim."

"Good morning to you both," Jon said, trying not to puke. "What can I do for you?"

"I heard that you come here early in the morning," she said nervously, "and I just wanted to thank you personally for your donation to Tim's fundraiser."

Jon looked at the smiling young man. "He has Angelman's—I remember."

"Because of you I can get him a live-in nurse for a year."

Jon shifted uncomfortably. "My donation was anonymous."

Lizzy nodded. "I know, but I couldn't take it without knowing—I mean, when I found out it was you I thought it was a joke." Her eyes welled with tears. "I'm sure you must...I just—I'm grateful. And I'm glad to know that the rumors and gossip about you isn't true."

She put an arm around her grandson. "It's been a difficult year for us—thanks very much."

Jon fought nausea as he stood up. He hugged the gracious woman, who burst into fresh tears when he embraced her. She kissed his cheek and ushered Tim toward the dolphin statues. When they were out of sight, he emptied his stomach into a trash bin.

Wiping his mouth, he straightened up and collected himself. He refilled his coffee mug at one of the cafés. Leaving Katina's, he crossed the boulevard. And once he was dockside, a gnarled boat captain tossed Jon a fresh cinnamon bun from a grease-stained bag before shouting at a dockworker getting tangled up in a mooring line.

A whiff of the sweet spicy aroma eased Jon's queasiness—a hearty laugh did too. Up ahead, on a dais in the heart of the marina, stood the bronze statue of a sponge diver—traditional diving suit, helmet in its hands, its fixed gaze frozen in silent watch.

At its feet was a sign: 'In Memory of the Spongers of Tarpon Springs'—a memorial dedicated to lives lost at sea. Its hues of honeyed ocher and goldenrod captured the essence of the men it honored.

Jon raised his mug in a silent toast. "Good morning, Nico," he said, biting into his sticky pastry. He knew the man whose young clean-shaven face stared back at him.

With a smile, he headed to Athens Street.

Nik's Knacks sat between Zorba's bistro/nightclub and a narrow alleyway that ran behind the main strip facing the river. Despite heavy foot traffic, tourists were less inclined to leave the view that the Sponge Docks offered to go shopping for trinkets—Jon's store was well off the beaten path anyway. Still, he managed to make enough now that he was selling more than just tchotchkes.

He stuck the key into his door, the bell jingling as he went inside.

His headache returned. Its dull throb had parked itself across his forehead. His skin had an achy tingle—sick skin, he called it. *God, I'm not strong enough to face this again. I promise to do good deeds, no matter the cost.* Jon focused on menial tasks. He took inventory. He restocked shelves and tried to bar all thoughts of death out of his brain.

No more fruitless prayers either—his head was crowded enough as it was. At least he had some control over what he allowed inside his skull. He meditated upon his night with Felicity—he smiled the whole time he set up the new display in his storefront window.

The bell jingle-jingled.

An elderly woman with large liquid eyes entered the store. The sound of screaming gulls passing over the building seeped through the door before it finally closed.

Jon felt as if he knew her—*why do I know her?*

She was not filthy in any conventional way. She looked like she lived her life moving in and out of bed. Her hair was a nest of gray yarn and bits of twig, as if she had been playing in the woods behind the fishmonger's shop, a wide graveyard of broken crab traps and boat skeletons near the river. Jon and Panos played there as boys, pretending to be pirates at war over beds of sponges.

The woman looked as if she had been playing there too.

Jon cleared his throat. "May I help you?"

She ignored him. She wore no shoes. She hopped from bare-foot to foot, stepping in time to a rhythm all her own. Odd people often appeared before him. He was accustomed to it.

Encounters were often surreal experiences that usually ended with him signing autographs, posing for pictures, turning down investment opportunities, accepting rounds of free drinks, or fleeing in terror. This woman looked puzzled, as if she were figuring out what equation had brought her there.

"Beverly," she finally blurted, almost imperceptibly.

Jon raised his eyebrows. "Beg pardon?"

Swatting at things over her head, she said, "Beverly Pink—you know my nephew."

Jon snapped his fingers. "I thought you looked familiar."

Beverly Disston Pink was one of Tarpon's wealthier eccentrics. At the sudden conclusions of both her tennis career and her marriage, she tucked herself into her three-story Victorian Dollhouse on the farthest point of the Golden Crescent—hers was one of two Disston manor homes on Spring Bayou.

"Jon Christakos," she said, snapping her fingers. "Are you deaf, boy?"

"Yes—I mean, no—how may I help you?"

"I heard you have paintings to sell." She was about to say something else, but opted for staring at him in uncomfortable silence instead. After a moment, she continued in a mumble. "Yes, sell your paintings to me. All the ones you don't like." She looked at her dirty bare feet. Then she walked around like a hermit crab. "Selling tourist crap—blech—you sell yourself too short by not selling your paintings in the open. You're better than this. No, don't argue. I know what you have in back."

"Did Adam send you? Or Evelyn Kouskoutis?"

Beverly sneezed. "I don't HAVE to tell you who sent me. Go get the artwork, boy!"

"Fine," Jon said. "Wait here—don't touch anything."

"I'll touch whatever the hell I want to touch," Beverly screamed, digging inside her fringed bedazzled clutch, taking out a wad of rubberbanded bills. "I want original Christakos paintings. A few sketches too, some drawings. Anything you want to get rid of. I'll wait here. I won't go in the back with you—I won't let you rape me, *Tripod Jon*. If I like the art you make, I may come back for sky rockets in afternoon delight flight." She crossed her arms. "GO! I got things to do!"

Nik's Knacks had dual functions: a kitschy boutique and private painting studio. Jon had spent many days waist-deep in oils, charcoal, ink, and watercolors—nights when his headaches made sleep impossible. He went into the studio and darted past recently finished mermaids—10-foot by 7-foot canvases, twenty in all.

I need to hire someone to help me manage this.

At the far wall, he grabbed stacks of pages covered in drawings. He sorted through sheets of scribbles, concepts, and studies. Here, an original acrylic mermaid. Here, a poster-sized watercolor, unfinished with too much green. Here, an inch-thick portfolio of doodles, fish tails and fins in motion, bodies floating in water, Ophelias drowning, and mermaids a-swimming.

His arms and hands full of mediocre work, Jon left the studio.

He learned a few things about economics and human behavior over the years. People wanted either what they could not have or what everyone else had, specifically what they were buying en masse. That made it easy to trick people into believing that what you had to sell was vital and important to own. Playing hard to get was part of it.

With a smile, he returned to the strange woman, who was spinning in circles like Maria Von Trapp in the middle of his store. "Beverly, keep this between us—it's a private collection."

She stared at him and sneezed. "MY private collection now—I'll be back for more."

"When? And why do you want my artwork?"

"I'll come back when I'm damn ready—why is none of your business." She wiped her nose with the back of one hand and shoved a wad of money at him with the other—his head pounded at the sight of it. "Big canvases. Those mermaids—I want them. New ones, old ones." She shuffled through the pieces Jon had culled for her. With a frown, she laid them on the counter and barked, "Sign them. Last name only. Bottom right corners. Christakos, yes. Sign all of them!"

Beverly paced back and forth until he finished. Jon put down his marker. She gathered her stack of signed Christakos art and bolted from the store. The bell smashed the glass. All that remained of her were footprints on the floor and a ringing in his ears.

Pouring more Irish cream into his coffee, he pocketed half of the money and tucked the other half in his safe. He opened his tattered volume of *Stranger in a Strange Land*. He barely finished two pages when a burst of yelping outside in the alley behind his store interrupted him. He tried to ignore the crash of an overturned garbage can. But the cruel laughter and bloodcurdling cries of a terrified dog in pain that penetrated the store's brick wall—that was another matter.

Jon slammed the book shut. He swore under his breath and went outside. Helpless cries became staccato shrieking.

In the middle of the alley, two teenage boys had cornered a tiny black and white dog. It was so caked in mud, vomit, blood, and refuse that it was hard to tell what kind of dog it was. The blond kid in the dirty overalls reared back a steel-toed boot to kick the animal.

But then he thought better of it. Quite suddenly too. And he kept shaking his head, as if he had glimpsed what kicking the poor creature would do to it—and to him.

Clapping with sausage hands beside the lanky one was a short doughy kid in a stained wife beater and jeans. "Do it—kick the hell out of her. Kick her! Do it!"

Guilty Lanky Blond shouted, "She can't breed if I kill her, you idiot!"

Dough Boy spat, "Then I'll kick her in the head, Chucky—I hate these stupid purebred dogs. I hate all of them. Even more than I hate people."

Jon knew the one in the overalls—*Chucky, what the hell are you doing, kid?* He did not know the other one—the fat psycho with the shrill voice.

Fueled by a righteous rage (and an agility that belied his current condition), he jumped and landed directly behind the two boys. He grabbed Chucky's boot and drove it into Dough Boy's hip.

Both of the little bastards went careening into three upright garbage cans, knocking them down like bowling pins. The dog quickly ducked inside one of them to hide. Before they had a chance to retaliate, Jon pinned them to the cement.

He punched Dough Boy's nose, which cracked open, spilling liquid red. Chucky held up his hands. "It's me, man."

"I know it's you!" Jon shouted, stepping back to catch his breath. "You know better than to do this—damn it." The fog of his headache made him dizzy. Leaning against the brick wall, he pointed to the mewling fat one. "I've seen you stuffing your face down at Hellas—what's your name?"

"D-D-Dickey—wait until I tell Spiros about this. He'll KILL you!"

Jon laughed. "Tell him to take a number." To the blond one, he said, "What's wrong with you? You got a little brother and sister. You know better, Chuck Parker."

Chucky spat. "We all can't be famous trust fund babies, can we?" He yanked his arm away when Jon tried to help him. "I wasn't going to hurt the dog."

"What were you doing to her then?"

Chucky did not answer.

"We have a history—I thought we were friends," Jon hissed. "You know that you could have come to me if you were in trouble."

Again, Chucky did not respond. But there was emotion behind his eyes. Turmoil. Anger, regret, shame. Yes, he did know better. Dough Boy Dickey was in the throes of a fit, replete with foaming at the mouth. His nose and lip were bleeding. "Wait 'til I tell Spiros," he sobbed, spitting out a tooth. "I know who you are, Jon Christakos—you're a dead man! And so's anyone who lifts a finger to help you!"

Jon gritted his teeth. "Dough Boy—threaten me again, and I'll rip out your tongue. Make trouble in my alley again, and I'll put the business end of a butter knife in your gut." He turned his attention back to Dickey's companion. "Chucky—either you turn your sinking boat back to shore, or I'll show up at your house and do it for you. Shame on you for doing this."

Jon crawled inside the garbage can. The dog was crouching behind some dirty diapers in the back of it. Shaking and trembling, her breathing labored, the dog snarled at him when he reached for her.

The smell filling his nose was beyond vile—*come on, girl.*

She yelped and shrieked when he pulled a leg to get a firmer grip. Carefully holding her in the cradle of his arm, he got to his feet and managed not to vomit when he left the alley. He rounded the corner and scanned the street—it was as empty. Not that he cared, but witnesses would have misconstrued events.

Jon opened the door to his store.

The jingling bell frightened the dog. He nearly dropped her as he took her into his studio. He cleaned his hands and face with soap at the sink. The stench from the garbage can was too thick to ignore, so he tossed his dirty golf shirt into the corner with the painting rags reeking of mineral spirits and turpentine. He plucked a clean shirt from a basket of extra clothes he kept in the broom closet.

"Easy, girl—you're gonna be okay."

He wiped the filth from her muzzle, eyes, and ears. She shrieked as he tried to free her front paw from a plastic tie that had cut into her skin. It was swollen and bleeding. But he managed to remove the tie completely. Using an old picnic basket as a makeshift carrier, he closed the store and headed toward the heart of downtown. There was a pet hospital two blocks south of Mother Meres Park.

This was one of those rare times that Jon wished he had a car. He was going to miss his appointment with Raj Patel—*God, remember this good deed six months from now when You are about to make the decision whether or not to save my life, with or without a miracle.*

Tarpon Springs was the Epiphany City—perhaps a miracle was not out of the question.

Jon waved to the passers-by who greeted him. Some whistled, some called his name. Some swore at him or spat on the ground as they crossed paths. A small group of young men saw him from across the highway. One shouted, "How's it hanging, Tripod Jon?"

Without missing a beat, Jon retorted, "Ask your mother, Ares!"

That drew howls of laughter from those young men.

Head pounding, Jon pressed on, the basket getting heavier with each step. The dog started whimpering again—*God, a little help here.* It was a long walk, about a mile, to the clinic. In the back of his mind, sirens warned him that events beyond his control were in motion now. There was little else he could do but to let them unfold and then try not to drown in the wake of their collective turbulence.

*

CHAPTER 03

Righteous Pathways

"Sins are more easily remembered than good deeds."
~ Democritus

Nico Cocoris was a descendent of the Greek entrepreneur who started America's sponge diving industry in Tarpon Springs. At 83 years of age, Nico was still a prominent figure in the community. He owned commercial buildings on Hope Street and Athens Street, including the buildings with Nik's Knacks and Zorba's. Nico's polished El Camino came rolling up Ada Street and turned into the parking lot of Mama Maria's Greek Cuisine.

"You walk too damn fast, Jonny," the old man said with his trademark smile. "I'm behind the wheel, and I'm the one out-of-breath. Get in—I'll take you to the pet hospital."

Jon slid into the passenger seat and set the picnic basket on his jack-knifed legs. Nico shifted the car into drive.

"Of course, you'd be the one to make worse trouble for yourself by doing something good," he said, pressing the accelerator. He patted Jon's knee with a deeply tanned hand. "BAH! Let the die be cast—you did the right thing."

"How do you know what happened? The alley and street were empty."

Nico laughed. "Were they now? Your uncle and I were hotheads. Sons of Poseidon, the two of us, selling sponges, fishing, fighting, and— well, we had women before we settled down." He laughed. "I saw what happened—the last part. How is your girl in the basket? Animal abuse is unforgiveable."

Jon opened the lid and peered inside. "She's still panting heavily—shaking like an alcoholic going through withdrawal too." He looked behind the driver's seat. "I'm stealing your towel—she needs a blanket. She's in shock." He closed the lid and swore under his breath. "I've got to report this. If I take her to the hospital, I'll have to report it. Dammit."

"The fat *malakas* is your problem—he's breeding dogs and running drugs for Spiros Zervos I hear." Nico spat. "How did that blond boy Chucky get mixed up with that boy?"

Jon swallowed. "I don't know yet—I told him that he needed to make a better choice," he said, "Spiros Zervos is just a rumor—he's just a boogeyman, Nico. Criminals have been saying they work for that man since Panos was a rookie."

Nico laughed. "Longer than that, Jonny. But who knows what's real these days? It's all made-up for circus television." He was silent for a moment. "That movie we saw, when Kevin Spacely pretended to be crippled, but secretly was the big flaming cheese."

Jon laughed. "Kevin Spacey was Keyser Söze in—"

Snapping his finger, Nico shouted, "*The Usual Suspects!* Yes, you sat between Evelyn and me. And I kept wishing you'd sit on the floor. Oh, she wore that perfume, not the number—hers wasn't so *apaití tikós.*" He turned them into the hospital parking lot. "No one knows this man, Jonny. Spiros Zervos is not just a man. His corruption spreads from Tarpon Springs all the way up to Weeki Wachee. Be careful about talking to the police. Be prepared for the consequences, rey. Don't forget that the crippled man was Keyser Söze."

Suddenly, Nico's tanned face cracked into one of his Anthony-Quinn-as-Zorba-the-Greek grins. "God smiles on those who protect His innocents, but you know the old saying about good deeds—don't think you won't be punished for this one."

Jon got out of the car and waved a trembling hand as Nico drove away. *Spiros Zervos,* he thought with a shudder. Real or imagined, secret or no, it was a name that parents in Tarpon Springs invoked to scare their unruly children into better behavior.

*

An hour gone and still no word about Jon's tiny rescue. The animal hospital lobby was a zoo too.

Horse-sized dogs jumping into the laps of strangers. Puppies wreaking havoc between legs and under seats. The unholy mixture of rambunctious canines and hissing felines. Annoyances in any vet's office, and easily ignored for the most part.

Today, however, there were kids who had not heard of Tarpon's boogeyman—and the parents of these brats had left them in charge of their family pets. One obnoxious mouth-breather was choking a sweet-faced Benji mutt and LAUGHING as the dog gagged.

Jon asked the monster's mother to watch her precious child. She told him to mind his own business. Mouth Breather did it again—Benji gagged and hacked.

Jon leveled his gaze and lowered his voice. "Ma'am, if you don't do something, I will."

The woman was a rather large specimen of trailer trash. She spun around with a surprising grace. Holding up a finger on each hand, she screamed, "Just because you're Jon Christakos don't mean you can tell me what to do! My dog is fine—my boy is fine. Shut your face."

"Ma'am, I asked respectfully—this is my warning shot before I grab the leash from your kid," he said. "I've rescued one dog from two bullies already. I'd be happy to repeat it."

Thankfully, the sweet-faced young woman behind the counter was there to cut the leash with a pair of scissors before whisking the dog to safety. Mouth Breather's Mama started barking about the cost of that leash and how she was going to sue this place and file a report of assault with the police.

Jon took a $20 out of his wallet and handed it to the woman. "Buy a new leash and show your kid how to make a dog heel, not choke."

Other pet owners started clapping.

Applause humiliated the woman enough to force her outside to wait for her turn. The sweet-faced young woman behind the counter returned to the lobby wearing a wide smile and twinkling green eyes.

She mouthed a 'thank you' and escorted Jon to a small room down the hall. He massaged his temples, mumbling curses under his breath for what seemed like hours.

The door finally opened.

In walked an attractive woman wearing a white lab coat. She introduced herself as Dr. Flowers and nodded for Jon to follow her down the long hallway that reeked of cleanser, wet dog, pet food, and sickness. She ushered him into a little room and closed the door. "Your dog is a lucky one, Mr. Christakos. Very lucky to have a white knight like you."

"I just want to pay for services, donate to the ASPCA, and go. I have a busy day. "

Dr. Flowers gave him a curt smile as she gestured to the corner. The dog was half-wrapped like a mummy and shaved to a fuzzy wisp of her former self. She lifted her head, blinked and yawned, and slowly lowered her chin to rest on her paws. "She cleans up nice, I'd say—let's see… Cuts. No need for stitches. Just two bruised ribs and a tiny half-centimeter hairline fracture on her back leg—she'll be wobbly in that splint and sore as hell for a few days. But she's healthy, all things considering."

"Really, Dr. Flowers, if I leave her—"

"Mr. Christakos, I think it's a sign—she needed you. You need her."

Jon was not biting. "I don't believe in signs. I can't have a dog."

Dr. Flowers looked at him for a long moment. "Lemme see those knuckles," she said, inspecting his swollen hand. "Put some ice on this when you get the dog settled. You'll be back in the ring by Saturday night, Clubber Lang." Jon was about to protest when she put up a hand. "This Pomeranian has had at least two litters in her traumatic short life."

"If you would allow me to explain my situation, then—"

"I don't give a rat's puckered poop chute about your situation," she said. "You WILL take the dog home with you. You WILL feed her twice a day. You WILL give her the prescribed pills. You WILL show her kindness two hours a day—three if you don't want to burn in hell. Understand me? One week, Mr. Christakos. Anyone can beat up two fools—the hard part's cleaning a mess that isn't yours."

"Great," Jon muttered, shaking his head. "This is just what I need."

Dr. Flowers nodded. "After one week, you will see that I'm right."

"Now what?"

"Now you may go to the lobby and wait. I'll bring her out after you've paid the bill, made a donation, and talked to the nice police officer waiting for your report. Animal cruelty is a cardinal sin in my book. Make sure your story is thorough. See you in one week, Mr. Christakos."

"One week?" Jon asked, failing to add a witty bookend.

"Yes, Mr. Christakos—one week."

Jon wore a half-smirk on his glassy-eyed face.

With a tilt of the head (and a bemused wrinkle of her button nose), the good doctor left before he tried to be clever—she doubted very much that he even had the ability.

Jon did not disagree. He sighed as he headed to the lobby, where Officer Neal Peruski was baby talking into a box of mewling kittens. After paying the bill and making a donation, Jon hefted the picnic basket, with his sedated rescue dog tucked securely inside, and followed the officer outside. The sirens in his head started screaming again.

Bur he could not stop thinking of Dr. Flowers.

*

The wooden swing Uncle Dmitri had built for Aunt Bessie creaked and croaked, asking and answering itself as it swept back and forth. Half the money that Beverly had paid him was gone—*why did this day have to be so long?* The dog was fast asleep near Jon's feet, the left one providing a ball-to-heel locomotion to the swing.

Creak, it asked, a sound lilting upward.

Croak, it replied, a sound falling down.

Warmth from the late afternoon had given way to a surprisingly cool twilight and a lovely view of a cloudless crayon sky over the bayou. On his lap were bills and a stack of Valpak coupons he'd never use. A new warning letter from the HHS was naught but scattered red bits behind his seat. And every HHS letter hereafter would be doomed to the same fate.

Creak...croak.

Jon absently reached down to pet the dog. She craned her neck and turned her head, offering each ear to his fingers. He chuckled as he massaged her scalp. Minnie seemed relaxed with him—one week, Dr. Flowers had told him. Jon smiled. Suddenly, he was having a hard time thinking about giving her up at the end of this one-week sentence.

Maybe Abigail Flowers, DVM, knew exactly what she was doing.

"Want some people company, Jonny?"

Jon looked up and grinned. Evelyn was halfway up the walk. Tonight she wore jeans and a frilly tank top. Her hair was up in a bandana. Her face was caked with pistachio-colored night cream. And still, she was a stunning-looking woman. "I heard about your acts of bravery and charity this morning—more myths for your growing collection of celebrity skatá. Did you reschedule with Raj?"

"Of course, I did—tomorrow. As if that will change the diagnosis."

Evelyn ignored him. "Look at the little princess puppy dog—what kind is she?"

"Shaved Pomeranian," Jon replied.

Evelyn climbed the stoop. The dog watched in sleepy curiosity as the woman sat down to pet her with gentle motherly hands. "Such a precious thing—what deadly cuteness. Hey, rey—watch this." Evelyn lifted her arms above her head and shook. "Think I put on too much powder? Oh, I'm coming undone underneath." Inch-thick blocks of talcum broke off from her pits like chunks of arctic ice.

Jon rolled his eyes. "I'll fetch you a gin and tonic, Evie."

"I'm still drunk. I spent the afternoon bleaching my teeth as I watched shirtless men rid our backyards of pests—yuck. Considering its start, my day ended well. Yours started great—and now? *Skatá.*"

Creak...croak.

"Yeah, and after I sold $4,000 worth of art to Beverly Disston Pink. I rescued a dog and paid a vet's bill that cut my earnings by half. I missed my appointment with Raj Patel to file a report with Neal Peruski, who thinks I'm in big trouble."

Evelyn ignored him, turning her attention back to the dog. "I love this Oreo face, you perfect little dunkin' dog. Markings like a baby cow." She smiled at Jon. "I hear Dr. Flowers is single. Oh, don't look at me like you don't know I got eyes and ears everywhere."

"I don't want to talk about Dr. Flowers."

"You lying liar," Evelyn accused. "Alright." She reached into her back pocket. "The photos you requested. Four nights, two weeks. What's going on? You haven't slept-walked in years."

"I think it's the pain pills I take at night for my headaches."

She patted his leg. "Oh, look at this picture. Your face is Hollywood gangsta."

Jon sighed. "Holy crap—is that a photo of my junk? What the hell?"

She laughed. "Well, you went Full Monty at the Heritage Museum—what can I say? You took off everything and sprinted for the amphitheater. Any thoughts as to why?"

Creak...croak.

Jon was not ready to speculate. It was unwise to toy with a Greek mother unless you had a death wish. Medea ate her children, after all. And Evelyn was worried enough as it was. "I'm taking enough pain meds to put down one of Hannibal's elephants—that's what's causing my somnambulism."

"You can't stop taking them if you're in pain."

"I need some weed," Jon said, pointing to the dog. "And I need a puppy-sitter tomorrow."

Evelyn turned her face away. "Six months. Not much time."

Jon shrugged. "Dr. Faklis says the same thing—she's a realist. But Raj refuses to put such a fine point on it—he's working through a new surgical method. I'm living as if I don't have an upcoming expiration date and letting others do the worrying. Have faith, Evie. Try to—"

"Shut your mouth!" Evelyn shouted before sobbing into her hands. She wiped her face with her gown. "Don't tell me what to do or how to feel, dammit! I'm angry."

"Evie, I'm sorry."

"You should be."

Keeping faith was one thing. Rolling around in the minutiae of day-to-day, as if nothing horrible was unfolding, was next to impossible. Jon knew that he was asking too much. That he was being selfish. Evelyn was the only mother he had—he was the only son she had.

They were family, period.

Having gone through this before, there was so much more to fear and lose this time.

Creak...croak.

"Six months might turn into six years," Jon explained. "I'm plagued with enough attention as it is—if my doomsday date comes and goes, the people in this town will go berserk." He sighed. "I won't tell you how to feel—but let's tell only people we can trust, Evie."

"Good," she said, absently wiping her cheek. "I'm glad you told Felicity. I worry about you keeping everything to yourself. It's no way to live, Jonny. You need people. People need you."

Jon looked away. "The good people of Tarpon Springs," he spat. "George died. Panos died. Aunt Bessie and Uncle Dmitri died. Our families were gutted by tragedy after tragedy, Evie, and the good people of Tarpon Springs accused us of having an affair all along."

"Not all of them, Jonny—you're generalizing."

"Generally speaking, they inspired me to leave town."

"And that inspired me to fix the problem," Evelyn replied. "The bad apples who started the rumors left Tarpon Springs. You came back a better man. You opened up."

"I don't know about that," Jon said. "It was enough to hear Adam Disston's suggestion that we give the good people exactly what they want."

"Until they wake up and see the truth—I believe they will."

Jon snorted. "That'll take a miracle."

Evelyn sighed as she patted his leg. "Even so—I'm glad you told Felicity the truth."

"Only after I blacked out in my bedroom." Jon smiled. "I should've played the 'dying of brain cancer' sooner though. Worked wonders for me last night."

Evelyn chuckled. "Felicity brings out your sense of humor. You were too serious to have one back then. Loveable, but dull and not funny."

Here were the facts. Jon was barely sixteen when cancer first donkey punched him. Benign tumors played hide and seek on his brain stem, producing an array of acute symptoms that hid his chronic condition. They had to hit it hard with chemo and radiation, plus a more controversial weapons system. It took almost four years, from start to finish. Jon won, in the end, but there were casualties—always.

"I still don't think you're funny," Evelyn teased.

Jon laughed. "And I don't disagree."

"I remember at one point you kept saying over and over that you had nothing to fight for, nothing to live for," she said, shaking her head to clear the picture. "I still have dreams about it."

"Chemo made the teenage angst stronger than it should have been, Evie—but I did lose the first girl I ever loved to my brother, who treated me like a leper," Jon said. "Panos avoided facing the truth that I was sick. Tarpon was covered in spit, sweat, and semen by the time he came back."

Creak…croak.

Evelyn blew her nose on the underside of her tank top. "Bentley Safford tormented Bessie and Dmitri while using his own daughter to drive you boys apart." She swallowed. "Hard to believe Panos abandoned you—if he were sitting here with us, I'd smack his head for breaking our hearts—the malakas. And if his father were here, I'd smack him too—how dare that man die on me."

In the silence, as she drifted on a sea of memories, she patted her chest softly, a thump-thumping rhythm over her heart. "*Georgie-mou*—I wouldn't have survived losing George without Panos by my side. I wouldn't have survived losing Panos without you by my side, Jonny."

She wiped her eyes. "My boys—I still ache from not having them here with us."

"God rest their souls," Jon said, knowingly.

"Amen," Evelyn said, crossing herself. "I'll watch puppy tomorrow—what's this?" She picked up the torn bits of HHS letter that Jon had discarded. "Oh, they'd better not start this up."

"Never rains, but it pours," he said. "The HHS doesn't have teeth since Bentley Safford put a pistol in his mouth. That came today. The one I got yesterday is inside. I'm ignoring them on principle."

Evelyn narrowed her eyes. "Close the store. Open a gallery. Maybe you need—"

"Maybe I need Beverly to fund it—your idea?"

Creak...croak.

"Beverly is crazy, and I don't do crazy." Evelyn sniffed.

"Yes, you do."

"Her nephew would do anything for you. Point fingers at Adam Disston. His new article came out." Getting to her feet, she pointed to the rusted letterbox. "I printed you out a copy. Puppy is coming with me now. Get your overnight bag and join us—you need supper and a safe place to sleepwalk naked without frightening the neighbors."

Jon rolled his eyes. "Who's running the HHS now anyway?"

"Alicia Safford—there's some crazy for you."

"*Skatá*—I might as well move to Tampa tomorrow."

Evelyn crossed her arms. "Alicia Safford doesn't want your house, but should you decide to stand up and fight the HHS, I'm there." She took Jon's hand. "Pity you don't love Felicity."

Jon would not argue that point.

*

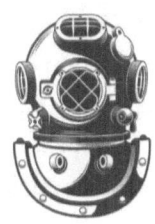

GULF COAST LIBERTINE
ADAM DISSTON

No More Love on the Run?

Last night, playboy Jon Christakos was seen cavorting with his sometime Caribbean Queen, supermodel Felicity Noel.

Witnesses claimed to have caught the two sharing the same dream until midnight. They were last seen retiring to Spring Bayou's infamous eyesore, the historic home Christakos now owns. Domestic aesthetics aside, there's no doubt those two hearts were beating as one well into the wee hours of morning.

We've seen this utterly stunning woman in magazines and on television. She's bright and funny, warm, and genuine. She's America's favorite supermodel for a reason, kids.

And yet, 30 minutes after sunrise, Felicity Noel was kicked to the curb in typical Christakos fashion—alone.

It's hard to imagine this gorgeously unkempt woman walking barefoot to her red Ferrari alone, clutch and spiked heels in one hand, keys in the other. Hard to imagine a man would be so cruel to someone so beloved.

It's said that the wounds Jon Christakos incurred after Tarpon socialite Alicia Safford rejected him decades ago are to blame, hardening his heart and making it impossible for him to fall in love. Safford's recent return to Tarpon may have inspired Christakos to rekindle the flames of his ancient passions.

If so, will Felicity Noel find the inner strength to be her own woman and find a better man? Only time will tell.

Don't you just love the smell of the Information Age in the morning? Until next time, make good choices, kids.

*

CHAPTER 04

A Crowded, Magic Number

"There are three kinds of lies: lies, damned lies, and statistics."
~ Mark Twain

Weekday mornings in downtown Tarpon Springs were lively in the summer months. What with all the beaches and parks, and the Sponge Docks (of course), filled to bursting with tourists and local kids freed from the shackles of school. Jon watched the hubbub of passing cars and pedestrians as he waited for his bus—waving at honking horns, catcalls, and whistles. He posed for selfies with passers-by. Sat for smartphone video interviews.

Soon, the bustling was easy to ignore. He allowed himself to get lost in thought—*Alicia Safford, the woman I love to hate.* Her sudden appearance filled his breadbasket with butterflies. His heart thrashed inside his chest from thinking about why she was back in town. The thought of seeing her again scared him more than his meeting with Raj Patel—*at least I know where his loyalties lay.*

A happy sound broke Jon's reverie.

Ding-Ding!

Jolley Trolley was a local bus service, with vehicles decked like San Francisco streetcars. A small fleet of them shuttled folks to and from Tarpon Springs and Clearwater Beach. Jon loved the service—he had an annual pass and knew every driver. He was often the first passenger to board, especially at this hour.

It was always a relaxing, smooth ride too. No jostling, no side-to-side sway—just the odd jerk of starting and stopping and easy-as-a-Sunday-morning acceleration.

Ding-Ding!

Jon laughed as the bus slowed to a stop. Other vehicles had a number—this one had a sign in bold letters that read, 'Hallelujah Line'. That meant only one thing—his driver was Leon Rain.

Leon was a twiggy man with night-dark skin and a pencil-thin moustache over a generous mouth with perfect teeth. His was a melodic voice marinated with the spices of gospel music, public speaking, and truth. His nature was akin to that of a wily monk with an overactive mind, unwavering loyalty, and acerbic bravado—forever juggling and riding a unicycle. He sparked admiration and controversy, as his was the only route christened with hallelujah.

Boarding the polished bus, Jon shook Leon's hand and made a bee-line for a bench in the back row. He slid over to the open window, thrust a hand outside, and waved. Most passers-by waved back—some shouted playful obscenities—one or two did and said things that Jon simply ignored. The bus rolled forward, and Leon Rain started talking about falling in love for the hundredth time last night. How hot the summer would be. And what plans he had made for the rest of the year.

Ding-Ding!

The kitschy moments of their crawl south made the ride worth taking. Landscapes of coastal views, parks lined with palm trees, mobile homes and RVs, Mediterranean- or Spanish-style homes, strip malls as far as the eye could see. Many of the bus stops due south of Tarpon were empty. Leon kept going and continued gabbing. Jon, who was in a blissful state of half-listening and half-watching, could not get Alicia Safford out of his head. He wondered how age and time had tempered her over the years.

Ding-Ding!

New passengers took their seats. When the bus started moving again, Jon let out a sigh. Thoughts of Alicia Safford invariably led to other thoughts. He had buried them in his past for good reason—to what purpose did dwelling on the damn things now serve?

He had trouble expelling her from his mind.

I'd rather look at X-rays of my brain tumor, he thought.

Not entirely fair to the cancer, as it did not have the ability to make better choices. But Alicia Safford consciously tried to drive two families apart—and very nearly succeeded too.

Jon passively noted the change in scenery. Breezes off the bay nearby, the warmth of the morning air, dapples of hide-n-seek sunlight—storms were brewing on the horizon over the Gulf. Clouds rolling inland were shaking the sky, promising summer rain. The off-and-on hopping of passengers did not annoy. Everyone on the Hallelujah Line wore a smile. Here were destinations found only on the Gulf coast, with views as eclectic as the beach-going folk seated snugly on the lacquered benches.

Ding-Ding!

The bus sputtered as it passed an empty stop. It lurched, languishing in a limbo of acceleration and breaking that made it difficult to think of anything. And that was just fine with Jon—he needed a moment to catch his breath. A summer shower summoned heady scents of moist asphalt and freshly cut grass.

Soaked passengers from the next stop, all in beach-or-bust attire and faces kissed with rain, boarded in clusters jostling for window seats.

Ding-Ding!

Alicia Safford dropped into his life like an atom bomb.

Jon fell in love with her. And then she left him for Panos. The two brothers barely spoke when Jon got sick. Or when he faced the fallout of his treatments—the radiation, chemo hits, spinal taps, and a surgery that left him paralyzed for a year.

For Panos, indulging in denial and spite was easier than facing the truth—that his breast-brother had cancer and was mortal.

Pretending the opposite was his only compass, as if forsaking Jon was keeping him alive. Panos had this epiphany after pulling the cross from Spring Bayou. It took all of three seconds—Father, Son, Holy Ghost—to realize what he had done to Jon. He climbed out of the water and shoved Alicia aside to get to his family. He fell to his knees and wept bitterly, begging for forgiveness.

In Tarpon's Greek community, it was a sin to forsake your family. But Jon chose his brother over his brother's sin. It was the right decision, without question. They had three good years before Panos was killed in the line of duty.

Ding-Ding!

Jon fixed his watery gaze on the blur outside his window. "You came back," he whispered.

"Who came back?"

Shaking the memories lose, Jon searched for the one who spoke. The Jolley Trolley was full of passengers headed to Clearwater Beach. Every man, woman, and child wore bathing suits. The woman on the bench next to him wore a pretty smile under a straw hat and owl sunglasses.

She poked his knee. "Mr. Christakos, who came back?"

Jon blinked. He knew the woman's voice—the rest of her was unfamiliar. The three other women next to her were all attractive too—and young and tanned and scented. Like the one who poked him, they wore bikinis beneath artfully arranged wraps. Then, it hit him.

"Dr. Flowers, I didn't recognize you without your lab coat and scowl."

"Mr. Christakos, I didn't realize you enjoyed talking to yourself on public transportation," she replied. "Kind of creepy—I hope you know that." She smiled.

"You have such pretty white teeth, Dr. Flowers—who would've guessed."

"I'm almost afraid to ask this, but where's the dog I left in your care?"

"Slow cooking in my crock pot," he said. "What? I grew up in Malaysia."

She tried not to laugh. Turning her head she said, "Cat's a much better roasting meat." She looked at him again. "Seriously, Mr. Christakos, where is the dog? Perhaps you had another date with Felicity Noel and left the poor thing in the supermodel's car?"

"I have an appointment this morning," Jon replied, "so she is currently being pampered at my next door neighbor's house. That house also belonging to—"

"The dog or the supermodel?"

This time Jon tried not to smile. "My mother, and—" The photos Evelyn had taken of him slipped from his fingers. He managed to grab all but one—it fell atop Dr. Flowers's surprisingly tiny (and cute) bare foot. With swift, unexpected grace, she picked it up. He tried to protest, but an icy glare told him to shut his mouth. She turned her attention to the photo. One of her girlfriends tried to steal a glance, but Dr. Flowers raised her shoulder to block the pretty blonde from viewing it.

Returning the snapshot, she simply said, "Disappointing."

Ding-Ding!

The Jolley Trolley decelerated—his bus stop was ahead. Jon excused himself and slowly made his way down the aisle, apologizing each time he bumped legs and arms in his path. Thanking Leon Rain, he disembarked and stuffed the photos into his pocket. He headed toward the cluster of medical buildings tucked under the canopy of pine trees. To the corner office, the door with 'Clearwater Oncology & Radiology - Rajeev Patel, MD | Althea Faklis, MD' in bold letters on the glass.

Ding-Ding!

Jon pulled the handle and went inside.

He was unaware that someone had been watching him intently.

As soon as he was inside the building, she was watching the Jolley Trolley roll toward Clearwater Beach without her. It was better that she was not on board—her friends hated the way she cried.

*

Jon was sitting in the waiting area an hour later. He had two halves of a teardrop-shaped agate in the palm of his hand. Another gift from Raj Patel, whose family once lived in the Pacific Northwest many years ago. He and his father would spend long days collecting agates near the Cape Blanco Lighthouse and Battle Rock City Park. Last week, he gave Jon a carving of Shiva—a lovely sculpture and apropos.

Raj Patel's female colleague was too professional to give tokens unless you were under 18. Althea Faklis became a fierce, doting Greek Mother Earth for kids fighting cancer.

Jon marveled at the stones. The revelation of their identical centers was a study in perfect gradation, from amaranthine to mazarine to sapphire. Like the split halves of an Everlasting Gobstopper—*this one is Willy and this one is Wonka.*

Raj Patel entered the lobby and sat beside his patient. He suddenly poked Jon in the center of his forehead.

"Beyond this portal lies the path to living life in the present," he said. "Six months of living life in the present can pass like seconds or years—the choice is yours."

Jon nodded. "I'll certainly try to remember."

"You must DO this thing, dammit—remembering to try to do something means nothing. It is setting a reminder to make an attempt. You're strong enough, stubborn enough. So, DO this thing I am telling you to do." He poked his forehead again. "Live in the present and these next six months will pass like years. I want your mind and body at relative peace when I return from India."

Raj Patel possessed a peculiar bedside manner. Mysticism coupled with a powerful knowledge of medicine. He inspired hope, renewed faith, and summoned courage—he believed it was important to challenge statistical inevitability with the proper spiritual tools.

Raj would not dare to foster unrealistic expectations in his patients, but he encouraged the possibility of survival, even when the chances of survival were not in their favor. His particular branch of neurooncology meant facing uphill battles every day—his partner was a dedicated neurosurgeon with a matching doctorate in Brain Science.

Together, Dr. Patel and Dr. Faklis worked miracles.

They treated nurses as indispensable collaborators—the waiting list to join the practice was backlogged two years. Patients under their care tended to beat unbelievable odds.

Jon sighed. "Six months—this sucks, Raj."

Patel patted his leg. "Have faith, my friend. You're relatively as-ymptomatic and should stay that way until it time for the surgery in November."

"What if something happens to you?"

"You have a whole team, Jon—let me worry about the logistics," Raj told him. "I think you should schedule an appointment with Sita. Talking about this might be a good idea. She's got books too."

"You just told me to live in the present—you poked my head."

"Yes, but the first Buddhist tenet is learning to accept that all life is sorrowful," Raj replied. "Come over for dinner tomorrow night. After-ward, I shall casually disappear into my study for an hour."

A session with Dr. Sita Patel meant one thing—six months was a death sentence.

Jon was not ready to admit that yet—*it's always better to hope for the best and prepare for the worst, but I'm not giving up.* He juggled Willy and Wonka. "And not one drug trial?"

Patel laughed. "Gives us license to do radical treatments. Think about dinner. Please."

"Only if you show Sita those naked pictures, Rajeev," Jon quipped.

The dark-skinned doctor hooted. "My people invented porn—your *lingam* is no match for mine. I am a Tantric god, you Polish-Greek mongrel."

Laughter shanghaied Jon into apoplexy—it felt good to laugh.

He opened the folder in his lap. Emergency contact numbers. His weekly schedule of vitamin drips and glutathione injections. Prescriptions for sleepwalking should his new pain management medication fail. Dr. Faklis put him on a strict no sugar or processed food diet for the next six months. "I'll starve before the cancer kills me," he groused.

Patel ignored his whining. "Sita and I leave next week," he said. "Fa-ther agreed to help me with your treatment—no one else knows your case better. It's a good sign, Jon. I hope to return by October unless this non-traditional glioma of yours decides to behave the way the textbooks say it should."

Jon swallowed. "Anything I should do while I'm waiting?"

"Try to meditate. Paint as much as you can. Go for long walks. Clean your house. Get organized—your bank accounts, living will, trusts, power of attorney."

"All that stuff is done—what else?"

"Make sure you see Dr. Faklis every week and don't be a jerk." Raj laughed.

"Then YOU make sure those gossiping nurses in back keep quiet. I'm serious—I don't want people talking about this—oh, Misty and Eric are here." A woman and her young son were standing outside just short of the glass door. The woman was upset. The boy at her side was comforting her, his hands waving and gesturing as she gripped the handle, unable to pull.

Jon got to his feet. "I'll call you about dinner."

Patel shook his hand. "No, you won't—see you on Skype in two weeks."

With a wave, Jon went outside.

Misty Harmon threw her arms around him when she recognized him. He held her in a warm embrace until she was calm enough to pull away. Jon crouched to speak to her son after spinning the boy around. Eric began gesturing furiously, his fingers moving with alacrity and precision.

Jon gestured for him to slow down.

"I'm old, Eric, and my hands are rusted with age." After some small talk via hand signals, he playfully knocked the boy's chin. "Go give it hell, rey." When Eric entered through the glass doors, Jon embraced Misty again. "He's so strong. Hang in there."

"Is your supermodel back in town for your birthday?"

"Ooh, I think jealousy becomes you, Misty."

She smiled. "With you, I'm always jealous—no paparazzi then?"

"In Tarpon Springs? Not unless she gets out of control at the Sponge Docks."

Misty laughed. "I'll see you around, Jonny."

Jon headed to the bus stop—*God, watch over Eric.*

The afternoon sun was oppressive—even the palm trees looked beaten down with the heat. Charcoal clouds filled the sky but provided no relief. In shade or in shadow, Florida summer temperatures were constant, always hot as a Gator Alley swamp shed.

An army of darker clouds marched inland from the coast. A low rumble shook the western horizon. It was all just noise. A storm would do little to cool things off anyway, no matter how loud it was. A spattering of fat drops, a gust of wind picking up dust and grass, a rumble from the gloomy gathering above—Jon ignored the saber rattling. He continued his slow walk to the bus stop as he scanned his files.

The images from his recent scans were clearer.

A ring of cysts were hiding a pocket of diseased tissue, a compacted core of cancer only the PET scans revealed. Those cysts were miraculously containing the cancer to one tiny spot on his brain stem and then keeping the cancer from metastasizing There was no way to tell how long this precariously miraculous situation would continue.

Suddenly, the colorful rocks weighed like three-ton boulders in his fisted hand. Six months—*ay hyessou.*

"Hello, Mr. Christakos." Dr. Flowers was sitting on the bus stop bench. "You could've told me," she said, fishing a tissue from her bag. "Figures you'd be a flipping saint."

Jon laughed. "I'm no saint. And who said that I have cancer."

"I know cancer."

Jon ignored her. "I come here to sit with patients getting chemo sometimes."

"My father died of cancer when I was nine," she said. "I won't tell anyone if you're trying to keep this private." She smiled. "In case the press saw me with you and wanted to ask questions."

"What kind of cancer did your father have?"

"Brain tumor," she said, sniffling. "It destroyed him. Destroyed our family."

"I'm very sorry, Dr. Flowers," he said, meaning it.

"That woman and her son—how sick is he?"

"Eric will be transferred to All Children's—it's terminal. His mother and I are old friends."

"And the sign language?"

"Aunt Bessie was deaf. I grew up signing. Eric's been deaf for four years. Tough world."

"Look, I want to apologize before the next bus takes me down to suck drinks and bully men at the beach this afternoon." The sky rumbled. "Or maybe not."

Jon waved a pair of mating dragonflies away. "The storm will hit it and quit it. Monsoon season is weeks off. You'll have plenty of sun to bake your skin to a golden melanoma, Dr. Flowers."

She smiled. "I was hoping you had a soul. I won't stop reading Adam Disston though. He's snarky and I love him. I'd marry him if he would have me."

People reacted to Jon's celebrity in unexpected ways. The unpredictability made life in Tarpon Springs dynamic, if nothing else. His biannual trysts with Felicity always kept his name on wagging tongues—brought him business to the store.

He could not complain too much.

The peculiar heat and brightness of his status was easier to manage now that he was in his 40s. Learning to live with being an object was a harder lesson when he was a younger man.

"You do have a soul, don't you?" Dr. Flowers asked. "I was right about the dog."

Jon snorted. "Maybe so. People see what they want to see—you believed I had something resembling a soul. You never would've put me in charge of a wounded animal."

"I'd like to take you out for dinner, Mr. Christakos. We might hit it off—she's kind of hot AND she's a doctor AND she's willing to pay for your company."

"I don't date."

"C'mon. It's not a date if you're a friend showing a new friend around town."

Jon rolled his eyes.

Spending time with a woman like Dr. Flowers was intriguing. Still, he wanted to keep her at arm's length for good reason—he actually liked her. "I'm really busy. I just got this new dog, and she's a bit broken at the moment, so..." He smiled. "Too complicated. Really."

"Fine, play hard to get. And my name is Abby," she said. "It's not the 1890s."

"Abby's a pretty name, Dr. Flowers—you may call me Mr. Christakos."

She shook her head. "It's none of my business, but if you ever need to talk—I mean, I don't know what's going on with you. Just putting it out there. Whatever IT is, I'm a good listener."

Jon considered her for a moment. "It was the naked photo, wasn't it?"

"Weird, famous, and naked? Right up my alley."

Ding-Ding!

"Looks like my ride to Clearwater is here," she said, getting to her feet. "I'm sure my girlfriends are dying to hear about the infamous Jon Christakos. I can't wait to tell them he's a pompous jerk."

Jon threw his head back. "FINALLY! Someone who gets me. Letting you leave suddenly feels like a really stupid decision on my part."

"Make it up to me then." She looked hard at him. "C'mon, you know you want to."

He smiled—*yes, I do.*

It would not hurt to have a friend, but he decided against it for now. It pained him. Deep inside, he protested against his own silence and set fire to the Great Wall around his emotions.

Now was not the time to get close to someone.

In silence, Jon watched her board the Jolley Trolley and waved as it drove away. How could he explain to Dr. Abby Flowers that he possibly was a dead man walking?

Well, whether that was true or not, six months did not give him enough time to make anything up to anyone. And her heart was much too beautiful to break.

*

Handsome did not do Brik Buckman justice.

Hippie beard, hair pulled in a douche-bag ponytail, boyish face with a lantern jaw, Superman physique, golden tan. He kept eye contact whenever he shook hands and spoke names. There were more than a few similarities between Brik and Panos that Jon noticed. Same height and build, same intense eyes, same confidence, devil-may-care spirit.

The difference being that one was a honey-hued Viking and the other was a dark brooding Spartan.

Jon kissed Evelyn before he sat down to eat.

Greek chow mein from Mr. Souvlaki—sautéed bell peppers and onions, feta cheese, spice-marinated pork. He dipped a warm slice of pita bread into a bowl of rich, garlic tzatziki sauce and wrapped it around a finger-sized slab of stuffed grape leaves. He shoved it into his face and made a plate of chow mein.

"So, Brik," Jon said, "did you work much without your shirt today? The Golden Crescent is all atwitter about you."

Evelyn poked Jon with her fork. "I will smother you with a pillow tonight."

Brik laughed. "I always work without a shirt, brah—half the people who hire me want the value added service of this healthy body."

Jon looked at Brik. "Really?" He then glanced at Evelyn, whose face was in her hand. And then he looked at Brik, whose face was fit to burst with laughter. Jon smiled. "Ah, you're another smart-ass. Well played, handyman. Well played. I too am a smart-ass thanks to my Greek mother here and not the Polish woman who gave birth to me. But I'd imagine you know all about that, don't you?"

Brik took a drink of his iced tea. "Rumors—I grew up in Holiday, so we rarely heard your name said much. Now that you're with Felicity Noel, I hear it all the time. Must be weird being famous like you cured cancer. You know? I've seen a celebrity or two, and it's not a motherfu—"

Evelyn smacked him upside his head. "None of that talk in my gazebo."

"*Hck*—sorry. I get carried away when I'm nervous," he said, knocking the table three times. "So, how did you meet her? Was it at one of those 'Night in the Islands' events?"

Here were the facts. During one of those Greek festival events, Jon and Evelyn were busy working the bouzouki music pavilion. A group of drunk kids showed up to see Tripod Jon dance. The girls kept posing for pictures. Their boyfriends kept trying to put Jon in his place. He got angry, smashed a plate, and left the tent. It became a Christakos legend as the years passed. Evelyn later explained to him that the notoriety was not real. That it was best to practice turning the other cheek and walking away. *Had it not been for Evelyn, I would've gone insane.*

"I don't attend public events," Jon replied, coolly. "Unless Evie makes me."

"You owe me Wednesday nights at St. Nicholas—any time you're ready, Jonny."

"Only if the Icon of Saint Nicholas weeps again—don't you believe in miracles?"

She threw a pita slice that landed behind him. "Heathen—I'll see you in church by Christmas," she said, snapping. "Minnie, don't eat that—"

Jon plucked the bread from between the dog's paws.

"So, Evelyn tells me you have a boat," Brik offered diplomatically. "I'm a photographer. I'd love to work something out in trade, brah. I'm dying to get out to Anclote Key to see the lighthouse up close again. Your boat's over at Belle Harbour, right?"

Jon narrowed his eyes at Evelyn. "Yes, it is."

"You know you really don't look very Greek to me, Jon—*Hck*—boom, boom, boom! Sorry, man. That was rude. See? I say stupid stuff when I'm nervous. Forget I mentioned the boat thing."

Jon smiled. "What's the deal with the, uh…what are those? Tics?"

"*Hck*—yeah, about those," Brik replied.

Here were the facts. Mild Tourette's at the age of six solidly trumped a stammer at four. The stammer he managed with music and singing. The tics were hard to manage without medication. His mother taught him how to live with the tics using as small a dose as possible. His need to do or say things in threes and his *tic*-cups, as he called them—all manageable until his mother and father split.

"I was sixteen when a heart attack put Dad into a cemetery—*Hck*—I dropped out of school and traveled the world with the money he left me. Canada, Brazil, Belize, Chile, Taiwan, Hawaii, China, Siberia, Croatia, Italy, Greece. Always had a place to stay or work to do. Picked up a hammer, a camera, a drafting table, keyboard, a sense of humor—*Hck*—I'm a handyman savant with great abs and a knack for landscape design, brah. Here's to my awesome self."

Jon raised his plastic cup. "*Na zdrowie*," he toasted.

Evelyn threw down her napkin. "Speaking of Polish—look who's walking up my driveway. Hello there, Neal. Want some baklava? I can hear your stomach begging for it from here."

Neal thumbed his belt. "Sorry, Miss Evelyn—just need your boy to take a ride with me."

Jon reached into his pocket. He handed the agate halves to Brik. "Close-up photos of those might be interesting—that one's Willy and the other is Wonka." He followed Office Peruski to his cruiser.

*

Two hours later, Jon was free to leave the police station. No citation, no booking, and no indication they were charging him for anything.

Neal offered him a lift home.

"What a waste of time," he muttered as they left the parking lot. "But dammit, did you ever kick a hornet's nest."

"What's happening? If I'm being accused of a crime, then why—"

"You DID commit a crime," Neal said, hitting the steering wheel. "Chucky's over 18—but he's saying nothing about what happened. The fat one's 16. Touched in the head doesn't begin to describe the level of crazy this boy is—he's singing like a bird about every violation imaginable." He swore under his breath. "Look, you busted his nose and threatened him in a public alley. Violent intent, assault and battery—that he's a minor is icing on this crap cake you baked yourself. But…"

"There's a 'but' in this? Really?"

Neal frowned. "Don't get too excited," he said. "Are you on any new medication? You've been acting strange for a few weeks—you're skin and bones. Medication affects judgment, behavior."

Jon silently berated himself for being dense. "Didn't think that was relevant, but yes."

"Is it back, the cancer?" Neal asked.

Jon blinked and considered his answer—*now was not the time.* "Just precautionary."

"Good. Guys get out of messes on that kind of technicality—that's one 'but' for you."

"There's more?"

Neal laughed. "Chuck Parker refuses to corroborate Dickey's story. Says they were trespassing and making too much noise. Basically insinuating they got what they deserved. Chucky's on your side."

"What the hell? Why?"

"Because Dickey is suggesting you forced yourself on them too."

"WHAT?"

Neal nodded his surprise too. "Without Chucky to back him up, Dickey's got nothing. And no other witness has come forward either. Well, Nico said that he saw the aftermath of a commotion that didn't last but a few minutes. His statement shines brightly on your case—makes Chucky's testimony cleaner too. Another thing working in your favor — Dickey's made false accusations in the past. That he won't submit to a physical exam isn't helping him. Anyway, here you go."

Jon laughed. "Neal, you brought me to Silverking."

"Babcia promised to load me up with food if I did. You could use a beer anyway."

"What am I supposed to do about this? Sit tight?"

"And watch your back. Don't skip town unless you tell me. If things start to happen, they'll get going quickly. I'll continue to do what I can to stall, and Nico's been a huge help. Old man, my butt—he's a rock star. I just hope he doesn't get burned for putting himself out there for you." He looked at Jon hard. "My brothers and I have long memories, despite our small numbers. Find comfort in that."

"Nothing you boys do is small—it's more than I deserve."

"Shut-up with that. Go tell Roman to bring out my food. Olga's ovulating, and she's got a honey-do list in the bedroom that I'm looking forward to checking off."

"Gross, Peruski—TMI."

"Bite me, Christakos—TTYL."

Here were the facts. Silverking Brewing Company was at the heart of Little Warsaw. Aleksandra Grelik (whom everyone called Babcia) owned the two blocks north and south of Lemon Street—well, the Section 8 housing notwithstanding. The place had a rustic, contemporary feel— hunting lodge meets Bauhaus fishing shack. All the furniture was varnished wood with metal accents. On the concrete walls were fishing rods crossed like swords, hooked spears, harpoons, wooden oars from old boats, mounted deer heads, fish paintings, black and white photographs, and the namesake Silverking trophy, a six-foot monstrosity mounted behind the main bar. A fair sampling of Tarpon Springs converged here.

Jon walked through a glass door marked with Silverking's fish logo, an image as unmistakable as its name. The co-owner of the brewery was a handsome Barney Rubble-type going to seed in a rugged devil-may-care fashion. Bret led Jon to the main bar, where his brother Roman waved him over to an empty stool. He poured Jon a pint of his favorite brew and left to fetch Neal's food. Jon always felt at ease with these people—today he needed the comfort of familiar faces.

Roman returned to the bar. "Bret, where's that stack of bags you brought in?"

From the garage next door came Bret's reply in garbled Polish. Curious language, Polish. Like Russian, but without all the sex, drugs, and Rasputin. Jon loved listening to the Polish-only conversations around him. Growing up in a Greek community prepared him for the vigorous, if alien, communication—he always felt at home here when the Grelik boys started barking at each other.

He looked at a framed photograph to his right. A smiling woman in a sparkling mermaid costume swimming in a water tank, a halo of light behind her head. The picture was one of several similar photographs on the walls of his house—*love you, Mother.*

"You are too skinny," said a gravelly voice. The old woman it belonged to grinned as he kissed each of her wrinkled cheeks. All 93-plus years of Aleksandra Grelik's life made it impossible for those younger than her ripe old age to make a difference. To make an impact or an impression. The old bulldog always got her way—even when she did not win, she always got her way. She suffered no fools. "Here, take the bags. Bread and kapusta. Golumpki and pierogi too."

Jon did as he was told. "*Dziękuję*—thank you."

He knew that he was Polish by blood (one of the few details he knew about his father). He suspected that his father was part of the Grelik family tree. He had no proof. Mostly hunches, bits of information and pieces of story he had connected over the years.

Babcia had always looked out for him. He never pressed her for the reasons why, having learned to graciously accept her mysterious vigilance. Patting his arm, she considered Jon for a long moment, eyes welling with tears as she rubbed his cheeks with gnarled hands.

"Good boy, strong face. You call if get arrested. *Pravda?*"

"I swear, Babcia," he told her.

And so, with plastic bags of food and beer, Jon left Silverking. With the late afternoon sun splashing his face, he could not shake the strange feeling that he was crossing the Rubicon, that he was moving beyond the Event Horizon of a Black Hole at the center of a universe he could not see.

*

Jon stood on the eastern arc of the Golden Crescent.

With arms aching and feet dragging, he trudged toward a familiar bend of trees—his destination was just ahead. He hiked up the driveway, put the food on the porch, and took a growler of beer across the street to his piece of the bayou. A private dock that was little more than a long rickety deck with a wobbly bench. Jon had the slip removed after his aunt and uncle's accident years ago. Upkeep for the dock matched his philosophy about it for the house.

Here were the facts. The winch and pulley system broke when their skiff was being lifted. The bow dropped, sending them careening into each other when it hit the surface of the water. The wreck took them under. They died less than 150 feet from their own front porch, 20 years after his parents died—to the effing day. A week after Jon was born, his mother's aunt and uncle adopted him, gave him their Greek surname, and enlisted Evelyn and George Kouskoutis to raise him alongside their infant son.

It was high drama that fueled years of wide-eyed stares and whispers about Irony and Fate having their way with Jon, who seemed to be a magnet for their frequent visits. Oh, did the gossipmongers have a field day when his aunt and uncle died.

Jon was neither religious nor superstitious, but he was a savant with intuition. Hunches filled him with dread. His gut screamed that changes were coming. And whenever he felt the weight of the world, he always came here to have a talk with his aunt and uncle, and his parents.

"Six months," he began, taking a drink from his growler. "A better prognosis than the last time, but even if I beat this thing again, I don't know if I can go through the recovery. Raj says that my brain function could be altered or damaged for a while."

His voice broke as he spoke.

Pieces of it skipped like stones across the surface of the water.

"I'm really scared this time, Aunt Bessie," he whispered, wiping tears with the back of his hand. "I love Evelyn, and I am grateful she's here, but I'm scared this time."

"Hello, Jon."

Clutching his chest, the soft female voice having stuck his heart like a bell, he turned toward the sound and swallowed. Alicia Safford was standing a few yards away. The dusk did little to hide the shape of her, which had not changed since first her body bloomed fully.

"Alicia, I'd heard you were in town," Jon said. "Out for a run, I see."

"May I talk to you?" she asked. "It won't take long."

Dock lights across the bayou flickered on. Street lamps followed. Even bathed in sickly yellow-green fluorescence, Alicia Safford was achingly beautiful. Tonight she wore a revealing outfit, the kind worn by rich cougars on the prowl at local gyms. Black sports bra, neon pink top, charcoal spandex bottoms, hair tie to pull her blonde tresses into an artful tail. The sheen on her face was a fairy dusting of perspiration perfumed with coconut oil. "Sorry for interrupting—walk me to the curb?"

Jon left the jug on the bench when he got up to follow her. They stood apart from each other just beyond the glow of the streetlight. "As head of the HHS, I wanted to personally thank you for alerting our office regarding our list of house repairs and landscaping."

"I didn't contact your office."

"Someone did, and earlier today I spoke to the contractor you hired, Brik Buck—"

"I didn't hire a contractor either."

"Oh, well then," Alicia said, her face twisted in confusion. "Are you certain?"

"Yes, I am—will that be all?"

"I'm sure I don't know what you mean."

Jon smiled. "Cut the crap and tell me what you really wanted, Alicia. I have late dinner plans with Evelyn, so make it quick, and keep the bitch level below three."

Alicia Safford collected herself as she considered her reply. "Evelyn Kouskoutis must have contacted my office after she hired Mr. Buckman."

Jon pointed at her and tapped his nose. "Anything else?"

"I-I-I just wanted…to tell you," she said awkwardly, apparently still unnerved by Jon's mocking coldness. "Yesterday morning, I saw you in the alleyway with those two boys and that poor dog. I saw very little to be honest. But I heard everything. I'm sure you had your reasons."

"Alicia, what are you talking about?"

"I heard the fat boy went to the hospital—don't know about that blond one."

Now it was Jon's turn to feel awkward. His heart began to race as he tried to put together how she could have known, let alone seen, what had happened.

"That's a lie," he finally said.

Alicia shrugged. "I was on my morning run. I turned down Athens Street from the Sponge Docks and saw a commotion in the alley. At first, I wasn't sure it was you. I took out my ear buds and recognized your voice. "I did not see the fight. I heard you threaten the kid though. And I saw his face afterward—he was missing a tooth. Busted upper lip, bloody nose. Wept like a baby."

Jon's hackles rose—*perhaps she's telling the truth*. All he could manage was a weak head nod.

"I understand why you did what you did—that poor dog looked worse that the fat kid," she offered diplomatically. "He got what he deserved in my book."

"Why tell me then?"

"The fat one didn't see me there, but the blond one did," Alicia said. "I was already running when we made eye contact—he knew I knew what had happened." She crossed her arms. "Jon, I didn't come back to town to stir the pot—I'd prefer that we keep separate lives."

"You haven't read Adam Disston's article then."

Alicia smiled. "I never miss his column," she said with a shrug. "It's trash, but very amusing." She cleared her throat. "I bear you no ill will. And I understand why you're still angry."

"No, you don't. You couldn't."

"Fair enough," she conceded. "Listen, if the blond kid says something to the police about seeing me there passing by, then I'll get invited to the station. That fat kid saw Nico Cocoris getting into his car. The police called him to the station. I just wanted to tell you that I've got nothing to say unless they come to me first—like I said: I saw very little." She cocked her head to the side. "Not that I'd presume to know what you're thinking, Jon, but you look either puzzled or troubled."

"Maybe it's both, Alicia." For a long unbroken moment, he struggled to measure the gulf between them. It had widened since that fateful winter in Atlanta. His memory of the four days they had shared was still clear to him. Jon had two collisions with Alicia Safford. Admittedly, the scar he earned at 16 was a hangnail compared to what he had earned at 23—*four days of snow.*

"I know how little I've meant to you over the years," he said. "So, I am puzzled."

Alicia opened her mouth to speak. Someone else did.

"Alicia Safford, if you don't go back to your evil castle, then I'll toss your butt across the bayou myself—*patsavoúra.*" Evelyn left the dark gangway of her private dock a few feet away. "Whatever scheme you're plotting, do not include him."

"I'm plotting nothing. I'm including Jon in nothing."

"Don't lie to me." Evelyn's glare was unwavering. "If I find out you are, then I won't be held responsible for my actions once the insanity clouds my mind. You're not worthy to lick his shoe."

Alicia Safford's face was a terrifying mask of Junior League witchcraft, one with delighted smile and twinkly eyes. "It's been nice seeing you again, Miss Evelyn," she said, adjusting a setting on her fitness watch. She neither spoke to nor looked at them when she jogged away.

Jon watched her bounce along the Crescent until her silhouette shrank into the darkness.

In the aftermath of her absence, he felt a familiar ache that refused to let go of the piece of his heart branded with her fingerprints. It was rather like the obnoxious rebirth of an ugly phoenix. But then, as if by some miracle, the rising pain suddenly died and grew cold.

With a shrug, he said, "That was odd."

Evelyn narrowed her eyes. "I'll save my lecture for a time when I can talk to you without scratching your eyes out!"

Heading back to her house, she shot-put strings of Greek epithets hot enough to superheat the air. She climbed the stoop and slammed the front door, her words filling the sky with storm clouds of obscenity that would drown the bayou with rain for days to come.

*

CHAPTER 05

Trials of Water and Fire

"Heat and hoary frost shall hold their course, till fire purge all things."
~ *John Milton*

Jon woke the next day face-planted on his bedroom floor without a stitch of clothes. Not a usual habit, but nothing out of the ordinary either. It was noon. Sounds of sawing, hammering, and myriad other carpentry noises rattled his brain more than they did the glass in his bedroom window. Focusing on the corner, he took a deep breath to right himself. The attempt failed miserably, as he ended up in the same spot curled on his side and drifted back to sleep.

The next alarm came 30 minutes later—a series of barks from the impatient Pomeranian dancing next to his face. He sat up on his knees and scratched her muzzle before falling again. His naked hairy backend went up as his head went down, a seesaw exercise in vulgar physics.

Minnie released her full bladder and trotted downstairs without any guilt about having done so. Jon woke an hour later to the sound of knocking and rank smell of pee.

Knock-knock-knock.

"You gonna sleep in piddle all day? Huey, Dewey, Louie—*Hck*—get up." Brik's voice was muffled, as if it were trapped behind glass.

A second burst of knocking prompted Jon to sit up (and stay up this time). He turned toward the window. He slipped in the pool of cool urine underneath him as he tried to prop himself up with his hands.

His eyes trying to focus, Jon saw the blurry outline of the golden-hued demi-god sitting in a scaffold outside the window.

"What is—why am I wet?"

The handyman laughed. "Minnie left you a present." The scaffolding tilted. "GAH—get up—*Hck*—seriously, brah, your third leg is giving me a complex. And you're disgusting."

Jon cleaned his sleeping spot and himself. He dressed quickly. Went to the kitchen and finished the Polish leftovers. Drank a liter of Gatorade with a handful of pills. When he was able to move around without vomiting, he catapulted himself outside and sat on the front porch swing with the dog.

Creak...croak...

Jon gently rocked back and forth using the balls of his feet. He absently scratched Minnie and watched the sweaty crew rake and saw, chop and mow. They bagged the refuse from the backyard into several fat black pouches and carried them to the curb. His property was no longer an eyesore—thanks to Hot Handyman.

With a contented grin, Jon said, "Suck it, HHS."

Shirtless, chiseled, sweaty Brik Buckman trotted up the stoop. He wore his dimpled damn smile for Jon and wiped his face and neck with a towel. The hot handyman opened a beer plucked from his red Igloo picnic cooler. He drank a third of it in one gulp. "*Hck*—fuzzy-wuzzy iz-your-hairy butt, man. You're like the missing link—boom, boom, boom!"

"I blacked out last night—did I sleepwalk?"

"You wobbled and drooled as I tucked you in bed. You must've got up way later."

"Where's Evelyn?"

"She left this for you—*Hck*—sorry it's smudged."

Jon took the folded envelope and turned it around. He traced his name written in Evelyn's elegant flowery script. His heart began to thrum as he opened it. The letter inside was short—it felt heavy in his hands as he read her words. He read again.

After he reading it a third time, he handed it to Brik.

Sending letters was a quirky habit that Evelyn had instituted after Jon ran off to Atlanta to be an actor for a couple of years. They took their letter writing seriously. In an age of perpetual connectivity and instant gratification, their horse-and-buggy communication method grounded them in a reality they had spent 20 years building.

It was their way of circling the wagons to defend themselves against a world that wanted to keep them like pinned butterflies in a shadow box diorama. Evelyn had since embraced the Information Age, including many of its technological advances.

Jon had not succumbed—in fact; he equated its power to that of the One Ring.

"I'm sorry about your aunt—*Hck*—she didn't have a lot of time to fill me in either," Brik said, returning the letter. "So, what does writing a letter do that a phone call or email can't?"

"Talking from the heart requires simplicity," he replied with a sigh. "Pen, ink, and paper—no whiteout. Cuts through the crap, you know? I've saved every single one of them."

"That's pretty cool, Jon—*Hck*—I've not written a letter since I was...I can't even remember the last time I wrote a letter." He put on a clean shirt. "So, cancer?"

Jon slowly nodded. "Yes, Brik—please don't tell anyone. Look at me. I mean it."

"Dude, I swear—I can keep quite."

Before returning it to its sleeve, Jon read the letter once more.

*

Jonny, my sister Fotini had a stroke last night. I'm flying up to Ohio this morning. Until Peter and I can sort things out, I'll likely be here for a few weeks. Poor Peter—as if he hasn't gone through enough since his father died. He's looked up to you all his life, so he'll need you for direction before long. Expect his visit once we see what his mother needs. I tried to wake you before I left—I didn't want to tell you this in a letter. Brik has promised to housesit. Please let him help you with Minnie or any medical issues that come up. I've told him about your situation, so try to be patient with him when he asks questions. He's a good man to have in your corner should you need something off the beaten path. Don't let your pride keep you from asking him for help. And ask Dr. Flowers out, dammit. I look forward to hearing all about it in your response letter. ~ Evelyn

*

Three was the final tally of Jon's sleepwalking events over the following week. The number of photographs taken was larger. After all, Brik was a photographer and he promised to document what he heard and saw. He even hid sheets and blankets in strategic locations around the Crescent in case 'clothing optional' was Jon's preferred attire. That Brik managed the task with such aplomb and efficacy impressed Jon, who found it hard to keep him at arm's length. With matters regarding the Pomeranian, however, Brik Buckman was neither handy nor man—in fact, he was a useless Nelly.

Take the day of Minnie's follow-up appointment.

The three of them were in the lobby waiting for their turn to see Dr. Flowers. Jon and Minnie were calm, cool, and collected. Then there was Brik, sweating, fretting, legs a-twitching, hands a-wringing, eyes darting furtively at strangers and *their* pets. Biting his fingernails and humming as he chewed. The dog was content to sit in his lap until his agitated moving sent her to an empty seat.

Jon refused to sit beside a grown man who sucked his fingers out of habit. He paced the floor instead. A young woman clad in scrubs marked with little paw prints—indeed, the same sweet female assistant who cut that kid's leash last week—waved at Jon when she clocked in and sat behind the counter. The unhappy male assistant sitting there looked miserable, as if he were in a constant state of chewing, swallowing, and regurgitating his puckered greasy face.

After the examination, which Dr. Flowers finished rather quickly, she had nothing but praise for the accidental pet owner.

"Nicely done, Mr. Christakos. She's healing. Seems happy. Weight's good—all in all, she's strong enough to have surgery."

Jon's face fell. "What surgery?"

"I want her spayed and microchipped today. I've slotted the time."

"I don't understand."

"Look, it's just a precaution," she said, keeping her voice steady. "Reports of stolen purebred dogs from wealthy neighborhoods in the area are rising. If Minnie's microchipped, then we can find her if she's ever stolen. And if she's spayed, then she can't breed. And no, I'm not—"

Jon raised his hand. "I get it—yes, go ahead and do it."

Dr. Abigail Flowers smiled. And her natural beauty sparkled in her eyes. In her intoxicating perfume—the scents of her hair, skin, and breath. In the dimple of her left cheek, a hidden diamond Jon had failed to notice until now. He struggled to remember why he was there, as he was involved with solving the puzzle of this woman. She had poisoned his rational mind and turned it into a mass of poetical non-sequiturs. He lingered there for a brief moment, stretching this small strand of time until the tingle of its taut tether ignited sparks between them.

"I'll bring Minnie to your place around 8 o'clock, Mr. Christakos."

"I leave her in your good hands then, Dr. Flowers."

Kissing the dog's wet nose, Jon quickly left the room with a wave and did not look back. Walking away from her pained him more than he would ever dare admit to himself or anyone else—and he did not much like leaving his dog either.

*

Brik looked at his watch. "She's late."

For the past hour the handyman had been filling the time waiting with telling his weird stories. He seemed to have an endless supply of them. In truth, his manic need to relay his life's episodes was impressive, even if the end results were inconsistent and awkward. Jon had never known a man of the world so close to his own age, so he appreciated the handyman's efforts. He was too quiet now.

Jon patted his arm. "Don't worry—she'll be here."

The wall clock said it was a quarter past eight. Brik's leg began to twitch. Biting his fingernails again, he wiped his wet eyes. "I only had one blood sibling, a twin sister. I have lots of brothers and sisters from other mothers and fathers. *Hck*—dude, I'm a baby-man over this dog. Shoot me in my ovaries. If something happened to her, I'd lose my mind."

A siren roared by—the third one this evening.

Sirens set Jon's teeth on edge. A fourth siren blasted as its vehicle headed for the Sponge Docks—like all the others, its screeching made the house shake. For the next ten minutes, shrieking horns came and went, the Doppler effect raising and lowering their pitch as the distance swallowed them. Other emergency vehicles—police cruisers and ambulances—brought up the rear of the parade.

"Jesus, Mary, and Joseph—*Hck*—this is jacked."

The house phone rang. Jon answered it. "WHAT? No, I heard you. On my way." He looked at Brik. "Nico said there's a fire on Athens Street. Zorba's is in flames, the whole building."

"Boom, boom, boom—*Hck*—what about your store?"

Jon shook his head. He did not know whether his store was in trouble or not—the building in which it sat was separate from the one burning now. He left the house in a blind run.

*

The car belonging to Dr. Abigail Flowers was sitting in the driveway. She very likely was parked on the hallway floor just beyond the front door as Brik played guitar to pass the time. Jon was content where he was. He liked knowing that the woman he liked was in his home. It comforted him. Gave him strength to hold out long enough before barreling in there with his melodramatic news.

Melodrama has been the flavor du jour of late—what am I going to say?

Jon still felt as if he were floating above his body. The night he just had prompted him to detach for a while longer. He was home. He had been sitting on his front porch for a while now. He did not know exactly how long he had been there. Listening to the music wafting from his house soothed his weariness and eased his anxious mind. He was not settled enough to get up and open the door, see his friends and pet his dog. Besides, the music was too delicate, too precious to interrupt.

Ganymede lifted the cup to the lips
Of the god who had cursed him with immortal strains
The beautiful boy broken down as he grips
To the chalice filled from his veins—hey, la
Ganymede crept from his prison one night
And ran to the edge of the river
He wept in the tide, and with arms open wide
Ganymede threw himself in

He leaned against a post and closed his eyes. It was a song he had not heard before, one of Brik's originals, from the sound of its haunting melody and lyrics.

And he drowns, he drowns—he drowns.
Hey, la—nobody knows
Hey, la—what this could feel like
Hey, la—you will all know my name
I'm not far away from the god in me

Jon got up and took a deep breath. He opened the front door and waved weakly. Indeed, they were both sitting on the hardwood floor a few feet inside the house—*just as I thought*. Minnie was sleeping soundly on a bed nearby, oblivious to everything. The concern on their faces when he greeted them indicated that his appearance was worse than a ripped shirt, bandaged hand, and torn pant leg.

And a missing shoe.

Jon looked at his face in the mirror next to the door. Soot, sweat, blood, dirt, myriad smears of unknown origin—*it's much worse*. He teetered a moment. The smoke on his skin and clothes sickened him—as he had nothing left in his stomach to vomit, he dry-heaved like a sick cat instead. Wiping his mouth, he asked about Minnie. Brik assured him that she would recover. He explained everything that had to do with the stitches, special food, and tender spots. "Snap, crackle, pop—she's fine, brah. Tell him, Abby."

"No worries," she said. "Tell us what happened at the Docks."

Jon did not know where to begin. He had seen fires, but never like what he saw tonight, and he told them so.

"Zorba's is a smoldering ruins, smoking concrete, charred rubble, warped steel—all soaked, hissing, and dripping. It's a miracle no other buildings caught fire," he told them. "There was some looting. The Nik's Knacks window was smashed. Nothing was taken. Some items were ruined in the display case. Someone left a pile of feces in a pool of urine there." He lifted his bandaged hand. "I got this cleaning when some glass cut me." He left out the details of pulling out a half-inch shard—his wound had bled through the makeshift T-shirt bandage. "The second fire was worse, I think."

"*Hck*—there was more than one fire?"

"Nico's house burned down. Took half of the one beside his." Jon pointed to his television in the nearby den. "It's all over the news—turn it on and pick a channel."

Abby grabbed his hand. "Jon, this cut needs to be cleaned and—hold still," she ordered, sucking her teeth at the full sight of his angry wound. "This needs to be stitched. Meet me in the kitchen." She scrambled to fetch an emergency first-aid kit that she kept in the trunk of her car.

Brik sat on the couch to watch the news.

Jon grabbed a bottle of Scotch from his liquor cabinet and headed to the kitchen. In the bright lights, he could see that his thumb needed medical attention.

The cut was as vicious as the skin around it was red. He was not supposed to imbibe alcohol—he did not care at the moment. He needed something to dull the sights and sounds, swirling about his brain like noisy eddies of fire and water. He drank the whiskey until his throat burned and mind cleared.

Jon wasted no time removing his clothes. He gathered his soiled things, which sifted soot into little filthy piles on the white floor, and took them to the large garbage canister outside. He returned to his bottle of Celtic hooch sitting on the counter. He had forgotten his nakedness by the time Abby joined him. She took his wrist without comment and led him to the sink. She immediately got to work.

Jon offered her a drink.

She took a swig and returned the bottle, refusing to make eye contact. "Smoky toffee, smooth finish—a hot smack of fragrant honey somewhere in the middle," she said. "So, it was arson yes?"

"But who did it and why are the real quest—ouch—"

"Oops—not used to so much naked human skin," she said, stressing the word naked."Alrighty then—hold still and keep it together," she added, a directive more for herself than for Jon. "Almost done—no, dammit, don't move or the stitches will tear. Lemme see you turn it to the side—slowly, Jon. Now, the other side. I think we're done." She pivoted away from him, squaring her shoulders parallel to the sink as she put her kit together. Trying not to snicker, she said, "Stitches should dissolve in a few days. It's not infected, but you should go to a minute clinic tomorrow."

"Why? Do you think I need a tetanus shot or something?"

"Or something," she said, adding, "like a robe—that kind of something."

"Dr. Flowers, are you blushing?"

"No, Mr. Christakos—I'm a professional."

Jon kissed her nose. "Thanks, Dr. Flowers."

She blushed as she took his non-bandaged hand. "You're welcome, Mr. Christakos."

They returned to the living room. Brik was too involved with the talking heads. And they were not revealing anything new about the fire. Jon offered the handyman the bottle. "Here, brah."

Brik accepted it. "You were there when it happened, so you have a *third* leg up on the reporters—*Hck*—tic-tac-toe. For the love of God, will you PLEASE cover yourself? There's a bathrobe on the recliner for you," Brik said, pointing to the chair, eyes fixed to the flat screen on the wall, face bright red. "You might want to take a shower soon—you smell like barbeque and feet."

Abby snickered. "You are naked and you do smell like barbeque, Jon"

Brik snapped his fingers. "This was arson—I bet this was arson!"

Jon rolled his eyes.

For the first time in a very long while, he did not feel so alone. Casually gliding over to the recliner, he donned the white terry cloth robe and returned to the side of the still-giggling veterinarian upon whom he was crushing. "Yes, Brik," he said, taking Abby's hand. "It was arson."

"Who would do this—why? I don't understand."

Jon had a good idea as to why it happened and who did it. It was retaliation for Nico's decision to help him, to come forth as a witness and discredit a damaging accusation as false.

And if Chucky had done the same thing, then he was facing his own punishment from Spiros Zervos.

*

CHAPTER 06

Cancer Is a Water Sign

"Sex and beauty are inseparable, like life and consciousness."
~ D. H. Lawrence

The night exploded as Jon stood on the porch with Minnie in his arms. Watching fireworks light up the bayou, waiting for Nico to stop by on his way to the airport to say goodbye, wondering whether Neal would arrest him, trying to remember to tell Brik about the rusted mail bin beside the front door.

BOOM! KkkkrrraaaAAAACCCKKKK!

The dog howled in response.

"Easy, girl," Jon whispered, stroking her head as he sang about how Minnie was brighter than the 'moon, moon, moon'.

He was hungry for chicken tikka masala.

Yesterday, before he and his wife headed to the airport, Raj Patel dropped off two large care packages. The box filled with Sita's amazing food, all frozen into perfectly portioned little meals, filled the freezer. The gutted second box lay on the porch swing, its innards scattered over the curved seat—months of supplements he was to start taking tomorrow. An enclosed letter listed explicit instructions to follow—the NO protocol would be in effect then.

Pop-pop-pop-pop!

No alcohol, no processed food, no sugar, no breads, no gluten, no fruits—NO FUN.

At least the 'no alcohol' rule did not kick in until tomorrow.

There was no guarantee this diet would buy him time or keep the disease at bay. But cancer fed on sugar like Augustus Gloop, so Jon was happy to oblige—starting tomorrow. Besides, he was still a free man (so far, so good). It was his birthday (yes, he was born on the fourth of July). And he wanted to enjoy himself (preferably with people, although his dog was fine company in a pinch).

Indeed, it seemed that Alicia Safford had not been taken in for questioning. Like everyone else in Tarpon Springs, she knew what had happened to Nico Cocoris. The images of those fires had the power to influence the hearts and minds of fearful folk. And yet, to her credit, she did not volunteer herself to offer testimony.

As for Chucky, the only true eyewitness, the young man had not said anything either (according to Neal Peruski, who was not directly involved and was getting his information piecemeal).

K-k-k-k-k-KRAAAACKKKkkkk-k-k-k! Boom!

Jon laughed. Watching fireworks alone was pathetic He did not mind solitude, but he wanted company tonight. Misty cancelled her self-invite after Eric was admitted to All Children's Hospital. Brik declined an invitation because he said he had plans for the night.

BOOM! Boom! Pop!

Jon turned to go inside. "Minnie, remind me to tell Brik about this mail bin," he said to the disinterested Pomeranian as he studied the rusty metal letter catcher. He had fished a stack of old letters beneath the porch earlier that day, and he had been meaning to tell the handyman to add it to his list—so far, nothing important slipped through the opening.

Boom! Boom! Boom!

"Moon, moon, moon," Jon sang softly as Minnie panted with excitement. She barked and howled again. It was amusing to see the dog's reactions to the explosions. She wasn't terrified and cowering under the swing. In fact, the tiny dog was excited, and kept contributing her own patriotic barks in salute of each baby rocket's red glare and bottle bomb's in-the-air bursting. Sudden screams of whizzing fireworks prompted Jon to start his off-key rendition of 'America, the Beautiful'.

FFFffwwwweeeeeeee-pop! Boom! BOOM! Pop!

One of the neighbors across the bayou had been playing the popular Katy Perry tune on repeat for the past two hours. Jon belted out his off-key version of 'America, the Beautiful' as the finale of explosions and brilliant colors rained sparks from the sky.

Minnie was not impressed.

She squirmed in his hands, growling until he spat the last line. He put her on the lawn, where she circled for a spot and peed, returning IMMEDIATLEY when a loud boom thundered overhead.

Jon rocked her until her trembling stopped.

Silence filled the air. People who had gathered nearby began to applaud before making their way back to their homes. Families from the next street over continued with their own fireworks display in the middle of the street. Adults drank beer and chattered in a circle of tattered lawn chairs. Older kids sent up shrieking rockets with loud pops. Younger kids twirled sparklers and tossed snap crackers.

Pop! K-k-k-k-k-KRAAAACKKKkkk-k-k-k!

Jon went back in the house. He replenished Minnie's water bowl and took a quick shower. After he dressed and brushed his teeth, he wandered around the house feeling sorry for himself.

Ding-dong! Ding-de-DING-dong!

Jon jumped at the sound. After a night of muffled thumps, booms, whizzes, pops, and fizzes, the sudden peal of a ringing doorbell startled him. His first thought was that Neal was there to take him into custody. A peek through the window curtains in his study told him otherwise—no flashing lights, no media, no angry mob, no protesters, no stalkers—*perhaps Brik's plans fell through,* he thought.

Jon opened the door.

To his surprise, someone else was standing on his porch.

The unexpected visitor had a bottle of wine in each hand. "I brought red AND white—hope you don't mind me inviting myself over," she said, brushing past him into the hall. "After the night you flaunted your smoky naked self, I decided that you were an informal kind of guy. I still can't believe you live in one of these monsters."

"Dr. Flowers, welcome—come in and make yourself at home."

"Thank you, Mr. Christakos," she said. "But be careful what you wish for." Click-clicking footpads made her turn and crouch. With fuzzy Muppet head cocked sideways in curiosity, Minnie panted with joy as the good doctor handed the two bottles to Jon before sitting on the terra cotta tiles. "Make yourself useful, Mr. Christakos, and use big glasses—don't you dare skimp," she ordered. "I'll have the white with ice cubes, please." Abby gently examined the dog after a few belly rubs. "Good as new."

Jon returned with two large plastic tumblers, each one filled to the top with wine. "I didn't have glasses big enough," he said playfully. "This Sponge Bob cup is yours—iced white wine."

Abby studied her cup. "Sponge Bob? Really?"

Jon raised his Ghostbusters cup. "We're classy in this house," he said. "I have toys around here too—a box in the den, one upstairs. Eric used to come over and play sometimes. I wanted to make sure he had things that made him happy."

"Then here's to Eric."

"To Eric," Jon toasted, changing the subject. "C'mon, Dr. Flowers—lemme give you a tour of the best house ever built on the Golden Crescent. The living room is just a larger version of my study—and those stairs will take you all the way up to the widow's walk. How about we just go up to the second floor for now and end the tour there."

"What's on the third floor?"

"Oh, just a loft and guest rooms," he replied. "My bedroom."

"Fine, then we'll finish on the third floor later tonight, Mr. Christakos."

Jon usually relaxed whenever he talked about his home.

His guest made that difficult now. Still, he managed to continue without stumbling or stammering too much.

Three of the four knotted pine walls were filled with photographs and bookshelves. Hanging on the entire fourth wall, from floor to ceiling, was an oil painting of a swimming woman, her shiny mermaid's tail hooked upward and fanned outward. Abby stared at the painting.

"Her smile's my favorite part," she finally said, toasting her host. "Cheers to you, Mr. Christakos."

"Cheers, Dr. Flowers."

"I'd apologize for showing up without an invite, but your opinion is moot," she said, moving toward the large colorful canvas. "So, start with this painting—I'm mesmerized. Who's the woman?"

"My mother."

Abby Flowers was taken aback. "Oh, and who painted it?"

"I did," Jon replied. "She's in most of the photos you'll see too."

She looked into her cup for a long moment. "You're unbelievably good, Jon."

He shrugged. "Evelyn says that I've captured her spirit. I wouldn't know."

"Evelyn knew her?"

Jon smiled. "Yeah, they were both Weeki Watchee Mermaids. Best friends until my mother fell in love with my father and Evie fell in love with George. Evelyn preferred belly dancing to water dancing anyway." He touched the bright dimpled face of his mermaid mother. "She lost her parents too. Aunt Bessie and Uncle Dmitri raised her in this house too," Jon said, looking at his cup and quietly adding, "I don't know why I just told you that."

"Why?"

"I've never told anyone that my mother was orphaned," he said. "Anyway, Aunt Bessie said that my mother swam like a fish, that she belonged to the water. I've never painted her outside of it."

"Your mother was beautiful, Jon—and she was famous, I hear."

Jon chuckled.

"My father was responsible for that. He took hundreds of thousands of photographs of her, including the ones in this house." He guided Abby to the second floor. "Evie refuses to talk about my father—even now. I suppose she'd talk about my mother if I asked about her. I never do. As far as I'm concerned, Evelyn Maria Kouskoutis is my real mother."

Abby nodded. "Do you know anything about your birth parents?"

"There's some Super 8 footage I've seen—a couple of reels that Evie once showed me years ago. All I know is that my mother wanted to be a mermaid all her life. I know my father adored her and wanted to make her dream come true—so he did."

"Is it true they both drowned a week after you were born?"

Jon nodded. "Which is why I visit Weeki Wachee Springs each year on the anniversary. The older mermaids tell stories about how my father loved my mother so much that he had to share her with the whole world—and when the whole world fell in love with her, she asked him to make her next dream come true, something she wanted more than anything else."

"She wanted a child." Abby took a sip from her cup. "How did he make her famous?"

Jon lowered his voice. "My father's methods were more about things happening in back rooms. He was smart, fearless, wealthy, and part of the mafia, from Tarpon Springs up to Weeki Watchee."

"Ooh, intrigue—are you kidding me?"

"I have no proof. The evidence I do have is circumstantial. But what my father did for Weeki Watchee Springs was akin to what Bugsy did for Vegas. A much smaller scale. He twisted arms, pulled strings, broke legs, greased palms until—BOOM—World Famous Weeki Wachee Springs," he said, sweeping his arm. "Let me direct your attention to my Tarpon Springs wing."

The second floor was dedicated to the history of the town. The way it was arranged made Abby feel as if these regional events were inextricably linked to the world at large.

And so, as Jon led Abby down the long hallway, speaking of history, geography, and culture, she slipped her hand into his.

He liked it as much as she did.

"This guy, Newt Perry," Jon explained, "he founded Weeki Wachee in the late 1940s. My father invested heavily for a decade until, by the time Kennedy was president, Weeki Wachee was THE destination. See? Here he is with Elvis. Half of the Rat Pack. HA! This is my favorite. Here he is smoking a cigarette with Mr. Walt Disney. I got one of my father and Don Knotts downstairs."

Abby slapped Jon's arm. "Are you kidding me? *The Incredible Mr. Limpet, The Ghost and Mr. Chicken, Hot Lead and Cold Feet*—he's Barney Fife, for crying out loud." Passing newspaper clippings, maps and schedules, and more photos, she stopped at a clipping from *The Salt Lake Herald*. "I know these names. Safford, Disston, Cocoris—wait, Nico?"

"Cocoris is Tarpon's First Greek Family," Jon said, guiding her to other clippings and photographs. "Nico's father died at sea during World War II—here he is before he left for the Mediterranean. Here's Nico at the funeral with Uncle Dmitri. Anyway, his grandfather was so overcome with grief that he piloted a boat alone beyond Anclote Key, to the really deep water. He removed his clothes, tied himself to the anchor, and jumped into the sea."

"That's tragic, Jon."

"Tragic depends on your point of view. What Cocoris did to honor the death of his son honored rituals practiced by divers in the Aegean Sea. It paid homage to the Epiphany festival, when the Greek boys dive into Spring Bayou for the cross. Most of the founding families are shells now—empty. Babs Cheyney spawned demons that tortured poor Greeks for years until a storm sank the family yacht—no survivors. The Safford clan all but vanished after Bentley's suicide 20 or so years ago. Beverly Disston Pink is one the good ones—crazy as a bed bug. She'd jump naked in the sea with a tiger shark."

Abby sighed. "When I was girl, I wanted to be a pro tennis star like Beverly Disston Pink," she said, touching a frame photo of Beverly on a clay court. "I regret to say I read Adam Disston's column."

"Yeah, join the club," Jon replied. "Complicated bunch of weirdoes, closer in spirit to Tarpon's Greek families. Here's Nico as a young man with my uncle. Here's Nico's wife, who had a stroke and drowned in their bathtub a few years ago."

Abby gasped. "The statue at the Sponge Docks. Oh, my God—I

can't believe I didn't see that it's Nico Cocoris—this picture, the statue. His face hasn't changed. Oh, these Greek men make me tingle."

Jon laughed. "Nico's one of the great ones. Uncle Dmitri was too."

"So, the house and store you inherited?"

"Small fortune too, which the house and store have since depleted."

"Did they really drown on the anniversary you lost your parents?"

Jon nodded. "You'd think I made it up to get attention, the way people around here have talked about me over the years. I've never been interested in keeping up with all the wealthier Joneses around the bayou. Most of them conduct their affairs as if they're acting on God's behalf, as if the Golden Crescent is the Holy Land and they are the Chosen People. Here's my wall of shame, Dr. Flowers." Jon pointed to photos from glitzy charity auctions and other over-the-top fundraisers. "I do have to play their game at times—if it means funneling money to places that need it, I'd eat a panda cub on live TV."

"You do look good in a tux, Mr. Christakos. Is this how you met Felicity Noel, at one of these charity auction galas? How did you meet her? She's so exotic."

Jon shrugged. "She was a bartender named Kendra Jackson from Sarasota—oh, you really bought that she was from Barbados? Spoiler alert. She was a professional actor who bartended fundraisers."

"You shut your face—it's all an act?"

"Yes, and here's the kicker—Adam Disston is responsible for her rise to stardom. I sent him a picture and he did the rest. Don't trust everything you read on the Interwebs."

"Shut-up—Adam Disston? The man who smears you twice a month?"

"A consummate marketing mastermind," Jon said. "He takes pride in being the perennial bastard turd in everyone's Tiffany punchbowl. Kendra Jackson's a supermodel because of Adam."

"Wrong, Jon." She looked at him. "What? You're wrong. Adam Disston may have had the money and connections, but you discovered her. You provided the spark. You sell yourself too short—and too much, I'd bet. Worst trait I've seen so far."

"Alright, Dr. Flowers—what's your worst trait?"

"That's easy, Mr. Christakos—I have a nasty habit of running away when things get rough," she said. "I know. It's horrible. But ever since Dad died, I cut my losses earlier than I should." She held up her left hand. "Otherwise, this would be a real wedding ring."

Jon smiled. "Then why did you pick Tarpon Springs?"

"I didn't—Tarpon picked me," she said with a playful smile. "I'm a great surgeon. I'm even better at logistics. I fix animal hospitals in danger of being closed. The one here has me stumped. I've never seen such bureaucratic tentacles in a facility this size. I like puzzles. I'm working with a woman at animal control who has her stuff together better than anyone I've ever had to do this kind of work with."

"Kiki Kontodiakos," Jon said. "She's an old friend—we go way back."

Abby looked in her cup. "Why are you still in Tarpon? You're bigger than this place."

"Ah, that's where you are wrong, Dr. Flowers."

"And why is that, Mr. Christakos?"

Here were the facts. Tarpon Springs was Epiphany City, the Venice of the South, the Sponge Capital of the World, a Greek jewel beset in the crown of Florida's Gulf Coast, and the only home Jon ever knew. He grew up in this house, which was a stone's throw from the Sponge Docks and less than a block from the spire of St. Nicholas Church, standing beyond the trees like a leg of Colossus. He went to school here. He went to church here. He learned to boat and fish in its waters—the Anclote River, the Gulf of Mexico, the estuaries, bayous, and marshes. His life began in Tarpon. And one day, in the plot beside his aunt and uncle, and his mother and father beside them, he will be laid to rest in Tarpon.

In six months, if things don't work out.

Jon shifted his feet. "Sorry, uh—I do that more often then I'd like," he explained. "Next time I check out, just hit me. How about a refill and something to eat?"

"Lead on, Birthday Boy."

They ended the tour in the kitchen. Jon nervously made a meager meal of cold turkey sandwiches and a half-eaten bag of kettle chips. They shared the second bottle of wine as they sat at the corner breakfast dinette, Minnie snoring loudly at their feet.

"Your father took a lot of photographs," Abby said.

"Is there a question in there?"

"Maybe." She wiped her mouth. "Do you really believe they drowned? I'm sorry if—"

Jon shook his head to reassure her. "I will never be able to answer that one—I've tried for years," he said. "I've learned to accept certain mysteries about my life. I was the one who found my aunt and uncle buried under their boat at the bottom of the bayou. Wondering whether my parents drowned too somehow didn't matter anymore—if something bad can happen, then it will happen to me."

"Murphy's Law," Abby whispered. "And I think that's tragic."

He fidgeted with the tablecloth. "Because it's true?"

She took his hand. "Because you're wrong and don't know it," Abby said gently. "If what's tragic depends on your perception, then it's tragic that you haven't changed yours."

"If something good can happen, then it will happen to me."

Abby smiled. "Yeah, to you—I think you're long overdue for something good. Or several something goods." When her phone buzzed, she looked at the screen and slipped the phone back into her purse. "It's time," she said, getting up and leading him out through the kitchen door to the lanai.

"Time for what?" he asked. "I can't see."

It was too dark to see anything. But then someone flipped a switch.

Bright lights flooded the porch and patio, extending across the lawn to the back fence. Hanging from branches and posts were ropes of soft Edison bulbs crisscrossing overhead in a web of artfully arranged draping rows. At the bottom of the stone stairs in conical party hats were Neal Peruski, Brik Buckman, and Nico Cocoris. Minnie barked playfully as the trio of men clapped and blew horns.

Neal gave Jon a warm hug. "Just here to say happy birthday before

I head back to the station," he said. "Next time you're at Silverking, the beer's on me."

"Why is that—beer's never on you."

"I gotta feeling it will be," he said, raising his eyebrows. "Y'all have a nice night."

What the hell was THAT about?

"Mr. Cocoris," Abby said when Officer Peruski left, "would you mind helping me?"

Nico's face split with a blazing smile as he offered her his arm. When they had gone, a pair of bottle rockets zoomed overhead. Minnie barked at the noisy sky as she followed them.

Brik took Jon by the elbow to show him around the newly refurbished backyard. All the damage from the grasshopper invasion was gone.

The area was perfectly manicured and pristine, but with a Frederick Olmstead flair that made it feel wild around the edges. A pool beneath its waterfall. Stones of all sizes surrounding it. Fragrant grasses, marble benches, a gravel path strewn with mushroom shaped lights. A long pergola with open lattice dripping with bougainvillea, confederate jasmine, and heart-shaped philodendron.

The air was sweetly perfumed (despite the lingering smoke). Rows of fresh herbs, key lime trees, olive trees, and bushes of camellia, purple hydrangea, and wild rose.

The men returned to the patio.

Abby was there to take the birthday boy off the arm of the handyman. She made a production of it being her turn to escort Jon around the yard. She took him for an intimate little birthday stroll, circling the lawn in slow silence. The sky did grumble a time or two. And there were still pops and whizzes of fireworks in the distance.

"Did you enjoy your surprise?"

Jon grinned. "I did—thanks for crashing my sad birthday."

Abby rolled her eyes.

"I'm beginning to wonder if you'll ever kiss m—"

And so, Jon Christakos did exactly that—he kissed her as if he had never before kissed a woman.

Well, that was how he did it in his mind.

Abby's mind, on the other hand, went totally blank when he pressed his mouth to hers. That the sky rumbled as he did it made the impression beyond indelible—it was life-changing.

"Wow, Mr. Christakos," she said, letting go of his hand to walk backward to the lanai. "Nico's waiting for you out on the front porch," she said. "And I'll be waiting for you in your bedroom—you did promise that we'd finish the tour on the third floor."

Grinning as he watched her go, Jon opened the backyard gate and walked around the side of the house. It started to rain as he climbed the front stoop. Nico was leaning against a column smoking a cigar and gazing at the bayou. "Dr. Abigail Flowers," he said. "She's the kind of woman a man ought to wake up to at least once in his life. Here, open your hand." He dropped a set of keys into Jon's palm. "You keep shut the mouth. I don't need a car anymore."

"Nico, your El Camino's a gorgeous automobile, but I can't—"

"Happy birthday, Jonny," he said. "I'd offer you a cigar but—"

"I'll throw up and ruin your good time," Jon said. "Thanks, Nico."

Every once in a while, a rat-tat-tatting firecracker broke through the white noise of the rain. Nico put his arm around Jon's shoulder.

"We're not so different—we both know life and death, water and fire. Water takes the ones we love and leaves us waiting for fire's judgment." He waved through a cloud of smoke. "Fire has baptized me, so I go to Greece, as I came to America, with ten dollars and the clothes on my back. Fire will baptize you too, Jonny—God will send you a sign."

A taxi pulled into the driveway, the headlights blinding them.

Nico embraced Jon and kissed his cheek. "The fire will know your heart is Greek before it consumes you, Jonny—the fire will baptize you. You will become a new man then, I think."

"I'm not Greek by blood—you know that."

Nico squared himself directly in front of Jon. "What does blood matter without the heart? It's just red salt water, yes? THAT is Greek, the strong heart pumping that blood, beating in here." He pressed a leathery hand to Jon's chest. "You were baptized at St. Nicholas—I was there to see it. You are Greek. Your heart is Greek. Your name, Jon Christakos, is Greek. God has marked you three times—in your soul, your heart, and your name, you are His servant. Think on what you must do to honor His gifts."

Jon did not know what to say. His eyes burned.

Nico fixed him with his own tearful gaze. "There's no shame in weeping," he told him. "It happens when the fires of a man's heart burns his soul—his tears must put out those fires. You should ask this woman to marry you, Jonny."

"What woman? Abby Flowers?"

Nico laughed. "Funny weather tonight—it's a sign, you know."

"Yeah, my sign. I'm a Cancer."

"A water sign—and it's raining," Nico said, tossing his head toward the house. "Your lady is a fire sign, Jonny. Like your Greek heart, eh? She is Leo." Nico pounded his chest. "A lion, like me."

"And she is the sign that God sent to me?"

Nico Cocoris smiled that brilliant smile of his as he climbed into the cab. Jon watched his friend go. It rained harder as the taxi drove away. The fire burning his heart was too hot to be quenched by tears.

Cancer is a water sign.

The thought of Nico being gone from Tarpon Springs bothered him as he headed back to the house. That he would never see the old man again was likely—but who can see the future, as Nico might say.

I didn't know Leo is a sign of fire.

*

First floor.

Soaking wet and unbearably sad, Jon Christakos sloshed upstairs to tell a most desirable woman that he had a headache. It was not a lie—his head was throbbing with pain.

Second floor.

Jon heard music from the floor above. He smelled sandalwood, maybe vanilla—a scented candle. He climbed the final stretch of stairs—a narrower case that seemed to squeeze him. Now he was not thinking about anything but how nervous and anxious he felt.

Third floor.

Jon felt like an idiot, a soaked-to-the-bone fool. His room was only a few feet ahead. The door was open. It cast a warm glow across the floor in the hall—the only light in the passageway. Maybe his headache was not so painful. Jon stepped inside his bedroom and dripped on the floor.

Abby laughed when she saw him. There were candles lit in a few strategic places—nightstand, corner dresser, wardrobe, which was open. An empty hanger hung on the cabinet knob. "I hope you don't mind," she said, "but I borrowed one of your shirts."

"You did," Jon said, wiping his face. "You should borrow more often."

Abby sized him up and shook her head, making a quick exit and return—with two bath towels. To Jon's surprise, and his own for not protesting, she undressed him. Piling his wet clothes onto one towel in the hallway, she patted his body dry with the other towel. She tousled his wet hair and ordered him to get into bed and lie on his back.

Jon was not ashamed of his naked body—well, not in a manner that most men were ashamed. His shame stemmed from the knowledge of what his body had been versus what it was turning into. That it was diminishing, weakening, becoming less. Deterioration was somehow an unforgiveable sin.

Abby Flowers was, after all, vibrant, naturally lovely with piercing eyes. And not a petite, slight-framed woman—she was strong and intricately curved. The sight of her was blinding.

Jon tried to flip over onto his stomach—*she can look at my hairy backside.* Abby would have none of it. She rolled up the sleeves of her borrowed dress shirt and got to work. "I was a masseuse when I was an undergrad," she told him, pouring the contents of a tube she plucked from a bag at her feet. She rubbed the lotion into her palms, warming them.

"Close your eyes, Mr. Christakos," she ordered.

Jon tried to throw his arm across his face. He did not want her to see how frightened he was, how vulnerable and exposed he felt. How gaunt and ugly. How burdened with pain and exhaustion—there was no hiding the truth now. He knew the moment he felt her hands cradle his left leg, bending him gently at the knee to work his calf. Her electric touch prompted a sharp intake of air.

"Hush. You need this. It'll help with the pain."

"You know I'm sick then."

"I'm not stupid. I don't feel sorry for you," she said, adding, "And I'm not here because I pity you either—are we clear on that? Good. Normally I start with the hands. Yours are—"

"Fat Mickey Mouse gloves," Jon said with a chuckle.

Abby smiled.

She continued to knead the thin stretched muscles of his legs. "No more talking," she whispered. "I want you to inhale and exhale." She switched between one and the other, from calf to hamstring to quad, front to back, front to back—one leg, and then the other leg. She pressed into him despite his non-verbal protests and clenching. Her fingers kept moving upward—she ignored his attempt to move. She poured herself into each motion until he finally relaxed.

"When I touch your hands, you may have a reaction."

As soon as her fingers and knuckles rolled inside his palms, Jon started laughing. It was a silly sort of guttural sound that bubbled up from some deep well inside his hollowed-out spleen. Laughter soon became tears of joy—tears of relief and release.

"See? I told you," Abby said, her voice breaking.

"Told me what, Dr. Flowers?"

"That you're in good hands, Mr. Christakos."

*

CHAPTER 07

The Body on the Trail

"I will not destroy myself in order to find a secret behind the ruins."
~ Hermann Hesse

S ounds of lawnmowers and weed whackers stirred Jon from his sound
slumber. With a sleepy smile, he opened his eyes. The other side of
the bed had a new occupant. Minnie yawned and stretched when the
man's large hand scratched her belly. On the pillow was a note that read,
*'Call me when you have another headache. I wasn't lying to you about my hands.
P. S. Your shirt's on the chair.'*

Instead of a signature, she had scribbled her initials—in the shape of
a lion's head and mane, twisted like upward flames.

Jon thought nothing of it—she was a vet, after all. He dragged himself to the corner and picked up the folded dress shirt. He brought it up to
his face and breathed deeply.

The scent of her perfume was intoxicating.

His heart began to pound, as the events of last evening exploded into
his mind. Indeed, she was not lying about her skill—his headache was
gone too. He decided to go for a long walk this morning.

After he showered and dressed, he fed the dog and went outside. Brik
and his crew were bagging up dead leaves, brush, grass clippings, and
sawdust. Two oak trees and a Queen palm had termites, so they came
down earlier. Chainsaws were grinding what was left. Jon patted the El
Camino and headed to the Sponge Docks through the Greek Village.

He had no interest in opening the store. He did not want to spend his day in the studio either. Brik installed a new glass for the display window, which gleamed as Jon strolled up to it. He noted how skinny he looked in the reflection—not quite Steve Jobs skinny, but not quite himself.

Jon felt too good to be cooped up inside all day. Nonetheless, he did need some things before he went out on his walk.

He unlocked the door.

The bell jingled as he went inside. He grabbed his backpack from behind the counter and loaded it with bottles of water from the mini-fridge. He slathered sunscreen on his skin and went back outside.

Locking the door, he jogged toward the water, crossing the boulevard and saluting Nico's statue as he hopped up to the sidewalk. There, that cadre of older men drinking coffee and arguing about something or other, sitting on the patio deck of Dimitri's on the Water.

Draco Bilirakis, Luke Dukakis, and Vasile Faklis bombarded him with questions. A server brought his specially prepared breakfast, which went into Jon's backpack.

The three men refused to let him off the hook, even after Jon filled them in about Evelyn and her sister. He made a quick exit before they started lobbing questions about Felicity Noel. He deflected them with lots of hand waving and good-natured raspberries until he was well out of view. Still, he could hear them carrying on until he was across the highway nearing his destination.

Here were the facts. The Pinellas Trail stretched from Tarpon Springs all the way down to St. Petersburg. Back in the 1980s, CXS Transportation acquired the Seaboard Air and Atlantic Coastal railroad lines. The State of Florida procured all the trackage left behind and then converted the corridor into a robust 40-mile path for joggers, hikers, cyclists, skaters, the walking dead—basically anyone with the desire to move from one place to another without the trappings of air pollution and rush-hour traffic. The strip of asphalt that cut through downtown Tarpon Springs was a narrow median dividing Safford Avenue into a pair of parallel one-way roads on either side of it.

Jon passed the Suncoast Primate Sanctuary. He waved to a shrieking chimp and a surly orangutan in the cage next door. A quarter of a mile farther south, at Wall Springs, he sat under a pavilion overlooking the freshwater spring there to replenish his fluids and cool down.

The heat had roughed him up today.

He watched the swirling eddies of cold water feed the nearby estuary. There were plenty of gorgeous fish to observe. And ducks nesting in the felled marsh grasses on the banks.

He thought about his night with Abby Flowers, of course.

Thoughts of her hypnotized him—he was making his way back up the Trail when he finally stepped out of his daydream.

Well, he also had the screaming monkeys to thank for that.

Jon stopped in the middle of the trail to watch them—*why are you guys so worked up?*

Up ahead in the grassy shoulder close to the perimeter fence was a man face down behind the bench there. Most of his prostrate body was tucked beneath the seat. He slowly moved toward the wall of links. He recognized the clothes—corduroy pants, a flannel long sleeve, a gray T-shirt, a Bo Jangles-shoe on one foot (the other was bare).

Jon reached down to check for a pulse. It was faint but steady—Mr. Willie, how the hell did you get out again? He managed to revive the man and get him walking. The man reeked of booze, sour sweat, feces, and piss, a fetid stink that punched the face with brass knuckles.

Willie Dancer Jackson used to be a teetering fixture on this part of the Pinellas Trail. As if he were a living piece, a section always in perpetual motion as it shook from one end of town to the other.

Before he found a place in a group home, Mr. Willie drank enough ripple to sink a sponge boat.

Jon threw up his breakfast—twice.

But he managed to get him to the Island Rock Bar and Grill. He situated the man on the picnic table beside the smoker and let himself in through the back door.

"Seamus! It's Jon Christakos!"

The proprietor of the bar was a tall, dark muscular man, a sweet-natured soul who always smiled. The moment he saw Jon, he clapped his hands and opened his arms.

"Jon-Jon—you need to put some meat on them bones."

He pointed up. "Talk with Him—it's good to see you, Seamus."

"You too—alright, let's see your catch of the day. Where was he?"

"Suncoast Primate Sanctuary," Jon explained.

Together they dragged Willie Dancer inside the hall and past the bar to a broom closet behind the small office. The tiny room had a sink and a concrete floor with a drain.

As they had done before, they stripped him and held him under a stream of water. They scrubbed him top to bottom, crevice to crack. They dried him off and dressed him in a spare set of clothing—the soiled clothes were chucked. They took him to the bar and propped him upright in a stool with a high back.

Willie Dancer looked fearful and confused. His rheumy eyes were glassy and rust-rimmed, and they darted back and forth. Then, when he finally recognized the faces smiling at him, he laughed with joy.

Seamus patted his shoulder. "How about some red beans and rice? Maybe a sip of beer?"

A touch of lucidity took hold of Willie Dancer.

Although his hands shook in violent protest, he spoke with a clear voice. "How you two fine young men doing?"

Seamus looked at Jon.

"Adam's new article is up the computer screen." Taking the hint, Jon ducked into the back room and sat at the desk.

*

GULF COAST LIBERTINE
ADAM DISSTON

Ode to the Suckers Born Every Minute

I have a confession to make: I'm not a decent guy. I'm a soulless SOB up to no damn good. And why? Because I use people. And by **PEOPLE**, of course, I mean you bold and beautiful kids.

Others who don't read this column can't possibly understand the dynamics of group psychology or the effect of critical mass. They don't have degrees in economics, philosophy, communication, politics, or marketing—I do.

For your benefit as well as mine, I build things up, knock 'em down, and build 'em back up again. In our modern world of gadgets, social media, interconnectivity, and hyperpopulism, what's a little exploitation between friends?

A political proxy war between the haves and have-nots is about to make the American Revolution look like a bad night at the frat house—who's going to get you through it?

Real people want someone to guide them—that someone is me, kids. Daily gossip and celebrity melodrama have produced offspring in this glorious Information Age—the future is now.

I provide the salve for you hard-working folk, a tonic for the rattled nerves inflicted upon you by modern society. It's obvious you kids have had it up to here with life. Look at our fast food political system. On the right is McDonald Trump. On the left is Colonel Bernie Sanders.

Let freedom ring, yo!

Earlier, I called myself out for being soulless—hell, I've insulted all of you by praising you. But I think you'll agree with me when I say that I am an honest broker.

I deserve the millions of fans reading my column. I deserve all of you as surely as you deserve me. Until next time, kids—y'all make good choices.

*

Jon thought it a peculiar article for Adam—this was filler.

What is he up to?

He was lost in thought when Seamus walked into the room and leaned against the door shaking his head. "Old man's gonna lose his son if he doesn't do what he's told," he said with a heavy sigh. "An orderly accidentally let him out—it's my fault for not visiting enough."

"What are you gonna do?"

"Take him back and pay the fine. Help me get the old goat."

Jon followed Seamus into the bar. "Spend any time with your sister when she was here?"

Seamus laughed. "Kendra Jackson is Felicity Noel now. She's playing up her Barbados Grace Jones act, trying to forget her father's a drunk. Trying to pretend he's not shucking and jiving on the Trail or face down at the monkey house. She's done with the man—I'm close too."

They got Willie Dancer into the back of the old sedan Seamus had hijacked from his alcoholic father. Jon hopped out at Silverking. He stood on the curb and watched the car roll east—the group home was at the far end near the police station.

Jon turned to go into the brewery. A young woman with curly blonde hair was standing in the garage looking at him. She was eighteen, maybe nineteen. He was about to introduce himself when the blip of a police siren goosed him. He jumped out of his skin.

Neal Peruski jumped out of his cruiser. "I told you," he said. "I'm buying you a beer, buddy. You can have a beer, right?"

"A sip, sure. What's the occasion?"

"You, rey—you are not going to jail. The charges are dropped. The case is dead—nothing to report or investigate."

"I don't understand. What happened?"

Neal laughed. "Well, aside from the fact that the boys and I have your back. No one wanted to see you in trouble. No witnesses came forth. And let's just say that you owe Chuck Parker big time."

*

CHAPTER 08

Mermaids and Orphans

"What you leave behind is not what is engraved on stone monuments,
but what is woven into the lives of others."
~ *Pericles*

July 13

Jonny, next time, please send photos of Brik with no shirt. And
please know that I'm thinking about you today. ~ Evelyn

*

Here were the facts. Weeki Wachee Springs was a plastic-wrapped relic born from a simpler era. A large white sign shouted WEL-COME in bold red letters, a retro roadside beacon for those in search of the park's fabled mermaids. From parking lot to ticket center, along palm tree-lined walkways, on pathways over streams and pools, around sandy beaches packed with sunbathers, beside stony grottos draped in water-falls—visitors moved backward in time. This natural wonder of the Gulf Coast was a prepackaged paradise for the TV dinner crowd, a manicured haven of family fun standing at the intersection of 1950s Disneyland and a reality television show. Beyond the blue curtain, beyond the glass sep-arating air from spring, there was an underwater fantasy world carved from limestone. An explosion of bubbles revealing turtles, fish, manatees, and otters—and mermaids bedazzled with smiles as they performed their ballet. Not quite the Rat Pack swinging show from its heyday, but swanky and daddio-cool all the same.

Today most of them were sitting atop boulders flipping multihued Lycra fishtails and posing for photos with fans near the visitor's center.

As soon as he saw them and they saw him, Jon was running over to hug each of them. Abby remained where she was. She was content to watch those shiny women smother him with so much affection, as if they all were his mothers. *Dear God*, Abby thought, *this is what he must've looked like as a little boy.*

Well, whether that was true or not, it was a nice image. Unable to control her emotions, Abby marveled at the sparkly ladies perched upon those boulders. Waving to boys and girls of all ages. Glimmering like fish-shaped female bottles of champagne. Their contagious effervescence was a new physics of bliss, and Jon was the catalyst.

He was at the center of it all.

The man's light was blinding in this moment. And it made Abby's skin tingle with strange electrici-ty as she witnessed his brilliance. Here was a man becoming his best self in the midst of teeming chaos. And it was contagious to see whatever he was doing—whether it was the cha-risma that oozed from his pores or the shocks that registered on the faces surrounding him.

Jon Christakos was a rock star to these people. And not to just a handful—everyone near him was lighter in spirit, more open, quicker to laugh. He was a miracle worker.

Abby felt small, so she decided to stay put until he came back. She was fine with waiting. She had a lovely view of the park from her vantage point. She could see the Weeki Wachee River over there. Beyond the trees was the spot where Jon's parents had allegedly drowned.

Truth be told, Abby had not felt this nervous and insignificant in all her life. She was a Leo, for heaven's sake—she was not used to watching someone else get all the attention.

Abby Flowers, you are being so damned petty.

Feeling a caress at her elbow, she turned to see an older mermaid at her side. "Hello, dearie—I'm Melinda."

"I'm Abby."

"We saw you come in with our boy," Melinda said, pulling the younger woman over to a bench. "Sit with me a few moments—he'll be back after the crowd has had their way with the boy."

"Is it always like this?"

Melinda smiled. "It has been for fifteen years now. Everyone knows that Jonny buys every ticket for every guest on this date—the whole park is free admission all day."

"I didn't know that," Abby said, craning her neck to see where he was now.

"Jonny knows people enjoy the free admission, but he has no idea how much everyone looks forward to his visit here too. Not just his mother hen mermaids either. His mother would be so proud of the man he's become—although I doubt she would approve of the celebrity he's garnered. Not entirely his fault, but then, what else is an orphan supposed to do to get close to his famous parents? Hmm?"

Abby nodded. "I never thought of it that way," she said. "He's not so tragic you know."

Melinda patted Abby's arm. "Oh, I know that, dearie—I do. But you can't deny the enjoyment on that boy's face. It's only one day a year, so what harm is there?" A circus of people crowded around the man responsible for their free tickets. Spontaneous group singing, music, sudden pantomimes, impromptu line dancing—Jon was a lit match for this powder keg of gracious joy. Here was a magician ignorant of the feats of magic he performed—the affection he engendered spread like wildfire.

"Did you know his mother well?" Abby asked, wiping her eyes.

Melinda chuckled. "Not as well as I would've liked—but Jonny's got his mama's spirit. She sparkled whenever she was in the spring. He sparkles whenever he gives—you'll never meet a more generous human being, dearie. When Jonny puts his heart to the grindstone, he'll bleed himself dry in order to help someone. Did you know Jonny's mother could hold her breath for five minutes without needing to suck the air pipe? Breathed life into that water whenever she was dancing. Best mermaid ever, dearie—God's truth. And just look at her son."

Abby swallowed a lump. "He shimmers like a diamond."

"Yep, just like his mother."

"But what is it?" Abby asked. "How does he do it?"

Melinda shrugged. "Don't know, dearie, but we've adored him for it since we first saw him. Jonny is the son of a Weeki Wachee Mermaid. We love him as our own. You're a nice girl, Abby Flowers. You got moxie. I can tell. But you'll never belong to him unless you risk giving him all of you. And even so, there's no guarantee that he'll accept all of you. Regardless, you'll never be the same, dearie." Melinda sighed. "You're either the sun above him or the shadow behind him."

*

Cycadia Cemetery. The historic memorial grounds for most of the Greek families in Tarpon Springs—not exclusively, of course, but visitors would be hard-pressed to find a headstone with the last names of Cooper or Smith. Uncle Dmitri purchased a big plot when he first married Aunt Bessie, with plenty of room to spare.

Jon led Abby down the winding path past the mausoleums and around the retention ponds, their fountains gushing reclaimed city water and storm runoff 20 feet into the air.

There were two stops to make.

The first was the black polished granite slabs where George and Panos Kouskoutis rested. Jon wiped the dust from the top of each headstone. He put two white roses into the vase between them and joined Abby on the bench nearby.

"So, which one warned you about me?"

Abby touched her cheek. "You really have no idea what you do to people," she said. "Oblivious Jonny—that's what I'll call you from now on."

Jon laughed. "Ah, Melinda—she's thinks I broke her granddaughter's heart."

"Did you?"

He shrugged. "Not intentionally."

The moment of ensuing silence unfolded organically. It wasn't uncomfortable, but it was full. Today was an ugly anniversary—what else could be said about it? When Abby took his hand, he stiffened.

A moment or two later, she let him go.

He smiled when he saw the Circle K sign. The building used to be a Burger King. Panos and he would grab burgers whenever they came here. Jon opened the silver flask in the paper bag at his feet. He took a drink and offered it to Abby. She scrunched her face in disgust. He laughed and took another drink.

"Ouzo, drink of the gods."

"How did Panos and George die?" Abby asked quietly.

"George was fishing in the Anclote one afternoon. It was low tide. He moored his boat off this huge spoil island south of the Sponge Docks. Thought it would be fun to climb the tangle of mangrove roots and marsh grass. He jumped off the bow barefoot. Landed on top of the carcass of some dead marine animal buried in the sand there. The tips of broken bones pierced his feet. George died a week later from septic shock." Jon took another drink—Abby did too. "Panos was a cop. Neal Peruski's partner. They got this random domestic violence call—Jasmine Road, just behind us. About a mile down the road there's a trailer park. Anyway, the wife was on a meth bender. She had a semi-automatic. Shot her husband. Would've shot Neal if Panos hadn't pushed him out of the way." Jon took another drink—his eyes watered. "Panos took two bullets in his neck and one in the back of his head. Neal lived. Husband lived. Wife went to prison. Here lies my brave brother, whom I miss every damn day."

"Now I see why Neal cares about you so much."

Jon shrugged. "He thinks he owes me because of Panos did—the whole Tarpon Springs police department thinks the same thing. It's a good thing I'm not a psychopath."

"You don't like it when others care about you?"

"No, I don't want them to feel like they owe me."

Jon extended his hand. Abby took it.

The second stop was the Christakos family plot. She wiped the tomb-stones and arranged the roses (save the one that Jon had given to her). He took out an envelope from his pocket—a letter to his mother. The words he had written were private—unpacking his heart in public was something he did not do.

He propped the envelope against the stone and stepped back.

"Paul Jones isn't my father's real name," he said. "Evelyn says that his coffin isn't down there either. Not one with his body, anyway." He wiped his eyes. "I know this isn't the fun date you might have hoped it would be. Thanks for doing this, Dr. Flowers."

She sighed. "You're most welcome, Mr. Christakos."

*

July 14 - 5:53 a.m.

It's funny—I never thought I'd be sending you this kind of letter, Jon, let alone immediately after a heart-heavy day for you. But I'm not one to beat around the bush either. I suppose that's why I refused to put the salutation up at the top of my letter to tell you I need a break.

I didn't mean for this to happen—me liking you as much as I do. I told you I have a nasty habit of cutting and running early. I know it's what I'm doing now. Why? Because I'm scared of how I feel about you. I thought I could handle it and how I think you feel about me. The truth is, quite simply, I can't handle any of it. It's too much too soon.

I'm a rather selfish person. I don't think I am capable of giving you what you need. I don't know, maybe I am. But maybe if I knew more about what you're facing, I'd run anyway. I know I'm a terrible person, but I care too much about you.

After the day at Weeki Wachee and the night we spent together—it was a nice night too—I woke a little before 3 o'clock in
the morning. Your side of the bed was empty. Minnie was sleeping on her pillow in the corner. I went downstairs hoping that
you might be in the kitchen making a snack. I was hoping to rub
your neck and head to help you sleep.

You weren't in the kitchen either. You and Brik had warned me
this might happen. I was still surprised. Anyway, I went outside
and walked to the curb. I saw a silhouette on your dock. I crept
closer, hoping you would be the one there. And sure enough, you
were naked as the day you were born looking out over the water.

I quietly put a blanket around you and shepherded you back
to the house. The whole time I kept wondering what was going
through your mind. I'm not a jealous person. I've never been.
But when I got you back in bed, you called me 'Alicia' when you
thanked me. I wanted to rip your face off.

But then, in the smallest voice, you told me you loved me—"I
love you, Abby Flowers." It struck me, the honesty of it. But you
weren't awake. You weren't aware. So, I gathered my things, said
goodbye to Minnie, and came downstairs to write this letter.

It's nearly dawn now—the pale light is peeking through the
curtains. I keep thinking about what Melinda told me. I keep
hearing you calling me by another woman's name and telling me
you love me—and I keep wondering what's real. Maybe you will
tell me after we have some time apart. Time to think about this,
about us. I know I will—I hope you will too.

I'm sure we'll see each other around town. I'm so sorry for doing
this, Jon. But if this is meant to be, then it will be. ~ AEF (twisted into the flaming shape of a lion's head and mane)

*

That was more than a week ago. The studio still felt empty. The space felt barren, bereft of life and color. Abby's letter was burning a hole in his pocket—*this is your fault, Jonny-baby.*

Jon used that as motivation to sling paint around, as if the motion was punching a bag too. He debated whether to sketch a new series of black and white mermaids or do ink studies for a series of nightgown-wearing women floating in bodies of water.

He abandoned both options.

His head started hurting again. He vomited into the studio sink, almost passing out as he drank his fill from the faucet. He poured himself something to settle his stomach. He stretched himself flat across the cold floor and took deep breaths. He had not felt a sting like this in many years—*this effing hurts.*

The bell jingled-jingled.

Jon looked at the wall clock—2:30 p.m. Wishing he had not opened for the day—but what else was he going to do? He nonetheless wiped his face with a towel and headed into the store space.

Alicia Safford was waiting for him. "Hello, Jon."

"Hello, Alicia—what do you want?"

"Wow—nice customer service," she said, clearing her throat. "Just wanted to tell you I am, funny enough, your new landlord. All of Nico's commercial properties belong to my company."

Jon smiled. "Yeah, funny."

She looked at him sideways and continued with her cursory inspection, scribbling into a notebook. "I take it that your inventory records are current and easily accessible? Electronic and hard copy."

"Yes, sweet Jesus, Alicia Safford—why are you here? What do you want?"

She put away her pen and notebook. "My father wanted your family's house," she replied. "I honestly had a hard time not wanting to continue tilting at his windmill when I came back to town—I understand what it was that he wanted—it took me a while to pick through the brambles of his psychotic mind, but it was there. Bentley Safford, the man who had everything handed to him all his life, broke because your family was stronger than he ever was. I'm not my father's daughter. After I left you in Atlanta that winter, I had every opportunity to play that part. To pick up where he left off before he blew out the back of his skull in my bedroom. Cruel thing for a man to do to his daughter."

Jon spat. "Only if the daughter had given that father her heart—I got a feeling you didn't, Alicia, so cut the crap. Besides, I doubt you ever had a heart—well, you had the one I gave you."

Alicia turned around. "I never asked you for it."

"You took it nonetheless."

"You knew better than to part with something so valuable—and yet, you did it again a few years later with the same person," she said. "I was more careful the second time."

Jon shook with anger. "Were you careful?"

He wanted to tear her pretty blonde hair out by the roots and make her eat it. He also wanted to rip her clothes off and have his way with her on the floor. Those two violent urges vied for pole position inside his primitive brain while another urge—the secret one demanding that he wrap his arms around her and tell her that he still loved her—worked to palliate the symptoms of his rising venom.

"Why are you here, Alicia?" he finally managed.

"I need to tie up loose ends," she replied. "Look, do me a favor, and don't be such an ass the next time I come by—I own this building, and I can be a real bitch about my properties." She headed for the door. "I have a heart, you know. I could've gone to the police and told them what I saw—I didn't do that, Jon. Let me repeat that: I didn't do it."

"Only makes me wonder why you didn't."

Alicia took a breath and counted. "In the meantime, Jon, this retail space is in MY building—that's right; I own it. Which means that it will likely be torn down in the fall."

Jon could not muster a snarky counterattack. It meant two things:

this was within her rights, and there was nothing he could do to stop it.

The bell jingled when she left the store.

He stood at the counter for several minutes.

Waves of nausea punched him over and over until he finally let loose the Kraken from deep inside his belly. The mesh waste bin at his feet did little to contain the contents. It acted as a strainer when Jon carried it to the studio bathroom, where he vomited again. It repeated, of course, when he cleaned the floor—he was dry heaving by the time he was done.

The cramps kept him doubled over for an hour afterward.

It was time to pay a visit to Chucky. The day was already a train-wreck—*what could possibly make things worse than it already was?* If he still needed help turning his boat back to shore, then they would do it as they haggled over the price for a quarter bag. Jon opened the safe.

Weeks and weeks of paintings sold—nearly $50,000 worth. Most of the cash was marked for Raj Patel's passage to and from India. He had to sell more large canvases just to cover the cost of the surgery—*if Patel and Faklis ever decide on a damn date.* "I gotta move this money to the house safe," Jon whispered. He grabbed a stack of bills and closed the safe. To move his paintings, he needed a manager with experience—*after I buy something for this nausea.*

He locked up and headed to the Trail. By God, he was determined to walk Alicia Safford and Abby Flowers out of his mind—they did not belong there. And the gnarly seasickness in his body too—that did not belong there either. His head was thick with memories. He pretended to be wandering the world without a name or a home.

I am Pale Rider.

The new drugstore looked like a giant beehive next to the Family Dollar. A wrinkled woman who looked like a hairless cat owned the boarding house behind them. Jon chuckled as he went down Lemon Street. Wiping his forehead, swearing as his arm brushed a hot lamppost. The nausea returned. So did thoughts of Abby Flowers.

The birds in the dying tree ahead flew off in a panic when a dog came running out from the corner hedge. The taupe-colored pooch trotted alongside him, but veered south.

At the edge of Little Warsaw, he thought of the sun baking his skull, its heat killing the cancer in his brain.

Rubbing his temples, Jon remembered a girl he met working the perfume counter of the Walgreens. She was peddling sunless tanning spray. Looked great on her. She assured him a spray tan would make him handsome and healthy—*the wonders of tans from cans.*

I am George Hamilton.

Jon's mermaid mother popped into his mind. She smiled as she swam in a clear tank of refreshingly cool spring water. His father was taking pictures and commenting about how much she favored Audrey Hepburn—*why didn't I bring along some water?* He made his legs take him to where he wanted to go—*and where's Willie Dancer when you need him?*

Jon kicked a pebble into a mailbox. The stone ricocheted over his head. He passed Silverking and stood at the street corner. This intersection was the border between the order of Aleksandra Grelik and the chaos of criminals. The house across the street, the one with the purple door—his destination was there.

Too focused on what he was doing, Jon failed to notice the pretty young woman watching him from the open garage of the brewery. That he did not see her made no difference to him now—that she saw him was about to make all the difference in Jon's world.

*

Here were the homes of Tarpon's derelicts, addicts, and street thugs. Noting that Chucky's place was just across the street, Jon struggled with what he was about to do. The house was one of many small ranch-style cracker boxes on the outskirts of Little Warsaw.

There was a strange membrane dividing the areas—two separate universes connected only by a thin strip of asphalt. Jon checked his wallet and made his way across the street. The house was a few yards away. He walked up the crumbling driveway.

Before he knocked on the purple door, Jon wondered if this was a good idea. His hands were pistons. His mouth was cotton. His head was pounding. His heart was broken. His mind was made up.

Knock-knock-knock.

He had to trust this thing he was about to set in motion. Without offering to purchase from Chucky, something he had not done in several months, the young man might not be willing to discuss whether or not he needed help.

Knock-knock-knock.

Something in Jon's gut told him this was wrong. He was about to turn tail and go when the door opened. The man who answered wore no shirt. He was tall, muscular, and tan. His head was shaved to a military wisp. His eyes were glassy and relaxed. A pungent herbal smell spilled onto the porch from inside the house. Not unpleasant—certainly not legal.

Glassy Muscle smiled. He invited the visitor inside to smoke a bowl. Jon entered, feeling off-balance when Glass Muscle shut and locked the door. Sitting in the far corner of a smoke-filled den along to the hall was Chubby Huffer puffing on a hookah with half-slit eyes.

I am Alice.

Glassy Muscle led Jon to the kitchen.

He had a curious look on his face until he slapped his leg and shouted, "Tripod Jon Christakos! You're that deformed guy from my high school gym class. The one with the third leg that scared all the jocks to death—holy hell, man! You're effing famous!" He offered a chair for his famous guest. "Jonny Christakos—you killed your parents? Or something? You're banging that smoking hot supermodel? House on the bayou too. Man, I hear about you all the time. Those articles Adam Disston writes about you—dude, you're a legend! And that's all true, right?"

"Every. Damn. Word."

"I am jealous, Tripod, lemme tell you. What the hell are you doing in this part of town?"

Jon pulled a twenty from his pocket and handed it to his host. "For your hospitality, man—I appreciate the invite. What's your name?"

"Mine? Oh, it's Tall Gary."

Tall Gary laughed as he packed a small pipe with a pinch of herb. He took a hit before passing it. Jon took a hit and nodded. In moments, his pounding headache and nausea vanished—*maybe this was a good idea, after all.* Tall Gary sat cross-legged on the floor. The two repeated the action until there was nothing but ash in the bowl. "Chuck gets the best," he said. "Say, does that hog scare the ladies?"

Jon felt relaxed enough to speak truth. "Most women don't want to sleep with me, Tall Gary. The fantasy they had in their heads doesn't match the reality. I wish I didn't have this thing."

Tall Gary nodded in sympathy. "That's upsetting."

"It's very upsetting," Jon admitted. "But do you want to know the worst part?"

"What, Jonny?"

Jon swallowed. "Brain cancer. It's why I'm here—something for my nausea, headaches, and insomnia. Is Chucky around? I'd be happy to buy from you if he's not."

"No, man. Chucky's not home."

His head a painless fog, Jon nodded. "Okay, tell him I stopped by?"

"Sure—here, let me walk you out," Tall Gary said, lifting his dazed visitor from the chair, as well as the wallet from his visitor's back pocket. "Lean on me, man. All your weight." He removed the hundred dollar bills and returned the wallet. "Thanks for the visit, Jonny Tripod," he said, unlocking and opening the heavy purple door. As soon as his guest was over the threshold, he closed the door.

Jon stood on the porch staring hard at the purple door.

He was confused. He stood there wondering whether anyone was home. He also wondered how he got there to begin with—*I must have knocked ten times.*

Did I knock ten times?

Deciding to come back another day, Jon left the porch and staggered down the driveway. He emptied his stomach in the grass at the end of it. He twisted his torso left and right until his spine popped.

From there, he began the long march toward the street corner. Silverking was just across the street, just a hundred yards away.

His knees buckled. He swooned and fell. Before he hit the sidewalk, someone was there to stop him from falling.

*

Jon woke an hour later. He was sore, cranky, and exhausted—*what happened?* There was a Good Samaritan that escorted him across the street—he remembered that much.

Or did his mind make that up?

He vaguely recalled collapsing onto a cornhole game flat that broke beneath him. He vaguely recalled hands lifting him up and voices cursing him out in both Polish and English. He remembered drinking ice water and feeling a washcloth against his forehead.

"Chucky? Is that you?" Jon mumbled. "My wallet's empty."

"Because you got mugged, you idiot," a female voice replied curtly.

Jon rubbed his eyes and sat up. "Wait, who are you?"

The pretty blonde woman refilled his glass of water. "How are you feeling?"

"I've felt better."

"You look better than you should—you were lucky."

Jon drank the glass of water. "Am I wearing one of Bret's bowling shirts?"

"Yes—his ugliest one."

"Wait, do I know you? I've seen your face before."

"We've never met, not officially. I'm Hannah."

"I'm Jon. Do you work here?"

"Just turned in my notice actually."

"Well, Hannah, it just so happens that I need help at my shop down at the Sponge Docks—Nik's Knacks, Athens Street. Stop by any time before noon."

"What do you sell at Nik's Knacks?"

"Crap tourists like to buy," Jon said, adding, "and mermaids. I need someone to help me sell some paintings, Hannah. Interested in making a lot of money?"

"Not really," she said, getting to her feet. "There's hot food for you at the bar. Go eat."

Jon emerged from the dark storeroom and sat with Roman as he ate. When he finished, Bret was there to escort him through the garage space. Twenty-five foot ceilings, big wooden block seats, pool tables, two corn-hole flats (one broken). Propped atop four aluminum beer kegs was a huge awning emblazoned with the Silverking logo.

Local bands played live music shows there.

They went through a door in the back. The room beyond had a wall air conditioning unit that blasted icy air as they settled into a pair of leather chairs around an old desk.

"Babcia's worked hard to keep her eye on you—to keep you out of trouble. She'll be disappointed when she hears about the stunt you pulled today." He leaned closer. "Next time you need to talk to Chuck Parker, leave a message with me. Got it?"

"Yeah, sure. I don't understand."

Bret shook his head. "You don't need to understand—and I think you know why you don't need to understand. Because if I had to spell it out for you, that would put our relationship into a wholly different category. Why did you go to Chuck Parker's old house? Tell me the truth."

"I'm sick again—I wanted something for my nausea."

"The cancer's back? After all these years? And your doctor can't snag it for you?"

Jon nodded. "I also wanted to thank Chucky for not ratting me out."

Drumming his fingers on the desk, Bret looked at Jon for a long moment. "So, you think it was all Chuck Parker's doing? Okay, that'll work. But don't go back to the house again, Jon. Brik Buckman has the herbal medicines you need. Home grown in Holiday—best in the area. Don't look so damn surprised—our relationship is not nearly as shady as it sounds. Look, I'm sorry you're sick. I figured the skeleton look wasn't for fun and games. Hannah will take you home. See yourself out. Oh, and Jon?"

"Yeah, Bret?"

"Unless you need to reach Chuck Parker, don't EVER come back here again."

It was a clear threat—Jon obviously had worn out his welcome.

But what had he done exactly? And why was it such a transgression that Bret exiled him? Jon refused to think about the tangled web of implications. He left the office with a deep pit in his stomach and a head full of yellow jackets. He stumbled across the empty garage and went to the curb where Hannah was waiting to take him home.

*

CHAPTER 09

Dog Day, Summer Night

July 26

Jonny, quit being a stupid malakas—you have friends who love and care about you. Don't make me come down there. ~ Evelyn

*

It had been months since *Tarpon Lady* last left her bed at Belle Harbour. There was hardly any chop on the short journey to the emerald waters of Anclote Key. The crystal sky was a dome of clear cerulean blue. Clouds were wispy white lines of powdered chalk streamers. Sea winds fat with moisture left a slick salty sheen on sun-kissed skin. Excursions to the Gulf of Mexico rarely interested Jon, but even he could not deny the idyllic pull of the surrounding beauty—a perfect blend of Caribbean, Aegean, and Mediterranean right in his backyard.

"*Lady's* a beautiful boat, brah—why keep her locked up?"

Ignoring the handyman's question, Jon ordered him to take the wheel. Brik had done enough boating in Hawaii that he skillfully maneuvered her close to the shoreline for a decent mooring. They found a secluded spot inside a copse of mangroves, a private beach perfect for sunbathing, picnicking, and picture taking.

Brik left to explore their piece of the island.

Jon built a sand castle. He searched for scallops, which he imprisoned in a deep hole behind a driftwood portcullis. It had been a long time since he had played. He could not recall the last time he had been so inspired. The past few months had drained his sense of wonder and all but murdered his inner child.

Jon lost track of time as he added rooms to his castle. Fortifications and turrets, and more prisoners for the dungeon—the Anclote Scallop Rebellion had been summarily squelched. "Long live King Jon," he shouted, as the rising tide began to consume his kingdom.

He packed up their things and prepared the *Tarpon Lady* for departure. Brik emerged from his solitary excursion, as if on cue. They shoved off and headed back to the mouth of the river.

"Get what you wanted?" Jon asked.

Gazing thoughtfully at the shore, Brik said, "I can't wait to come back."

"We're not done, rey."

Jon took the boat around to the other side of the island. The waters were choppier without the spoils of mangroves and shallows of suddenly shifting sandbars. Fewer people, more isolated areas, better chances to spot bald eagles and osprey.

Jon pointed to an arid strip along the shore that looked like a Martian desert, replete with albino sand and stark bony trees.

Brik declined an invitation to explore. He unzipped one of the side pouches of his black canvas camera bag. He took out a small glass pipe and a rolled sandwich bag. He took out a pinch of green and stuffed the bowl. "Why haven't I seen Abby?" he asked, lighting and puffing. "You gonna—Hck—keep your cards close? Or you gonna tell me the damn truth for once?"

"Has ANYONE ever told you that you talk too much?"

The handyman's smile was the second lighthouse of Anclote Key. Brik knew that he was a specimen, that his chiseled face had charismatic power—he wielded it with a boyishly nonchalant confidence that would have come across as grossly arrogant in lesser men—*it's the tiny cleft in his damn chin.* The sun began its descent.

The sea rocked *Tarpon Lady* like a cradle between the waves. The sky erupted in a furious array of fiery hues of blood orange and militant red flecked with gold. Brik passed the pipe to Jon. "A little bit's all you need for this one—*Hck*—you'll eat like a horse and sleep like a baby."

"She wanted a break," Jon said, returning the pipe.

Brik thought for a moment. "It's that supermodel. I bet she got jealous—*Hck*—hell, brah, I'd be jealous if I were Abby." He puffed and passed. "Come on, man—talk to me."

Jon smoked the last of the bowl. "Abby suspects I'm sicker than I'm letting on."

Brik's smile disappeared. "And are you? I mean, I know you have—"

"Five months, Mr. Buckman. Wow, you weren't kidding. Nausea's all gone." Jon smiled. "Why don't you drive? I think I need a moment."

The handyman nodded sadly. "Aye-aye, Skipper."

Truth be told, it was time they returned *Tarpon Lady* to Belle Harbour anyway. Brik had a gig that night at Cap'n Jack's, the restaurant next door. A quick trip home to freshen up, and they were back an hour later pulling into the parking lot.

At the hostess kiosk, Jon hissed that he was either going to gnaw the giant plastic shark at the entrance. They sat in a booth on the main deck overlooking the river. Brik looked around anxiously. "Think we'll have a crowd? It's usually dead the nights I play here."

"I called in a favor to the owner. You'll have your crowd."

The drinks Brik had ordered arrived. He tossed them back. "When is Kiki coming?"

Jon got to his feet. "She's already here."

Kiki Kontodiakos was a hugger. Well, she was more than a hugger, but that was as good a word to describe her as any. And when she saw her Jonny-baby, she screamed in delight and wrapped her arms around him, squeezing until he cried uncle. She was a strong, curvy, independent, vivacious woman, and one of Jon's oldest friends. Kiki was the sister he and Panos never had.

She sat down and ordered a round of drinks for herself and the handyman. "Brik, I hear you've written a song about my boy's third leg," she said. "You know the story? Alrighty then. Freshman year of high school, puberty pressed Jonny's peeper one night and it broke the sound barrier. I swear. We all heard it—the sonic boom woke up the whole city."

Jon put his hand over her mouth, but promptly removed it when she licked his palm.

"After gym class, mid-way through the semester," she said. "He's in the shower, and the older boys see this thing and start throwing dirty jock straps at him. 'Tripod Jon' was born. Rumors spread fast too. My favorite was how his junk gave him scoliosis."

"Jon chuckled. "I was getting lots of attention from the girls too."

Kiki pushed him. "Yeah, but you were hung up on the wrong one, you dolt. All the blood from your brains done drained deep down into darker areas. Like that summer Panos kept finding his True Love each week. Talk about blood in other areas—that boy."

Jon laughed. "You wouldn't believe the stains Evelyn was bleaching out of his sheets."

"Oh, yes, I would. He was such a *zinkolo!*"

"Yeah, like you don't have your list of regulars."

Brik slapped the table three times and got to his feet. When the handyman left, Kiki draped herself around Jon and kissed his cheek. They hooted and cheered when Brik took to the stage. He introduced himself, welcomed the gathering groups of people, and dove into his set.

There's something on your mind—
I can see it in your eyes
You say you got a list of things to tell me
Might save our love from lies
Well, I'm the kind of man
Who ain't afraid of changing
Sometimes love needs a little hand
Lay it on me, girl
I could use some rearranging
I'm always trying to be a better man

Kiki took Jon's hand. "How are you feeling? Still got the cancer?"

"It's the gift that keeps on giving."

"How are you and Abby doing?" she asked. "Or not doing? What?"

"She wrote me a 'Dear Jon' letter. It's in my wallet. Wanna read it?"

"Gimme," Kiki demanded. "What kind of question is that?" After returning it, she said, "If you didn't look like one of those Star Wars space bears with an elephant tusk pound-for-pounder, I'd date you, Jonny-baby. Sounds like she's feeling too much too fast—be patient."

"Maybe—I think the cancer's scaring her off," he replied.

"You look better with some color—I'm glad you spent some time in the sun."

You make it hard to play
You make it hard to be
Ooh, you make me wanna say
Girl, that ain't right with Jesus
Now gimme peace
'Cause you're witchin' with my dipstick
Baby, now set me free
Yeah it's comin' from deep inside me
Girl, you know I can't hide me
I'm gonna give you all I got

Kiki cocked her head as she watched the women watching Brik. "Now I know why Evelyn hired him," she said to Jon. "Don't look at me like that. A girl has needs. And I needs to shave that boy's dreads so I can lick his bald head—ooh, new song."

Jon started tapping his feet. This was one of his favorite Brik Buckman originals, definitely in his top five. He told the handyman it needed to be recorded. That, of course, led them to a day of musical exploration—of all the songs in the Buckman catalog, which ones were good enough to make the cut for a full album?

And then, what would the album be called?

So pack a light lunch and walk to the sun
You'll get a broken heart if she's not the one
You'll get a little dizzy, girl, but try to have fun
You'll be fine when you're all done
You'll feel alive when you're all done
Live for the moment—live for today
Set yourself on fire when you run into your fear
Burn your name into the blue and you will see
Flying blind in your own sky is the only way to be

At the end of the set, Brik announced, "I'd like to call Tripod Jon to the stage."

Jon made his way to the handyman with his middle finger raised. There was a crew of big-boobed college co-eds sitting at a table close to the stage. Moving between them and another table of loud frat boys was like Odysseus navigating Scylla and Charybdis. While Brik played his new song, Jon handed out free tequila shots—it was the price set by the owner of Cap'n Jack's.

All you hungry, single gals you got to be on the lookout
For a strong man, dressed to kill and looking damn fine
He might be short, dark and handsome
And his teeth might glow fluorescent white
But don't give him a minute of your precious time
Don't get me wrong—I know that he looks so fine
But he got this strange condition

Amazing what a few simple chords and clever naughty lyrics could do to a bunch of drinking folk. Brik was milking the moment for all of its nutrition, hamming his every expression as he sexualized the concluding stanzas to his instantly popular song.

"I'll be damned," Jon said—*my one night out in public and she shows up.*

Abby Flowers was standing at the end of the bar looking up at a man who only could have been her date. She smiled politely whenever her eyes met his. Still, she looked as bored as a rich reality televi-sion housewife when she looked away.

Sad Mystery Date clearly had deduced the same ugly truth. He looked rather desperate in his at-tempts to make her laugh. Abby excused herself to talk to Kiki, who waved apologetically to Sad Mystery Date. The poor man downed his drink and looked dejectedly at his empty glass. Sensing that he was be-ing studied, Sad Mystery Date narrowed his eyes to cat slits when his gaze met Jon's. And he nearly dropped his tray of cheap te-quila when Brik started to wrap up his song.

You may think my story's steeped in urban legend, myth, or make believe
Because you cannot picture what this monster looks like
Beware of Jonny Dimples-Kisses-Long-Eyelashes
Hairy-Nipples-Crazy-Famous-Pokémon and his 10-foot pike
But don't get me wrong — I know that he looks so fine
But he got this strange condition

Everyone in the bar had quieted down to hear the finale. When it was time to sing the chorus, the servers lifted poster boards with lyrics over their heads. The raucous crowd got to their feet. Arm in arm, shoulder to shoulder, hand in hand, rocking (and spilling)—they sang and cheered as the handyman's hysterical homage to Jon reached a satisfying end.

He's got Chronic Colossal-Psycho-Phallus Genitalis
It might be fun to look at but don't put it inside
Chronic Colossal-Psycho-Phallus Genitalis
You had better wear a helmet if you go for a ride
Chronic Colossal-Psycho-Phallus Genitalis
His Willie calls shotgun for a night on the town
Chronic Colossal-Psycho-Phallus Genitalis
He killed a nun in Fresno just by turning around

"Let's hear it for Tripod Jon!" Brik shouted. The crowd erupted into applause that continued for several minutes. Ones and fives rained down on Brik (something Jon secretly set up with the bartenders earlier). The handyman was thrilled at the staged generosity, but then the audience got into the spirit and added to it.

Jon had lived in Tarpon Springs long enough to expect only the unexpected, but he was surprised that tonight was so positive. Well, except for Sad Mystery Date. He looked like he was sucking on dead sponges reeking of rotten fish.

On a crazy whim, Jon hopped onto the stage next and grabbed the microphone. For a moment, he was not sure it was a good idea—the effects of Brik's weed were wearing off. He shouted to Kiki and jumped (carefully) to the floor with a flourish of his hands. He began a slow series of steps that gradually increased in speed and complexity, and in repetition. Kiki joined in, mirroring the steps beside him.

Feet together, body facing right, right foot prime.

Slow step right on right.

Quick step right on left, behind right.

Quick step right on right, alongside left.

Traveling step right, left foot prime...

The kalamatiano was easily recognizable as Greek—it had been Jon's favorite dance since he and Panos were boys.

A young man named Alexis joined the duo as the crowd began clapping in rhythm. Then it became a mad rush to join the fun. Dozens of people moved tables and chairs to make the dance floor bigger. The Cap'n Jack's crowds were not known for their cardiovascular abilities, but they danced the kalamatiano vigorously several times before Brik took the stage again.

Jon had to fend off the advances of those lusty co-eds when he helped them put their table back together. Abby had been watching the scene, but when it became painful to witness their frenzied carnal offerings, she decided to mount a rescue. She swooped in and hauled Jon to the end of the bar where it curved outside into the warm night sky.

"Of course, I'd pick the place you'd be tonight, Mr. Christakos."

He smiled. "I'm like a bad penny, Dr. Flowers."

She smiled too. "How have you been?"

"Thanks to Mr. Buckman's herbal medicine, I'm nausea-free. I've been eating every kind of fresh fish imaginable tonight—and I'm holding my vegetables down too."

"Think you'll be able to sleep tonight?"

Jon shrugged. For a moment, he gazed into her eyes. Then, without warning or permission, he slipped an arm around her waist, pulled her close, and kissed her passionately. Abby leaned into it for a moment before realizing what was happening. Pounding his chest, she pulled away and shook her head, as if the gesture would erase the past 20 seconds completely.

Jon took a step toward. Abby raised her hand and backed away from him. Her face was a mask of conflicting emotions. She touched her bottom lip, unable to decide what to do or say, whether she should stay or go.

Refusing to watch her go home with the wrong man, Jon made a beeline for that table of co-eds—*I can go home with the wrong person too.*

But Kiki blocked his path.

Without saying a word, she yanked Jon by the arm and hauled him out of the bar. Pulling him toward the spillover parking lot, she muttered under her breath about always saving him from doing stupid crap. Pointing to her Jeep, she ordered him to get in.

A few minutes later, when she had pulled into his driveway, she pushed her passenger out. "How about call me more than once a month?"

"I know—I'm a horrible person."

"No, you have effing cancer and your entire life is on hold." After leveling a hard look at him, Kiki gently said, "I know I'm constantly on the road, Jonny-baby, but I'm here if you need me. I'll start coming over more often, with or without your permission. Understood?"

"Evelyn has talked to you."

Kiki said nothing.

Instead, she blew a kiss as she drove away.

Here were the facts. When he was a teenager, Jon had crippling panic attacks. Kiki made him sign up for a series of classical performance workshops at the Heritage Museum. Rehearsing in the outdoor amphitheater was Kiki's idea. Dramatically reading Shakespeare (something he loved) in public (something he hated) somehow made the panic attacks stop. He faced fear and found joy, a miracle quiver stocked with Time's arrows.

Jon was vaguely aware of Kiki's impact upon his life. But he had yet to understand its magnitude. Her tidal influence went beyond the realms of reason, coincidence, and fate.

Without Kiki, Jon would not have started performing.

He would not have fallen in love and have his heart broken for it. He would not have joined the Atlanta Shakespeare Company for two years. He would not have been in the right place at the right time, when the stars aligned over four crucial winter days—a key moment that Jon would have missed had it not been for Kiki.

Jon did not know this, of course—in fact, he was blissfully unaware that another one of Time's arrows was fast approaching its target now.

*

CHAPTER 10

Survival Methods

"Full fathom five thy father lies; of his bones are coral made;
those are pearls that were his eyes: nothing of him that doth fade
but doth suffer a sea-change into something rich and strange."
~ William Shakespeare

Jon despised festival events at the Sponge Docks. He had ever since the night those drunk teenagers crashed his music pavilion and bullied him for no other reason but that he was well known in town. He attended plenty of other Greek-themed events throughout the year, not to mention fundraisers for every cause imaginable, as long as those events were at the community center.

A 'Night in the Islands' event was happening just over there—Athens Street, as in the street upon which he was now standing, was the detour route for cars and trucks.

At this very moment, in fact, Jon was signaling the malakas in a white delivery truck for the seventeenth time.

Beep-beep-beep-beep.

The truck was wedged between the corner of his building and the one across the street. Its driver had been doing a 73-point turn for thirty minutes now. The number of men directing the gumpta behind the wheel had tripled in the last ten minutes alone. The scene reminded him of a joke Panos and George loved to tell.

How many Greeks does it take to change a light bulb?

Four: one to change it; one to sell T-shirts under it; one to open a gyro stand beside it; and one to tell them they're doing it wrong.

Beep-beep-beep-beep.

Jon looked up when several of the men in the street shouted and clapped. The truck was no longer wedged, but headed back from whence it came. No doubt the driver made a wrong turn—not the first one to make that mistake. Every summer, it happened at least twice. Heading back inside the store, Jon began to close early. He wanted to go home.

The bell jingle-jingled.

Alicia Safford entered the shop.

"Hello, Jon."

"Hello, Alicia."

"How's business?"

"What do you want?"

"For you to stop despising me—that would be a good start."

"I fell hard for you—and when I got sick, the torch I carried was keeping me alive. Which is why I welcomed our short four-day sequel seven years later in Atlanta."

"By chance, Jon—it was a coincidence."

"I distinctly recall you telling me it was destiny."

Alicia took a deep breath. "I'd like to purchase a mermaid painting from you. Beverly Pink showed me her growing collection—she's been showing everyone she knows. She put her tennis memorabilia into storage and converted that space into a gallery of your artwork. It's stunning, Jon—I mean that."

"Why now?"

She smiled. "It took me a month to realize I wanted one," she said softly. "Please."

"Alicia, my paintings are not for sale just because—"

"I'll pay you whatever you want to charge me," she said. "I came back to Tarpon Springs hoping that... I mean, in my head I knew what I was going to say to you. Now, I don't know how. Please, just let me buy a painting, you stubborn ass. What can I do to prove myself?"

Jon laughed. "Try another tactic."

"Another tactic? Fine. How about destiny? Or fate?"

"What the hell does that mean?"

Alicia did not answer.

The bell smacked on the glass when she left the store.

Jon stood at the counter as he watched her go. A part of his heart, as it often did, went with her. And for that, he wanted to kick her in the shins and whack his head with a ballpeen hammer.

Something strange had just happened. He could feel it.

His mind played traffic cop to emotions coming at him from every direction. His skull buzzed with their teeming, dangerous conference. Indeed, the one who publicly broke his teenage heart (and then his adult heart privately years later) had returned. As if her sole motive was to vex him—*well, at least I'm not blubbering over Abby Flowers at the moment.*

So, there was that.

Jon was in the studio when he heard the bell again. He looked at the clock—it was almost closing time. Brik would be dropping in to help him haul some of these paintings into storage. Maybe it was the handyman—uncharacteristically early.

Jon popped into the store space. A young woman with blonde hair was walking around. Looking into the bins, maneuvering around boxes of sponges and T-shirt racks. She did not see him—her attention was focused inside the display case now.

"May I help you, miss?" he asked. "Miss?"

The young woman turned. "Sorry it took me so long to stop by." She muttered something about the outdated décor (not to mention the number of items that had taken up musty residence there).

"Hannah, it's been a while."

"Jon, why are you selling shells with googly eyes? Cheap plastic snow globes with manatees?" She spied the hallway behind him. "What's back there?" She quickly maneuvered around him.

"Hey, that's my private studio!"

But Hannah was already walking through the studio door. She played hopscotch around the square canvases scattered over the floor. Most of his finished work was stacked in the corner or drying on pegs in the back wall. The canvases on the floor were for a new series of paintings—bold lines covered each of them—he tried to block her from viewing the new paintings. "Please, get out."

She pointed to the photographs of his Willy and Wonka agates. "Good pics—not quite at the level of your mermaid paintings, which are exquisite—wow." She picked up a small one he finished earlier that day. "This— masterful work, Jon. Why aren't these up front?"

"It's not what I want people to gawk at."

Hannah frowned. "I have a scary instinct about art—yours needs to be seen."

"My work is worthless unless—"

"Be quiet—you offered me a job. I'm here. Let me help."

Jon crossed his arms. Listening to freely given advice was more frustrating than the unexpected invasion of his personal space—and yet, he felt powerless to stop this Lilliputian force of nature. Sudden emotional stirrings made it hard for him to demand that she leave—*what the hell am I doing?*

Hannah was snapping her fingers. "I said that I'll take this one." She headed for the door. "I'll be back tomorrow to make you stop this googly-eyed madness. You need a bigger space too—so, I'll get to work on finding you another place."

Mouth working like a fish, Jon followed her.

The bell jingled as Brik opened the door—sans shirt, skin glowing in a sweat that made his lean muscles ripple. He smiled like an idiot.

"You must be Mr. Buckman," Hannah said, strolling past the handyman. "I'm sure Jon will tell you my name after I go."

She waved goodbye.

*

The next day, Jon woke to the smell of bacon and eggs cooking.

Well, he was already awake—he had been staring at the ceiling since an hour before sunrise.

It had been a night of strange dreams, most of them about Abby as a mermaid. Or Hannah and Abby—or Alicia and Hannah. The permutations were endless as they were strange and unsettling. Not nearly as unsettling as the anxiety gnawing at his intestines—the thought of another long day at Clearwater Oncology always made him sick to his stomach—*maybe that's why I had so many weird dreams.*

He was hungry too. Brik's herbal medicines were still doing the trick. Pity it did not have an effect on his weight loss. He was one month and a black turtleneck away from the Steve Jobs look.

Bacon and eggs—is that coffee AND toast?

Jon could not remember the last time he smelled those aromas coming from his kitchen. He heard Brik's voice—the handyman had a resonant baritone. He was talking to someone in the kitchen, but he could not hear the voice of that someone. After he showered and dressed, Jon went downstairs. He was expecting to find Brik having a light one-sided conversation with the dog. "Evelyn!"

The woman who helped raised him turned around—she was actually there. "About time you woke up, Jonny—hey, what's this?" She barely had time to speak before he was wrapping his arms around her, squeezing for all his worth. "Surprised? Good. I figured this was the only way to see how you're doing. Brik's more loyal to you than he is to me now." She shot the handyman a look, which he happily ignored by toasting her with a syrup-coated bacon strip. "At least I know someone has your back."

"How's Fotini?" Jon asked. "And Peter?"

"My sister's not improving fast enough for Peter, who wants to make everything better now and solve it all right now—he was the same way when his father died," Evelyn said, pulling away to look at Jon once again. "Oh, you've lost so much weight, my sweet boy." Her eyes brimmed. She wiped them quickly. "Anyway, I only have a few hours before I fly back to Ohio. I had to see you."

"Kiki called you, didn't she?" Jon asked.

"Of course, she did—I wanted to go with you to Clearwater today." Evelyn patted Brik's cheek. "And you get to play the part of my chauffeur—no need to dress. A hat and nothing else is fine."

"*Hck*—how about we let Jon eat before we go?"

Jon frowned at Evelyn. "Suddenly, I've lost my appetite."

And so, an hour and a half later, Evelyn, Brik, and Jon were seated side by side inside the office of Dr. Althea Faklis, whose normally soft-spoken manner had disappeared the moment her childhood friend had walked in with her patient.

Evelyn and Althea were speaking in Greek so quickly that Jon had trouble translating. Most of their exchange was about finding facts and allaying fears, about easing Evelyn's worried mind, which was already taxed and stretched beyond capacity. Dr. Faklis explained how her pragmatic approach balanced the philosophical/metaphysical approach of Raj Patel's. Evelyn did her best to rein in her emotions, specifically her anxiety over Raj not being there.

By the end of their discussion, only one tear managed to escape.

Dr. Faklis looked at her watch. She pointed to the large flat screen mounted in the wall above her desk. She adjusted the microphone and the speaker volume, as Brik positioned the camera.

"Hope we have a better connection this week," the handyman muttered. "Last time was bad."

Evelyn squeezed Jon's hand. "Is that a problem?"

Panic had tinted her voice.

"Despite the inconsistent connection strength," Dr. Faklis said, taking Evelyn's hand, "his excursion has been worth it. With this technology, I'm in the operating room during the surgeries that Raj believes are key to fighting Jon's brain cancer. My primary role is monitoring overall health—pain and inflammation management, diet and supplementation, blood and urine analysis. Thanks to Mr. Buckman's assistance, we've been able to cut out some harmful medications."

A series of bubble sounds announced the start of the video chat.

Moments later, the smiling face of Raj Patel, live from India, filled the screen. After small talk about the monsoon season, the two doctors tag-teamed as they relayed information and explained their overall strategy for treating Jon.

They spoke of upcoming shifts in their plan of attack, which would remain passive and preventative as long as Jon remained relatively symptom-free. They spoke of managing expectations about the prognosis, which they reluctantly suggested was not as dire as their initial assessments indicated. The image of Raj flickered on the large monitor—the speakers blared static.

"We lost the connection—*Hck*—dammit."

Jon chuckled. "It lasted 30 minutes longer than I thought it would— those rains are fat and heavy and last for days at a time."

Evelyn frowned. Smiling with all the strength she could muster, she blew her nose on a tissue that Dr. Faklis handed her. After taking several breaths to calm her inner storm, she looked at Jon and nodded, an indication that she understood things.

"Of course, you'd have the weird brain cancer that required your doctor to fetch your treatment on the other side of the world."

Them without warning, Evelyn slapped Jon's face—not hard enough to rattle his teeth or make him see stars, but hard enough to sting and leave a red mark.

No one in the office moved.

Evelyn raised a finger. "You will fight this with every breath in your body, do you understand me? No, Jonny—I don't want to hear your voice. Nod your head and mean it. Good. Because if you leave me alone in this world, then I will raise you from the dead and strangle you."

Evelyn pointed at the computer screen. "If Raj Patel comes back from India with nothing but a new diet of herbs and veggies, Althea, then I will strangle the both of you. Radical, dangerous, experimental—if you have to remove Jon's head to save my son's life, then so be it."

Again, no one moved—no one spoke either. And then, as if nothing had happened, Evelyn calmly rose from the chair. She kissed Dr. Faklis sweetly on her cheek and walked out of the office.

It was a 40-minute drive to Tampa International Airport, which was not particularly busy at that time of day.

Jon fetched a small bag from the trunk and waited on the curb for Evelyn to finish saying goodbye to Brik. After a discussion that dampened the handyman's mood, she kissed him on the cheek and whispered something in his ear. She pulled away and looked in his eyes until he nodded.

Evelyn climbed out of the car and took her bag from Jon. Neither one of them spoke—these kinds of farewells made them too emotional. They preferred the simplicity of silent departure, which spared voices from breaking and eyes from shedding tears.

Evelyn cupped Jon's cheek, the same spot she smacked earlier. "I love you," she mouthed, holding her hand to his face as she looked into his eyes. And then she walked through the glass doors of the terminal.

*

Jon was not feeling talkative on the drive home. And the handyman, who usually shouldered the responsibility of filling stretches of silence, was not his effusive self either.

Brik talked about the store and Hannah's ideas for selling the paintings. His ideas for a new series of photographs and some quirky landscaping that Evelyn had requested. He mentioned the retail spaces for lease on either end of the Sponge Docks.

At the downtown Tarpon intersection, Brik directed the El Camino north and said, "Mind if we take a quick detour?"

Jon shook his head no—besides, his curiosity was peaked. After they crossed the bridge over the river, the car veered onto Anclote Road, which sent a shiver through Jon's body.

Anclote Road was a dangerous stretch of serpentine highway that snaked along the coastline. From Tarpon Springs to Holiday, it wrapped around salt marshes and estuaries, slithering through unruly forests of mangroves and pine trees. Twisty and narrow, the road was all coils and bendy angles—a real hazard by day and a terrifying menace by night.

People died on Anclote Road.

Jon was a rational man, but it was easy to believe the highway was haunted with the ghosts of its victims. He wondered if the handyman would go into one of his nervous stories about lost souls hitchhiking along the shoulder, but he kept silent.

The El Camino rolled to a stop over a patch of gravel next to one of the state parks. Brik got out and started walking toward the road sign a few yards ahead. Jon got out and followed the handyman's lead, moving along the shoulder in lockstep behind him.

They stopped at a clearing that dipped into a growth of mangroves. A makeshift cross was crammed into the grass. A wreath of faded silk flowers hung around it. The name on the plate had been burned into the wood by a carpenter's dexterous hand—Rebecca Mathis, with dates of birth and death on a separate line below it.

Rebecca Mathis, Jon thought—*why do I know that name?*

Brik took out a bright yellow streamer from his pocket. He draped it artfully and strategically, so as not to fly away or hide the name. He stepped back. And stood in a contemplative silence that could have been two minutes or ten.

He coughed into his hand. "I wanted you to know something about me that not many people know," he said, cryptically. "It's important that I tell you—to show you I trust you. *Hck*—when my parents divorced, they split everything. Dad took me out west. Mom stayed here with my twin sister Becky. I kept Dad's last name. Becky took Mom's maiden name. Dad died. And then Mom died. We decided it was time to be a family again, her and me. And the two reasons that Becky and I came to Florida," he explained, "were to spend the month of August being a family and visit Mom's grave every day until it was time to go. See you next year, Beck—see you next year, Brik."

Brik smiled at the memory. "Becky always went off the grid whenever we parted—after a year, she'd reappear out of the mist—*Hck*—veni, vidi, vici." His voice cracked. "She was a free spirit. Wore the same clothes every day until they fell apart. Believed in reincarnation. Loved men, hated relationships. Believed *Jonathan Livingston Seagull* was the most vital spiritual text ever written. Loved Pez and elevator music pop covers. Hated television. Devoured tabloid newspapers and pulp fiction novels. She dreamed of being paid for climbing trees." Brik looked at Jon, who had never known his friend to be this emotional. The handyman's tears flowed freely now. He struggled to talk. "Evelyn told me to talk to you. At the airport, she told me to bring you here and show you. That it would—*Hck*—that it would be okay to t-t-tell you."

Jon stared at the little wooden cross. He searched his memory for the name of Rebecca Mathis—he had heard of the name.

But what was the connection to Brik?

The handyman wiped his nose. "I never stopped searching for my sister when she disappeared—Hck—the county messed up the investigation and tried to cover it up," he said. "When I figured out what had happened, what they had done, I found her over there." He pointed. "It took two years, but I found her. Today's the anniversary. I just needed some company. Thanks, brah."

Here were the facts. The Pasco County Sheriff's office had jurisdiction at the time of her disappear-ance. Discrepancies in the reports filed by two deputies tasked with coordinating search efforts in the marshes were uncovered years later. As it turns out, no searches were conducted in the areas to which they had been assigned. Two years after her disappear-ance, it was reported that a cyclist spotted the rusted frame of a Vespa in the salt marshes during low tide. A further search uncovered the remains of a young woman twisted beneath the wreck.

"Mathis was your mother's maiden name," Jon said. "Rebecca Mathis was your sister. All this time I assumed her last name was Buckman." He put an arm around the handyman's shoulder. And when he did, Brik finally let go and wept with racking sobs that shook his whole body.

*

CHAPTER 11

The Trouble with Hannah

"In Hebrew, Hannah means, 'God's given gift to the world', or
'God has favored me...with a child'."
~ Wikipedia

Jon could not remember the last time he enjoyed working at the store this much. Daily doses of marijuana and weekly vitamin drips made life enjoyable. And then there was Hannah. Born in Tarpon Springs, but never a resident. She was only here for the summer and then she was off to the University of Florida to start her sophomore year. Tenacious, combative, salty, clever, charming, vulnerable, intuitive, bold, confident, mysterious—all orbiting moons of Hannah's beautiful Saturn soul.

Brik could not keep his eyes off Hannah, who suffered from the same ocular malady. Jon secretly wished they both would find someone closer to their own ages. But Hannah was powerless against the variety of experiences Brik had at the ready, like sexy tools from a well-worn leather carpenter's belt.

Hannah genuinely enjoyed hearing him talk about his adventures, his tales of odd jobs and rootless wandering in foreign lands. The sweet recollections of Becky tempered Jon's irritation—but it was the strange jealousy that he did not understand.

Yes, the jealousy was the real problem.

Perhaps knowing the handyman's history with women made Jon feel protective of Hannah. Perhaps the gap between their ages made him uneasy about their little crushes. Until he could figure out the problem and find a solution, Jon preferred their separate company.

Brik had his own business to run during the day. That meant plenty of time spent solely with Hannah. And the time went by in a rush of hours and days—two weeks gone in a blink.

Changes, changes, changes—there was nothing left of Nik's Knacks, as the store had once been.

The walls and shelves were bare.

The display case and bins and racks were empty. Old inventory had been sold at clearance or donated. Jon suggested they keep a live manatee in the display case. A dumb joke, yes, but it eventually inspired his idea to hire Weeki Wachee Mermaids as greeters for the new space.

That alone was enough to expedite his decision to close. Evelyn thought the same thing when he told her—she even volunteered to make the call to Alicia Safford.

And yet, the empty store nonetheless was swallowing customers and spitting them back out into the street with arms full of artwork, prints or paintings, rolled or framed. A limited edition run of prints sold out in two days—the demand for more was growing.

They were turning away customers now.

"You'll be free to start again in less than a month, Jonny!" Evelyn bragged in her letter offering to speak to Alicia's office. "And that should give you a little more hope, don't you think?"

And Jon's reply to her?

Hope is too precious a commodity to waste on leasing a new retail space.

Soon, the only offerings were the largest mermaids, and most of them were several feet in length and height—the price tags were astronomical. That did not stop wealthy buyers like Beverly Disston Pink, who made her own purchases and referred new customers.

One afternoon, the bell jingle-jingled.

Jon was in the studio painting more canvases. Hannah was up front with Minnie, who greeted every guest with her happy yippy growl. When he heard the bell and the dog, he washed his hands and left the studio. A woman and her two daughters had come into the store. The girls made a beeline for the fuzzy little dog. While they cooed and giggled, their mother rapped the counter.

"I'd like to buy an original Christakos mermaid," she said to Hannah, who shot a look at Jon to go fetch one. He snickered as he went to the back again, hovering near the open door to eavesdrop. "These mermaids are all the rage—I hear they're selling for tens of thousands apiece in Seattle! The artist ought to make his work available online."

"Christakos has no plans to sell his originals online," Hannah said, "but I'm sure he'd appreciate your suggestion as a compliment. Now, this is a catalog of currently available works. I'm afraid we are only down to these two paintings."

"How on earth can he sell them for so little when they're worth so much?"

"I wholeheartedly agree," Hannah said. "Now, which painting—"

"Both, young lady," the woman replied. "Please ship them to this address."

And like that, Jon's store had nothing left to sell. Only when the woman and her girls had gone did he join Hannah at the counter.

"End of an era," he said. "Well, as soon as I finish the two paintings you just sold, it'll be the end of an era. And now I just need to find a—"

Hannah shook her head. "You just need to rest, Jon—or use the studio until it's time to leave it. Take a sabbatical—you've earned it. Don't you think? Now, why don't you go finish up back there while I wrap things up in here? Close up early and walk home?"

*

It was on the walk home that Jon contemplated the effect that Hannah was having on his life. It was not just forgetting about his cancer when she was around—it was that she inspired him to think about life without the cancer. To feel hopeful again, which made him feel unexpectedly joyful. He still could not explain his jealousy toward Brik—he loved his friend.

Jon had zero romantic feelings for Hannah—the thought turned his stomach upside down. She was too young—WAY too young—and Jon preferred women his own age, thank you very much. He preferred women with experience, with life around their edges and curves around their hips. Women like Abigail Flowers—*it's her birthday today, August 20.*

Jon sent a card and some flowers to the pet hospital earlier. He had made her a card using her signature, flames and letters and lion's mane. He doubted that he would hear back from her—deep down, he hoped that he would. Something, anything—a word from Abby could very well temper the surges of wariness and suspicion toward Brik.

Jon had not seen her nor spoken to her since the night at Cap'n Jack's. His constant ache for Abby eased his worries about secretly wanting Hannah, who always made him think about his mother for some reason.

And again, Jon could not explain why.

"Tell me about your parents, Jon?"

Hannah's question startled him at first—then he laughed. "My mother was a fish. My father was a mobster. They drowned a week after I was born. What can I tell you?"

"On purpose, on accident?"

"Yes," he said with a cryptic smirk. "And your parents?"

"Mom's a high society gal," Hannah replied. "Never knew my father until quite recently. Mom didn't tell me anything about him until this past February. She suggested that I meet him—she just didn't bother to tell me how difficult that would be. Mom has her good traits, her bad traits. I understand why she never wanted to tell me about him. He lives here in Tarpon Springs."

Jon's curiosity was piqued. "So, what's the problem?"

"How do you tell a man who doesn't know you exist that you are his adult daughter?"

Jon considered her words. He enjoyed the surprising depths that their particular silences offered him—they were comfortable. There was honesty to be mined in such stillness. There was meaning to be found in the spaces between sounds. Wisdom resided there, strength even.

"Have you tried reaching out to him yet?"

"I've been here since June—I'm going back to school in a few days," Hannah said, clicking her tongue when the dog dallied. "Hey, rey—I'm your secret sudden daughter! Yeah, no—I totally chickened out. Not like me to do that either, but...well, there you go. I'm an infant."

"What about your mother?"

"Mom's no help. I give her a pass though—despite everything, I don't fault her."

"Why's that?" Jon asked.

"Well, she wanted me aborted and changed her mind on the table," Hannah explained. "There she was, all prepped to have that vacuum death machine shoved insider her. She told me that a lightning bolt went through her—she had an epiphany. Because of the man she loved. It was his face that popped in her mind. His smile. At that moment, Mom got up and left. That's some real courage, what she did. Mom's my hero. She mustered all the courage left in her broken soul and pulled she back from an event horizon. Broke free of the gravity of a black hole. She told me she'd had three abortions before then. Several miscarriages between them. She miraculously made a different choice. For me. The greatest gift she ever gave me, besides life, was telling me the story of that choice. Because now I believe there's no such thing as being too far down a dark path that you can't turn around. That you can't take a different road." Hannah wiped her cheek. "Mom's story usually gives me strength when I'm scared—it's not working for me now, of course."

"And why is that?"

"Because I've always wanted a father. And feel like I was his little girl."

"Have you seen this man?" Jon asked.

Hannah looked at him. "Yes, I have—everyday I see him at least once."

"I don't understand why you're terrified."

Hannah shrugged. "I don't understand your insecurities either, Jon. I understand your art though," she added, changing the subject. "Your mermaids are transcendent. Every painting I've seen. The landscapes change, the companions change, the colors and compositions change, the media change—the only thing that doesn't change is your mother's face and that half-smile of hers."

"You're the only one who's ever noticed," Jon said. "I wanted to create something like a Mona Lisa smile, you know? Hanging on my wall at home, is a photograph of my mother taken after she found out that she was pregnant with me. That's the smile I always paint—the look on her face."

Hannah threw her arms around him. "We should celebrate tonight," she said. "Celebrate the sale of your paintings and my genius." She was crying and laughing into his chest, which prompted Jon to ask her what all the tears were about. She did not answer him. And of course, that was the real trouble with Hannah—well, as far as Jon was concerned.

She was just as stubborn and mule-headed as he was.

*

Minnie was not in her bed.

Unusual, considering the dog never stepped foot away from him whenever he was in the room. She could be in the kitchen, if her water bowl was empty. He poked his head into the hallway. Her bowl was filled. Jon called for her. There came no reply. Not a whine. Not a bark or a yip. Not a jingle of her pink collar. Nothing.

Jon looked at his watch.

Moving from floor to floor, he called her name. He went to the kitchen, hoping that she had wiggled her way into the pantry again—the door was so easy for her to open.

But she was not there.

He searched every room, nook, and closet—twice. After the search in his home yielded nothing, he headed for the cottage house. He refused to panic when it was possible that Minnie was staying with Brik. He smoked a lot of pot last night—his memory was fuzzy at best.

"Minnie! Minnie!"

She was not outside, thank goodness—*please, God, please let her be safe with Brik.*

Jon let himself inside the cottage house. As soon as he shut the door, he heard a familiar jingling and a click-click-clicking of soft paws. And then that sweet fuzzy dog rounded the corner and ran to Jon the moment she saw him. Circling his legs and wagging her tail in joy.

He dropped to his knees and kissed her muzzle and wet nose. He teared up a bit as he held her. And told her how glad he was to see her. How relieved he was to find her safe and sound.

Speaking of relief—after she emptied her bowels and bladder, Jon made her a breakfast out of some leftovers in the refrigerator. To calm his rattled nerves, he breathed deeply as he slowly paced the kitchen—*why can I not remember last night?*

Brik was a fastidious housekeeper. Not a stray hair or a dust bunny on the floor, which was spotless. Everything was in order save for the bathroom. Scattered on the sink were his toiletries. And on the floor were two bath towels.

The main bedroom door was slightly ajar.

Not knowing why he was doing what he was doing—truthfully, the compulsion to snoop was impossible to ignore—Jon poked his head through the open door. He did not know what he expected to find, perhaps Brik snoring or passed-out in his clothes with a woman he met at one of the local bars. He was not expecting, however, to see Hannah wrapped in his arms.

Jon shook with rage. The thoughts running through his head were bloody and psychotic. It was all he could do to pull himself away from the scene. It was none of his business.

They had done nothing wrong.

But Jon's vision was a bloody sheet. He left the room and returned. He repeated this action several times—*I have no choice but to confront him.* He had been so consumed with his internal debate that he did not realize the couple in bed were sitting up and looking at him.

"Is there something you need?" Brik asked, slipping into his robe. "If you're looking for Minnie, she's probably on the kitchen floor. Here, you look pale. Let me help——"

Jon punched Brik in the face.

The handyman went spiraling comically backward over the corner of the bed. The robe ripped open when he landed in a naked heap on the floor. His lip and nose were bleeding all over the white terry cloth.

Hannah screamed for Jon to get out.

He did not know how to move from the doorway.

Aside from shaking his hand to ease the throbbing pain in his knuckles, he just stood there staring at the scene, uncertain that he had done what he just had done.

"What's wrong with you?" Hannah screamed, mopping up Brik's face with the robe. "Get the hell out of here before I call the cops."

Brik somehow diffused the situation in a miraculous swirl of comfort for Hannah and compassion for Jon. In a matter of minutes, his bleeding had stopped. He had donned a new robe. Hannah was no longer shouting at the top of her lungs. Jon found that he was being escorted into the kitchen, where the handyman patted his leg and urged him to stay put.

"Don't move from this spot—I'll be back."

Jon did not know how to deal with the fallout. He had no idea why he was feeling so violent, but he wanted to punch Brik again—the urge was maddening. He actually thought about killing him, yes. Fantasized about it. Enough to make him sick to his stomach. A man he genuinely cared about—*what the hell is wrong?*

His jealousy was infinite—all his life he had never felt this. With a renewed urge to commit violence, Jon went back to the bedroom. "Brik Buckman, you should know better—she's barely legal, you pedophile," he spat, pointing at Hannah. "As for you, he's old enough to be your father."

Jon nearly doubled over in a pain that shot through the center of his head. It passed just as quickly. His balance returned. But the fire burning a hole in his heart was consuming him—that is, until Hannah spoke.

"Well, he's not my father, Jon Christakos—you are."

"What are you talking about?"

"That's nothing I'm willing to discuss with you at the moment," she said, calmly. "Brik seems to think you took the wrong medication or something—I'm not so forgiving."

"Hannah, why didn't you—"

"Get out, Jon!"

Jon gathered Minnie and stormed across the lawn. He marched into his house through the kitchen door. The dog wanted nothing to do with him. As soon as her paws hit the cool tiles, she was off to her hiding spot.

"Minnie, come back!"

The clock chimed eleven times.

Jon put his hand to his chest—his heart was still racing. Sweat oozed from his pores. His body burned and vision blurred. The Hyde to Jekyll transformation had begun. He headed to the living room and sat on the couch. He counted breaths, moving numbers forward and backward until his pulse slowed—it was not enough.

With a groan he went upstairs to his room. Blinking back hot tears, he reached under his bed for an emergency kit. Taking his blood pressure was a nightmare. He could barely squeeze the rubber stopper. If his numbers remained this high for much longer, he very well could meet his maker before lunchtime.

There was a protocol for this.

Jon opened the lid of the kit again. There were pills to take. The right pills in the right order. He took them and waited horizontally on the floor, breathing and counting, breathing and counting. Finally, the waves of irrational thoughts and violent urges began to subside—his pulse was no longer racing. His body felt cooler now. Clarity returned. Some lucidity followed. And then he was awash in shock, guilt, and regret.

The shroud covering his mind—this smoldering veil of night-black crazy—lifted like a theater cur-tain. Skin, head, throat, and heart—all pain-free. Only tears of shame pained him now. There was noth-ing he could do about those except allow them to do their job.

Jon closed his eyes. Minnie licked his ankle. He smiled when she crouched toward him along the length of his leg. She snuggled into the gap between his neck and shoulder. She licked his salty face and would have continued had he stayed put and let her. He sat up against his bed and looked at his swollen hand—should I go apologize now or later?

Later, he decided, would be best. Later would give everyone time to cool off. Later would give him time to process the truth about Hannah's bombshell. If indeed, what she had told him was not a lie—if it was not something told to make him flee.

If anything, the thought of being her father made sense—it explained the jealousy, the fierce need to protect her. A residual bit of jealousy still crept along the back wall of his mind, like Gollum searching for his precious. And then it was gone.

He took a shower and dressed. Clean body, brushed teeth, combed hair, fresh clothes, maybe a walk around the Crescent and back—just what the doctor ordered.

If I'm Hannah's father, then who the hell is her mother?

Jon could not even begin to trace the possibilities leading to that revelation. He opened the front door and—Hannah was sitting on the top step of the front porch. She was staring out at the bayou. She did not move. Nor did she turn around when she heard the door open and close.

"Hannah, I am so sorry—"

"You don't get to talk to me right now," she said, slowly rising to her feet. She brushed her hands and turned to face him. "Brik suggested that I give you the benefit of the doubt. For his sake, I will. You have a lot of work to do to earn your way back into my good graces, Jon Christakos." She looked around the porch with a sigh. And then she looked hard at him, taking one step toward him.

Then, with tiny balled up hands, she flailed her fists against him. "How DARE you! You had NO RIGHT to do that. None! You hit the sweetest man—your best friend who adores you!" Hannah began to sob, but she would not let Jon console her. "No, you don't get to do that, to be nice and kind—your privilege is revoked for the time being. Brik and I are consenting adults. What we did in his bedroom is none of your damn business. How we feel about each other is also none of your business. NONE. And here's the crazy part: Brik defended what you did. Because he thinks you were right to shame him."

"That's what he told you?" Jon asked.

Hannah did not know what to make of that. "What else is there?"

Jon did not answer—his shame had deepened exponentially.

"You have no clue how much you affect people," Hannah told him. "You wield a lot of power without thinking about the way you use it. You don't deserve these feelings I have for you. Or the feelings Brik has for you. My God—or the feelings my mother has for you."

"Hannah, I'm sorry."

"Don't touch me." Her bottom lip quivered. "Do you even know who she is? The woman who saw your face in her mind when she was about to kill me? The face that inspired her to save my life? Do you know who she is, Jon? The mother of your daughter?"

Jon took a step back. He did not know. "Maybe we can—"

Hannah raised her hand. "For the record, Brik wanted to keep our relationship platonic. I was the one who decided to take things to the next level." She took a deep breath. "As for the identity of the mystery woman—it looks like you have some detective work to do."

"Hannah, please." Somehow, Jon felt that his chance for Grace, if ever there was such a thing, disappeared.

*

Jon did not remember how he got to the Sponge Docks. He had been on autopilot since Hannah left yesterday. Brik helped arrange for a moving van and cleaning crew—men pilfered from his own landscaping team. The handyman needed time away to sort out his head, which was understandable.

Still, Brik was kind enough to make certain that the store would be ready to close in time. He also left a month's supply of smoking herb in a Carter Hall tobacco can, which he had strategically positioned on the shelf above the liquor cabinet. Admittedly, the extra herb was helping Jon manage the closing of his store.

In the end, when it was all done and he was standing at the empty counter, staring blankly ahead as he waited for Alicia Safford.

He was not ready to go.

Not yet.

"Maybe Beverly Pink will take the notebooks," he whispered, casting a glance at the one box left to take home—*I'd give them to her for free.* It was time to go home, take some pills, smoke more weed, and get some sleep—that was the prescription.

And so, Jon turned off the lights in the studio. Gathering his phone and keys, he slowly made his way down the hallway to the front.

The door opened. The bell jingled.

"Hello, Jon."

"Hello, Alicia."

She wore a serious look on her face as they signed documents. She took his keys and slid an envelope across the counter to him. He held it up and shrugged. "I'm buying you out of your lease, remember?" She smiled sadly. "Looks like all you need to do is walk out of here now. Unless you need help with that box—no? Okay then."

Jon picked up the box. Alicia held the door for him as he listened to the jingling bell for the last time. He dragged himself over to the El Camino parked across the street. He put the box into the trunk and turned around to look at the store one more time. The silhouette of Alicia Safford turning off the light was the last thing he saw before going home.

*

CHAPTER 12
Leo Is a Sign of Fire

August 30

Jonny, things are progressing slowly—between physical therapy, packing and moving boxes into storage, and trying to sell a house that no one wants. Peter and Fotini have been going through Michael's things. He was such a clutter bug, my brother-in-law. The only good thing to come out of this is that my nephew and sister have a chance to mourn him fully. Letting go is so damn difficult. I hear you let go of the store finally. I can't tell you how proud of you that makes me. Now, try to get some rest and take things easy. I hope my letter finds you well. ~ Evelyn

*

A week of thunderstorms nearly put Tarpon Springs underwater. The rain had not stopped since Jon left the store on Athens Street. The river was at flood stage now, so high ground or not, the Sponge Docks had zero visitors. Jon and Minnie spent those rainy days curled up on the couch watching movies—it was the closest thing to going on vacation. He decided that a break would be good for him—he would start painting again when this monsoon ended. A new storm already had replaced the previous one.

Knock, knock, knock!

The dog growled after a second set of knocks and a crack of lightning that shook the house. Jon got up and answered the door.

Standing on the porch in a yellow poncho was Abby Flowers. She shook out of her slicker and brushed past him. He handed her one of the towels he kept in the hall. "Sorry to show up like this," Abby said, patting her head, "but I had to see you."

"Why? Is something wrong?"

She shook her head. "I never thanked you for the flowers and card, for one—it was a pretty sad birthday. I mean, the office threw me a party and all, but..." She looked distraught. This woman who handled any situation, always in charge of herself, always able to control her emotions— here she was, lost in the middle of a storm. She wiped her eyes. "I've just missed you—this has been the worst summer and I—I'm sorry. If you're busy, I understand."

"Busy doing what? I have no store."

"I heard."

"I have no desire to paint."

"You should."

Jon laughed.

He did not feel the humor, but he laughed all the same.

Without thinking, he put his arm around Abby. The moment he did, she wept uncontrollably, sobbing as hard as any rain, matching it tear for drop. Somehow, she found the strength to smile. She did not feel the happiness, but she smiled all the same.

"Are you hungry?" he asked.

"No," she said, taking his hand and pulling him up the stairs.

"I can't—this cancer, Abby."

"Yes, you can, Jon—you will."

"But I—you'll just leave again."

"Probably," she said, still leading him. Then, stopping on the step above him, she turned around and took his face. She kissed him. "But I'll be back, Jon—I'll keep coming back to you until you tell me to stop coming back to me."

"I would—I mean, I'd never say that to you."

Abby smiled. She patted his cheek.

"So, that means you'll come back to me," he said.

She had tears in her eyes. She nodded. "Of course, Jon—what do you want? A medal?"

"No, Dr. Flowers—just you."

"That's good to know, Mr. Christakos."

An hour later, they were still in each other's arms. There was no thunder. No sound of rain. The house was silent save for the wind blowing. They did not speak as they dressed and went downstairs.

Abby tried not to cry as she opened the door.

Jon fell in behind her.

In silence, he walked her to her car and waved goodbye as she drove away. His heart was heavy as he went back in the house.

Jon tried to paint.

He sat in the den gazing guiltily at a blank canvas board. He had one propped up on a temporary easel. He stood before it, hoping that an image would appear on its own. Now that Abby Flowers had come and gone, his thoughts were a sea of rogue waves.

"I need some inspiration," he said to himself.

He surrounded himself with notebooks. Several were stacked at his feet. Others were opened to select pages, hanging from tacks pinned to the wall. Simple and minimalistic were not his style when his mind was so tempest-tossed.

Over the years he had mastered how he replicated the vagaries of his creative mind, distilling the pixels of imagination into drawings and shapes. His methods of rendering were bold. His lines were solid, and stark, and unyielding. His hand was quick and confident, his lines always sure of themselves.

He was rarely in control when instinct took over.

Tonight, he wanted to try his hand at making studies for a series of large ink paintings. In the kitchen sink were huge bamboo brushes he had fashioned from horsetail hair. He had a collection from a farm up in Ocala. The brushes looked like Olympic torches. They would make dynamic swaths from one end of a canvas to the other—well, when he was ready to move from his easel to the cottage house garage, where dozens of wall-sized canvases waited for him.

He could still smell Abby's perfume on his hands and arms.

If he could have painted that scent, he surely would have done so. Instead, he was painting her initials over and over, in that same flaming script that formed a lion's head and mane.

Flames. Fire. Lion.

Leo, a sign of fire—*is Abby Flowers my sign of fire?*

Jon rubbed his eyes and whistled for Minnie. It was time for bed.

*

Lightning shook the house.

It was well after three o'clock in the morning. Jon headed down the hall. A second crack and boom sent the dog scurrying after him. Face washed and hands dried, he picked her up and went downstairs to get something to eat.

From the second floor, Minnie growled.

Even as the rain poured from the flashing, booming sky, she kept growling. Someone was in the house. There was a shadow lurking at the bottom of the stairs—Jon recognized the silhouette.

"Chucky, how did you get in here?"

"You left the back door open—you said to could come to you if I needed help."

"Not at o'dark-thirty in the effing morning—what do you want? Minnie, easy girl."

"I need to borrow some money."

"Money? Right now?"

"Yes, right now."

"How much?"

"As much as you can give me, Jon. I'll pay you back, with interest."

Jon did not feel like fighting—he was too tired to protest. He had a fair amount locked away in his safe.

The money was not going to cure his cancer. It would not save his soul or extend his life. It would not bring back his dead family. It certainly would not summon Abby Flowers back to his bed. He had lent money to plenty of people over the years.

Something in his gut told him that he had to help. He kept plenty in the safe for emergencies—this seemed like one. Besides, he owed this young man for not ruining his life.

Jon nodded for Chucky to follow him to the den. He opened the house safe under the liquor cabinet. He transferred most of the stacks of bills into a plastic bag—*I can't believe I'm doing this.* He closed the safe and handed the bag over.

"I'm taking a leap of faith here—what's it for?"

Chucky looked down as tears filled his eyes. "It'll save my life, maybe a few others. I wish I could tell you something else to put your mind at ease—but this is business you can't know about, Jon. Do you understand me? Please say that you understand me."

Jon sighed. "I understand the implication—not the reason."

"You have to trust me—you can turn me over to Neal Peruski if I don't make good on this. And he wouldn't blink if you did. He knows what crowd I run with—well, maybe not my new crowd of associates." Chucky started to go. He got as far as the front door. With a hand on the knob, he stopped to say, "Dickey wasn't happy that I refused to rat on you. He's been unhinged since the charges were dropped. I mean, he was always unhinged, but he's lost his grip now."

"Unhinged?"

"Well, he burned down Zorba's—Nico's house. On behalf of Spiros Zervos, which may or may not be true. He kept making a mess for people like me. I got out, and he's unhappy that I did. I got a feeling he's got pay-back on his mind. He'll come after you too, Jon. He won't need a reason or plan. Dickey is addicted to drugs, food, power, and trouble—he loves chaos. Causing pain."

"So, he'll burn my house down? Take my dog away?"

Chucky opened the door. "Maybe, maybe not—his appetites change."

"I've always had a target on my back," Jon said. "I'm a big boy—I can take care of myself."

"I hope you're right," Chucky said, nodding sadly as he closed the door.

*

Lemon Street.

Four blocks past Silverking Brewery.

An unassuming beige—or perhaps taupe with a tint of warm gray? Beige and gray? Gray-brown, warm steel gray? No matter. The color of the painted cement blocks of the halfway house facility was muted and neutral. Willie Dancer Jackson was a resident there.

Jon had not visited since Seamus took his old man back here. Some of Tarpon's forgotten souls spent the rest of their days in this place. He felt a tinge of shame for having not come sooner.

He meant to visit weeks ago.

He parked in the lot and walked toward the entrance. Reflected in the glass door behind him was his El Camino, gleaming in the afternoon sun like a golden yacht. He stepped into the lobby and frowned. The nurse's station looked like the waxy rind of a hollowed-out cheese wheel. Flyers, pictures, and pamphlets were pinned all over its face.

The donut-shaped desk was unmanned, as per usual.

Jon shook his head as he wended his way around the station toward the hallway beyond—*no wonder Mr. Willie made it outside.*

Despite the fluorescent lights, the facility did feel homey, like a favorite school wing repainted in warmer colors. Residents were transients—veterans, runaways, and sex workers mostly—drug or alcohol addiction was par for the course. Still, having a place to sleep, regular meals, and safety made abusing substances a less attractive option. Mr. Willie stayed off the bottle as long as he was here. The only reason he ever left was because it was woefully understaffed.

And the staff was woefully underpaid. Like many municipalities the size of Tarpon Springs, they paid a few dollars above minimum wage for the folks in these health-related service jobs.

Over the years, Jon had funneled enough of his own money to keep this place afloat—he needed to do more for the staff. Sometimes he despised the way the world worked—how fast food workers felt justified in complaining about their low wages and got press for all their whining.

Nurse Walters was the blunt-talking down-to-earth administrator. Utterly dedicated to this job. Never married. Never clocked the inordinate amount of overtime she worked. She never complained.

Jon reached his destination. The last thing he wanted to do was make Mr. Willie feel shameful. Still, it was evident the man had self-control. He was in his room and the front doors of the facility were wide open. When he saw he had a visitor, the old man got up from the sofa chair in the corner. Hands shaking and body rocking, he turned off the television set and offered his guest a seat on the bed.

"How are you doing today, Mr. Willie?" Jon asked.

"I've been getting better every day since Seamus brought me back. I'm such a terrible burden for my children," he replied. "What I've put Seamus and Kendra through grieves my heart." Fat tears streamed down his face. He wiped them without fanfare. For all his demons, here was a man whose heart was intact. He knew that his sins weighed heavily upon those around him.

"Seamus loves you," Jon said after a long pause.

"Kendra's done with me—my daughter won't return my calls."

Jon's phone buzzed.

With an apologetic look, he glanced at the screen.

"Boy, you look like you just seen a ghost," Mr. Willie said. "What you got there?"

"It's a message from my, uh..." Jon could not finish the thought. He started at the screen and blinked, unsure what he was supposed to do. He looked at Mr. Willie and said, "A few weeks ago I found out that I have a 20-year-old daughter. She came to Tarpon this summer to seek me out and tell me who she was. I scared her off. Made her leave." He shook his phone with a tearful smile. "She just sent me a message. She forgives me."

"That's good news," Mr. Willie said softly. "Family is God's answer to prayers He can't attend to right away. Remember me telling you that?"

"I do remember," Jon said. "There's time to change Kendra's mind—just because she's Felicity Noel now doesn't mean she hates you. She's hurting because you weren't here when she stopped by to see her father. She's ignoring you because it hurts too much."

"What should I do then, Jon-Jon?"

"That depends on you, Mr. Willie. You're the one who chooses to stay when you know damn well you can walk out." Jon cleared his throat. "So, don't walk out anymore."

Willie Dancer nodded. "God gives me strength when I stay put. I wish I had His strength when I find myself walking down that hall. When there's a bottle in my hand."

"You're the one who puts it there."

The old man balled his hands into fists. "I just wish I knew His plan for me."

"NO man can know God's mind," Jon said gently. "You told me that too."

"What else did your girl tell you, Jon-Jon?"

"She wants to 'text' me later—it's how these kids talk nowadays. Her name's Hannah."

"That's the name for an old soul—strong-willed," Willie said thoughtfully. "Hannah was mother to Samuel, who anointed Saul and David, the first two kings of Israel." The man demonstrated a keen mind when he was lucid. "Old soul, young man. Best to keep that in mind—and respect her mother for naming her. Is she in town, the mother?"

"Hannah won't tell me the name of her mother."

"Oh, my. Your reputation—least, as I knew it when you were a younger man—always sewing your oats you were. Lord have mercy on you, son."

Jon raised the phone again, like a bible. After a lengthy pause, he managed to say, "Mr. Willie, neither one of us can keep doing what we've done to put ourselves where we are."

Mr. Willie's wooly eyebrows knitted toward his nose. "Boy, are you lecturing me?"

"Someone has to do it. Don't walk out that damn door again. If you stay put, you'll keep your family. If you leave again, you're the only one to blame for losing them. Let's go see Nurse Walters."

As soon as they stepped into the hallway, an orderly the size of a Dodge charger stopped them. "What the hell do you think you're doing?" the orderly asked. "Where's your badge?"

"We're going to speak with Nurse Walters," Jon replied calmly. "She's expecting me—I would have spoken to her earlier, but no one was at the nurse's station."

"Is that why you don't have a badge?"

"Yes—Mr. Willie, would you mind informing Nurse Walters that we have a situation?"

With a smile, the old man shuffled down the hall.

Jon rocked on his heels with his hands behind his back. He stopped when a bout of vertigo nearly toppled him—his phone buzzed and rang again, but he ignored it. Already had it been a long morning. The last thing he wanted to do was go mano–a-mano with someone twice his size, but he was feeling smart at the moment. He did not like being bullied. "Generally speaking, I always found gingers to be pleasant and not aggressive. I see that I've been prejudiced."

"I'm not being aggressive."

"Okay, Danny Bonaduce."

The muscular man stepped toward Jon, as if to grab him by the shirt and drag him out the front doors. Rounding the corner with Willie Dancer at her side was Nurse Walters. "Stop, you boneheaded idiot. I warned you about this yesterday. Or do you not recall me mentioning that we have a special guest who stops by this facility once every week or so to visit Mr. Jackson? See, this is why training is so important," she said, snapping at Randy and directing him to leave. "Front desk—now."

The redheaded man burned with shame and left.

Jon hugged the large woman. "Just in time," he said, squeezing her. "Thanks, Janine."

"Anytime, Jon—what the hell is wrong with you?"

"What do you mean?"

"You know what I mean—dammit," she said, tearing up as she wrapped her arms around him again. "Damn, damn, damn—not again."

"Which is why I am here," he said, uncomfortably. He slipped away from her long enough to take out a folded check from his back pocket. "That should cover things for a while." Nurse Walters looked at the piece of paper and burst into fresh tears.

"This is too much, Jon Christakos—this is—"

"It's enough to take care of this place," he said, putting an arm around Willie Dancer, "the staff and residents for another two years or so." The phone in Jon's pocket vibrated and rang. "I gotta take this," he said, excusing himself to answer it. "Brik? Are you home?"

"Just now—*Hck*—listen, you need to come home right now. I've called Kiki and Neal, so they'll be getting here about the same time as you. I started clearing out the garage for your painting studio, and I thought I'd check on Minnie for you—I wanted some company anyway."

"She was in the kitchen when I left," Jon said. "I've only been—"

Brik interrupted. "Hang on, let me go see if—*Hck*—oh, no. No, no, no—the kitchen door's smashed open. Minnie's collar's on the floor. Someone broke into the house—she's gone."

Jon was already running to the parking lot.

*

FALL

Last night, I was walking the railroad tracks
Almost too drunk to stand
My baby's gone and she broke my heart
She left me for another man
But I can smile with a tear in my eye,
I gotta case of your favorite beer
You know I'll drink myself half-blind
Daddy, how I wish you were here
The fog is clouding my weary brain
And the stars are all cold in the sky
Momma's waiting 'cause it's suppertime
And I was just passing by
Things'll never be the same again
'Cause I keep trying to bring us way back when
Daddy, you know I have to go, so
I'll pour you a sip of beer
Momma said to tell you that she loves you so
Daddy, how I wish you were here

—Brik Buckman, *Song of the Wonderworker*

SEPTEMBER

CHAPTER 13
The Two Favors

*"Every good act is charity. A man's true wealth hereafter is the good
that he does in this world to his fellows."*
~ Moliere

Two paramedics were hoisting Jon into the back of an ambulance. Brik was leaning over him, holding his hand as he climbed into the truck. The handyman's voice kept trembling as he explained what had happened—how the store had been robbed, his house had burned down, his aunt and uncle had drowned with his parents. His wet eyes were rimmed with red as he said that Kiki was handling the funeral arrangements for Hannah, Evelyn, and Panos, but that Alicia was handling the arrangements for Minnie and Chucky. And then, as the double doors of the ambulance closed, Brik squeezed Jon's hand and said with a smile, "Spiros Zervos took all your paintings and money—*Hck*—but I'll be the one to finish killing you at the hospital." Jon shook his head in confusion, but he could not make a sound—his voice did not work. Brik kept reassuring him that things were fine, that he was taking care of everything—that Jon would be better off dead. "If you think I don't know what we sometimes must do to ensure a happy reunion—*Hck*—*well*, you're talking to the guy who gives you weed, brah."

*

Jon woke with a start.

This was not his first dream about Minnie's dognapping. And not the first dream about losing eve-ryone else along with her. It was, however, his first time falling asleep on the Jolley Trolley. The bus was packed. He had done his best to ignore the passengers, but too many recognized him. Some greeted, some ignored. Some giggled and tittered. Three gorgeous young women asked to take a picture with him.

Brik warned him not to go to Clearwater on the bus.

He should have listened to the handyman—he had been nothing but a devoted friend, especially since Minnie was taken.

Neal Peruski was concerned for Jon's safety.

Brik was more concerned for the dog's. Jon had told him to go to Silverking and leave a message for Chuck Parker. If Spiros Zervos was responsible, then they needed him. Brik already knew how to get in touch with Chucky. He said it was a good idea and swore that he would find Minnie and bring her home safely with Chucky's help. Jon implored him to be careful, but Brik just smiled.

"You know me—*Hck*—stop, drop, and roll."

That was three weeks ago.

Ding-Ding!

Jon yawned.

The people behind him were whispering about him. How his mother died giving birth, how his father killed himself. How Felicity Noel was his girlfriend. He endured it, as per usual.

Today, the audacity of his fellow passengers bored him. He simply fell asleep as he stared out of his window trying to keep his temper in check, to keep from weeping over everything else.

"Attention! I have an announcement to make."

That was Leon Rain—Jon had forgotten he was on the Hallelujah Line. "The young man behind me is Mr. Jon Christakos, a resident of Tarpon Springs." There was a smattering of applause, and some boos for good measure. "Like you, he's going somewhere today. Some of you are treating my friend disrespectfully. I have two rules on my bus: Be Jolley and Be-have. Lady, excuse me—yes, I'm talking about you and your rude friends—are y'all for real?"

The passengers in trouble were suddenly looking at their feet, their hands, their beach bags, their hats, their phones—Leon Rain went a step further. "You're getting off my buss in beautiful Dunedin. If you have a destination farther south, you'll have to wait for the next bus OR call a cab. All give you the name and number of my supervisor as you depart. Refunds are gladly given!"

Jon looked in the driver's rearview mirror and smiled.

Leon Rain tipped his hat. At the next stop, 11 men, women and children exited swiftly and quietly. None asked for the name and number of his supervisor. Only three asked for refunds. When the bus started moving again, the passengers applauded. And then, when Jon got up to depart, they applauded once again.

*

After an uneventful hour with Dr. Faklis, Jon was waiting for the next bus to take him home. The bomb ticking inside his head, according to both Raj Patel and Althea Faklis, was still dormant. The good luck they had in June was still with them.

Lost in his thoughts, Jon did not notice the woman approaching him. He did not hear her footfalls or throat clearing as she stood behind him. Only when Misty Harmon gently tapped his shoulder did he look up.

She was crying.

"I was hoping you'd be here on Vitamin Drip Day," she said. "I tried calling you, but I should know better than to think you'd answer the phone." Her hands shook as she wiped her cheek. "Would you mind coming with me? Right now?"

Jon did not mind at all—in fact, he was grateful, even happy, to accept a ride. Driving through Dunedin, Misty said, "Eric's at home now. In his room, with all his things. His aunts and uncles are watching him for me now. His grandfather will be coming down soon. Aside from his morning nurse and me, no one else can sign that well—they can barely make hand pidgin talk. I wish I could stay awake—it would make things easier. Look, I know you have your own struggles at the moment. And I know it's not the best time to be asking you this—"

Jon took her hand. "Misty, you and Eric are my friends. Okay?"

She smiled through fresh tears.

Jon hated the capricious nature of this horrible disease. To an adult, it was a cruel biological terror that debilitated body and spirit. To a child, it was a metaphysical, almost biblical kind of evil that murdered hope as it eradicated a new life from existence. He and Misty were sixteen when they fought their versions of it. She recovered quickly, missing only three months of school. His recovery took two years longer than it should have—emergency brain surgery had left him paralyzed.

"Jon, I know you've made it your personal mission to help people like us," Misty said, clearing her throat. "Eric was hoping that you'd find some time to sit and talk to him before... uh, before he has to go. And I think that'll happen this week. We both do." She struggled to finish her thought. "You talk to him like a regular person. You always have. You know, you would've been a good father."

Jon always regretted not having a family—but being a good father? Lately, he was not good at much of anything.

He lost the store.

He lost the woman he loved.

He lost his dog.

He nearly lost his best friend.

Minnie was still missing, but Brik swore that he was close to finding her. Hannah left and then came back into Jon's life—Brik was responsible for that too. Hannah since had started a benign daily back and forth with him via text messaging. It was something, if not exactly a 'Father of the Year' connection.

"Jon? Are you alright?" Misty asked.

"Yes, of course." He took her hand, giving it a firm squeeze.

As Misty drove, his thoughts returned to Hannah—his long lost little girl. For the life of him, he could not figure out where he should start his search for the identity of the woman who gave birth to her. A string of careless trysts in his past dampened his prospects. He could not remember half the women who slept with him.

It was a messy bed of his own making.

*

Disston Avenue was not known for having many of them, but Misty's charming bungalow glowed with the bustle of visitors.

Despite the pall of death, she kept a beautiful house.

Jon stood in the living room as he waited for Misty's signal. From where he stood at the window, he could see every detail of the long white-washed vehicle sitting on the front lawn—and it made him smile. Years ago, the First United Methodist Church of Tarpon Springs rebuilt an old ambulance junker into an evangelical recruitment mobile for—wait for it, wait for it—the Holy Ghostboosters.

Had he not known any better, Jon would have rolled his eyes. But Eric loved that rolling trademark violation all his young life—after all, it looked like the car from his favorite movie. On the passenger-side door, there was even a cartoon ghost inside a red circle overlaid with a banner that read, *Acts 1:8.* It usually sat in the church parking lot next to the pumpkin patch every October.

Sometimes it went elsewhere for special events.

Misty waved Jon over. As he made his way to the back room, he put on his best smile, took a deep breath, and entered the bedroom. The machines and tubes. The drips and metal rods. The beeping and whirring. The clicking and ventilating. The rhythmic cacophony of sickness and hospice care. A dying boy's End of Days Play-set, cruelly crafted by an Evil Toymaker.

Misty stood next to the wide tilted bed in the center of the room. The pillows almost swallowed Eric. But he sat when Jon sat on the stool beside the bed. The boy was thin, gaunt, a shell of pale skin over brittle bones. Eric had trouble keeping his hands up as he signed. His normally agile fingers shook as he swept and pointed.

"Took you long enough."

Jon laughed.

"I was doing donuts in the yard with the Ecto-mobile."

Misty wiped her son's forehead with a wet cloth. "We spent the morning coming up with questions that he always wanted to ask you," she said, handing Jon a piece of paper. "If you're comfortable."

Jon scanned the sheet—Misty still has gorgeous handwriting. He looked at Eric and pointed to the paper. "Can you read my lips? Good." He narrowed his eyes. "You're a nosy little weasel." Without skipping a beat, he stuck out his tongue and flipped him the bird. "They're all are too good to ignore."

Why are you famous?
What's it like to kiss a girl?
What's the worst thing you ever ate?
What is your favorite thing to do?
If you could make one wish, what would it be?
Do you think my dog will be up in heaven?
What do you think angels eat?
If I miss the train to heaven, will I have to take the bus?
When you were sick before, were you afraid of dying?
Do you believe in God?

"Would you mind giving me time to think about these questions?" Jon asked. "How about you pick one for me to answer now?"

Eric nodded. "Were you afraid to die when you were sick before?"

Looking at Misty, Jon thought for a moment.

"I did die for a few minutes," he signed. "It was the week before Epiphany, when my brother got the cross." He smiled. "I actually died twice, nosy weasel. But I was only scared the first time—once I knew what to expect, the second time was a breeze. Besides, God's with you when it happens—you just gotta look for Him."

Eric struggled to breathe. "He's there so you don't get scared?"

Misty turned away. Jon nodded—*God, please keep me from breaking*. "I can only tell you based on my own experience—for me, it was like being on the biggest sailboat in the world all by myself. And it's got dozens of cabins below deck—and I got to go into each room and talk to people who loved me. People I really loved too. It's like God was the Captain, but

He made sure the sailboat didn't crash into an island or sink in a hurricane or something. He made sure the sails were filled with wind and the seas were smooth. The rest was up to me—so, I went through all the cabins and talked to people I loved."

Eric smiled, struggling to breathe as he signed that he liked that idea. "How hard?"

Jon gritted his teeth—*I will not fall apart.* "Remember when I took you and your mom around Anclote Key? You wished that you could keep sailing forever toward the sunset? It's just like that—after you close your eyes, you just imagine yourself sitting in a boat. It can be as big or as small as you want. All the pain goes away. And you can talk to all the people too. It's your sailboat—you have a voice."

Eric signed something to Misty.

Jon couldn't quite make out the shorthand. She simply kissed her son's forehead and reached for a box on the shelf over his head.

She handed the box to Jon and said, "The butterfly diorama that Dr. Patel gave him last year—he wants you to have it. He'd like to ask a favor. It would mean the world to us."

*

It was raining the night Evelyn's nephew arrived.

The whole business would have put an ordinary young man into a surly mood by the time he got to Tarpon Springs.

Not so, with Peter.

Fresh out of high school, built like a bird, three inches over five feet, thick black wavy hair, he had the most infectious laugh and always wore a smile. Peter was a humble young man. Eager, helpful, vibrantly aware, perpetually positive, loyal to a fault, charming, sweetly naïve—Peter possessed an innocence that inspired people to treat one another with a little more dignity and a lot more respect.

Jon was not surprised to find him standing on the front porch, as the airport taxi was driving away in the pouring rain behind him.

Brik lugged his bags next door.

Peter ate a reheated supper in Jon's kitchen. "I've got good news and bad news," he said, chewing and swallowing. "Which first?"

"Bad news first," Jon said. "Or you'll sleep in the rain."

"Aunt Evelyn and Mom are staying up in Ohio a while longer. Mom's not well enough to travel just yet—not even by car. And the good news is I'm down here to stay."

Jon was taken aback. "Why didn't Evelyn mention this in her last letter?"

Peter shrugged. "Surprise."

He explained that, after reading his essay and receiving recommendations from all the other young men and boys diving for the cross, the church allowed him to participate in the next Epiphany festival. Officials acknowledged that he was a member and that the last two years had been hard on him—hence the exception. Besides, he was generally considered to be non-threatening to the other strapping diving competitors twice his size. In other words, no one believed that he had a chance.

The morning of Eric's funeral, Brik was surprised that he did not have to threaten to ship Peter back home in a Ziploc bag. He was up and wearing his best suit before the handyman's early wakeup call.

The rain was sweet and light—more than a drizzle, not quite a shower—as the trio walked to the church in it.

They shared a large golf umbrella.

During the mile-long trek under it, they each spoke of personal sorrows—the losses they all had endured over the years. "That's a lot of people," Peter said when the lines of cars came into view. "Are you sure we have a seat? I'd be happy to stand outside if I have to."

"We have seats in the back," Jon replied.

There was a gauntlet of greeting ahead, which the three managed with humility and agility—they were seated inside the church sooner than he thought.

As expected, the affair was somber.

Misty sat in front with her parents and in-laws—she wore a look of serenity and peace.

It was time for Jon to speak.

As he made his way down the aisle to the altar, he took note of the numbers of mourners packing the First United Methodist Church of Tarpon Springs—*why did I volunteer to sit all the way in the back?*

The 15 yards between him and the dais seemed like a nightmare road with no end. He stumbled as he wended around the small coffin blocking his path. He nearly knocked over the easel holding the large photo of Eric's smiling face, and the arrangements of flowers and wreaths of sympathy around it. Of course, Eric would have thought it hysterical.

Somehow, Jon managed to reach the lectern without fainting. He gazed out across the sea of faces before him. They gazed back at him with the same sadness. Knowing that everyone gathered here was feeling what he was feeling was a comfort to him.

Swallowing the lump in his throat for the 173rd time, Jon found the strength to begin speaking. He released the sides of the wooden podium and smoothed the pages of his eulogy.

And then he raised his hands to sign in sync with his voice.

"Eric was four years old when I saw him twirling in Craig Park with his mother. His father had just passed the week before, so I went over to sit with Misty and watch her son spin. I'd never seen a child so full of life—he'd lost his father and was slowly going deaf. Misty volunteered me to teach him sign language. It felt more like a Big Brother-Little Brother arrangement. We had our schedule, but Eric was impatient and liked to show up at two hours early. My door has a heavy iron fish knocker, and it was too high for him to reach, so he would let himself into the house. He knew where I hid the key. A rather logical solution to his problem, I thought. But he knew he had an open invitation. No need to knock, just come in. And I always felt the vibration of his incredible spirit moving through the air before him and after his arrival. When he was there, you felt whole. When he wasn't, you felt empty."

Jon gripped the edge of the lectern.

He took a sip of water and looked at the glass.

"As you can no doubt see, my hands are shaking. I'm sure that you can hear my voice breaking too. I'd apologize, but Eric preferred things to be messy and honest. He accepted life the way it was, death included. It was always a privilege to be with him—he was a wise old soul."

Jon looked at Misty, who wiped her eyes and nodded encouragement. He moved over to sit down on the top step, directing his attention to the casket below.

"About a week ago, Eric gave me a list of questions," he began, signing in tandem. "He was a curious kid, but he was also smart and funny—I told him I needed time to think about my answers. I didn't have a chance to tell him last week, so I wrote them all down to read for him now—here goes.

"*Why are you famous?* Eric, I think I'm famous because I'm so very handsome, but everyone else seems to think I'm famous because of Adam Disston's outrageous articles."

No one laughed—well, Misty did, but she already knew what he was going to say.

"*What is your favorite thing to do?* Eric, my favorite thing to do is helping others that can't help themselves. If you believed the gossip about me, you'd know that my favorite thing is to look in a mirror and kiss my reflection. I don't do that as much since I started looking like a hairy Iggy Pop."

A few older men and women chuckled.

"*What's it like to kiss a girl?* Eric, besides your mom and mine, and Felicity Noel, girls are smelly and have stinky rotten shrimp lips. Dogs do too, but they kiss better."

A few more guests, mostly pre-teens, laughed.

The mood lightened.

"*Do you think my dog will be in Heaven? And if I miss the train to Heaven, will I have to take a bus?* Eric, as you already know, Bubba was waiting for you at the train station to Heaven, and that's because dogs, as everyone here knows, hate buses more than they hate cats."

The entire congregation laughed—the sound seemed to ripple and bounce.

"*What's the worst thing you ever ate? If you could make one wish, what would it be?* Eric, the story I'm about to tell you will answer both questions. It's an embarrassing yarn, but I won't lie. You see, when I was four, I made a wish to be Popeye. Yes, THE Popeye—strong to the finish, eats his spinach. Anyway, I remember the onion grass grew thick that summer. Instead of asking my aunt to cook me real spinach, I pretended the onion grass was magic spinach that would turn me into a cartoon sailor. This is because kids are inherently stupid. Uncle Dmitri saw me eating the onion grass, and started hollering at me to stop. I wouldn't stop. I wasn't Popeye yet, and I made a wish to be Popeye. Uncle Dmitri had no choice but to grab me by the arm and give me a smack on my backside. Not because he was angry—but because I was eating onion grass covered in dog poop. To this day, I hate spinach. Toot, toot."

That was what turned the valve—the pressure had to be released. The laughter was loud and full, constantly renewed. It lingered longer than it would have under normal circumstances.

Jon got up and walked down to the small casket.

"One more question," he said softly. *"Do you believe in God?* Eric, it's a good question, but you know the answer already. All I can say is this: 'The Lord is my refuge and my fortress; in Him will I trust. His truth is my shield. Terror shall not come near me; and no evil befall me. He shall give His angels charge over me, to bear me up, lest I fall.'"

Jon kissed the top of the coffin and did his best to return to his seat with dignity. It was a challenge, considering he was on the brink of weeping uncontrollably and people were pointing and whispering. He overheard one pasty young man in a faded secondhand suit tell his friend that he was always hogging the spotlight from others—that he always had and always would.

Several people actually smiled as he passed.

One or two shook his hand.

For the rest of the service, after Jon sat with his friends, he quietly observed, and mourned, and prayed, and rejoiced—with everyone else.

Peter and Brik were content to do the same—no, they did not know the boy well, but they still felt the sting of his loss. When the service was over, four pallbearers hoisted the coffin onto their shoulders and carried it through the front doors of the church.

The sky was not finished with its waterworks.

Jon said goodbye to Misty and her family before rejoining Brik and Peter on the sidewalk. He did not want to go to the gravesite ceremony. He only wanted to walk home in Eric's rain as it fell.

*

OCTOBER

CHAPTER 14

Let It Shine, Let It Shine

"No one after lighting a lamp covers it."
~ Luke 8:16

Brik had taken *Tarpon Lady* out into the Anclote River to help Peter with diving, swimming, and holding his breath—they went every day this week and planned to continue training for another. As long as the weather cooperated, and it likely would. Jon was happy to let them go without him. He wanted to be alone—since the funeral, it's all he wanted. Besides, he was often too exhausted—the slightest amount of activity was enough to put him in bed for hours.

That was the goal today.

The late afternoon sky was semi-cloudy.

There were few birds. No squirrels. The torpid air hung about his face, thickening with each breath and step he took. And then a breeze would blow and clear the space about him.

Jon was in no hurry. He had no place to go, no one to see. But he was tired of walking. Air conditioning sounded nice. Ballyhoo's was just over there—food, folks, and fish sounded fun.

Well, at first—not so much now.

The Kontodiakos family home once occupied the restaurant parking lot. Jon and Panos would stop by on Saturday mornings to grab Kiki before their long day of adventures began. With pockets full of allowances, they would head over to the Sponge Docks to buy gum and ice cream and annoy tourists—*we'd dangle our feet over the water and talk smack for hours.*

The memory made Jon smile.

A kid could do so much with so little back then.

He passed the house of Vasile Faklis, who was sitting on his porch smoking a pipe and reading a book. "*Kalispera*, Vasile."

"*Yassou*, Jonny—how are you this evening?"

"Can't complain. What's the book this week?"

"*When the Tree Sings*," he said, tapping the cover with his pipe stem. "Important book about the Greek civil war—have you seen Draco or Luke today?"

"No, sir—should I go to Dimitri's?"

Vasile threw his hand. "Nah—next time you see us there, we'll talk," he said. "Jonny, you don't look so good—white as a tarpon's belly. You wanna cold beer?"

"Your daughter has me on a strict no-beer diet. Rain check?"

"Deal," Vasile said. "Kick that cancer in the face, *rey*."

Jon smiled—*I'll do my best.* When he reached the curve of the Golden Crescent, Jon spied a familiar car parked at the end of his drive. Rounding the bend of trees, he waved to the man sitting on his porch swing. He crossed the yard and climbed the stoop.

"Disston, what the hell are you doing here?"

"Good to see you, Christakos."

Jon opened the door. "What the hell happened to your face? You get in a fight?"

Adam smiled. "That's a story for a later time—c'mon, man. I'm thirsty."

Here were the facts. Adam Disston was the wealthy great nephew of Beverly Disston Pink. He was a genius, with advanced degrees from Vanderbilt and Yale. He owned property in Connecticut, Vermont, New York, and Florida. He was an avid art collector. Rugged and handsome, Adam possessed an old-fashioned grace and a timeless optimism that belied his modern proclivity for snark. He had a whimsical fascination with sensational journalism. Over the years, he ran several magazines and newspapers, online and traditional. His reputation as being a king maker or breaker was not accurate—Adam Disston was an alchemist who transmuted lead people into golden gods.

Adam lit his cigar and waved the smoke. "How sick are you, Christakos? How long?"

Jon shrugged. "Very, I suppose—and beats me."

"Why in the blue blazes is Raj Patel in India?"

"He's trying to save my life here from over there. There's a surgery technique he's going to use with the targeted treatments Dr. Faklis has prepared."

"Where's Evelyn? You really shouldn't be alone, Jon."

"Her sister had a stroke. And I'm not alone—Peter's down from Ohio. He and Brik are next door. Kiki's a phone call away. Neal Peruski—well, he's not as available as he once was."

"Why's that?"

"He's either on call for baby-making or he's trying to keep the department from falling apart—he's hinted that shake-ups are coming. I don't know whether that's true or not, but there are coordinated neighborhood watch committees all over town. Peter and his Epiphany diving buddies walk the streets of the Greek Village at night—Guardian Angels of Tarpon Springs."

Adam laughed. "It's about time this town stopped being the bitch of Spiros Zervos." He raised his glass. "To the good people of Tarpon Springs—God give them strength and courage."

Jon pointed. "Is that why you look like potted meat? C'mon, cheer me up with a story."

Shaking his head, Adam leaned back in his chair. "When is the surgery, Christakos?"

"Second week of November."

"I hope Raj Patel doesn't repeat the same mistakes that his father made. It would be a shame for you to put all your eggs into this one basket and things don't work out."

"This cancer's not your typical glioma," Jon said, motioning to his body. "I know I look like I'm auditioning for a Holocaust musical, but I'm healthy otherwise. Well, the headaches are bad. And the mood swings and memory gaps. Exhaustion. There's a ring of cysts around my brain stem trapping the cancer inside. Bizarre blessing in disguise. Glacial growth. Zero metastasizing. My blood's clean—my tissues, my lymph nodes. No one can explain it—and no one wants to do anything to trigger something. That's why they're so willing to wait for Raj to get back. They have more time to study me."

"Keeping the cancer at bay," Adam whispered, amazement in his voice. "How often do you go in to be poked and prodded then?"

"Once a week—I get another spinal tap in a few days."

"Wow—you hit the cancer jackpot. Wish I could get a spinal tap."

Jon smiled. "Thanks to Brik Buckman, I'm not as nauseous. I eat like a pig and sleep through the night. That's why Evelyn's not here. She's needed more in Ohio."

"You're going to beat this thing, Christakos. I can feel it."

"Disston, not even you can summon the kinds of miracles I need."

Adam choked on the cigar smoke, trying to make the cloud dissipate as he laughed himself into a happy contented sigh.

He still wore a bright crimson face with heavy creases around his mouth—the color almost made his wounds look healed. But then, when his natural hue returned to normal, the bruises and cuts on his face regained their previous shades.

"Your worth is priceless, Jon Christakos—like your paintings, you are one of a kind. You're long overdue a miracle or several."

Jon narrowed his eyes. "Son of a bitch—you're the private collector Hannah told me about."

Adam Disston raised his glass. "And Aunt Bev was my crazy partner in crime—it was her idea to scare you into selling your work." He reached into the sleek man bag at his feet. "And now you are in next month's *Art in America*. Just a blurb about some upcoming exhibits in New York and Seattle. Look, Kendra Jackson didn't become Felicity Noel in a day. It'll take time for you to become Christakos."

Jon looked at the magazine on the coffee table. He clearly saw the bright yellow tab marking the page—he would look at it later.

"What do you want?"

Adam said nothing.

"Tell me something."

"I'm here for a few reasons. A: I wanted to know just how sick you are—I got what I needed on that front. B: I wanted to give you proof that your artwork is known—the look on your face was what I needed on that front. And C: I wanted to encourage you to make peace with Alicia Safford—as soon as possible." Adam tamped out his cigar. "Jon, if you knew what was at stake, you would." He got up, pointed to his own face, and smiled. "I need to start writing my story before I forget the details."

"What story? A, B, C, and D—tell me Reason D, you godless bastard."

Adam smiled. "Don't get up. I know my way out. Don't disappoint me, Jon. Don't die before you make me millions of dollars. And don't make me write your eulogy either." He was already walking down the hall when he said, "Alicia Safford—call her up. The sooner the better, my old friend."

*

When Adam had gone, Jon cleaned up and then wandered around the first floor. He sat beneath the painting of his mother hanging on the stairwell wall. His head rested somewhere on the bit where her mermaid tail had swept over a turtle swimming beneath it.

He smiled—*Art in America*.

The house was a lonely place without his dog in it. It was like a body devoid of its soul. Here a ball, there a toy—here a half-chewed stick of rawhide, there an empty bowl of water.

I must trust in Brik and trust in Kiki.

Jon was filled with a gnawing fear. Not about dying—he and Death were old friends. No, he was afraid of losing more people he cared about.

He thumped his head against the staircase post. The irrational thoughts that flooded his brain were starting to spin. He thought about Eric and Misty, and Hannah—YES! He took out his phone to read their last message exchange.

H: hey, u there?
H: wanted to say sorry about Eric
　　J: thx, hannah
H: need a hint about my mother?
　　J: thought you said no hints
H: << impatient << girl = mind-changer
　　J: okay - lol
H: hint 1 of 3 – golden –
H: if u don't figure out with that
H: then I want a different dad
　　J: very funny

He hovered his thumb over the number for Hannah. No, a quick walk around the Crescent would clear his head—*it's getting dark outside, you nimrod.* "I could go visit Alicia," he whispered, before practicing what he might say. "Adam told me to stop by, Alicia—if I'm disturbing you, blame your ex-fiancé."

Jon got to his feet and did a raspberry.

He hopped down the stairs and headed for the front door. When he opened it, he screamed bloody murder at the shadow standing there, with hand raised either to stab or smack or—"Turn on the light, you goofy malaka—you scared me to death."

Kiki Kontodiakos reached inside the door and flicked a switch. When the light came on, she spread her hands, as if to say, *it's only me.*

Brushing past Jon, she closed the door and dragged him to the kitchen. He sat at the dinette as she poured a glass of water and made a sandwich. "I ran into Adam Disston at the Tarpon Tavern just a minute ago," she said, frowning as she rummaged through his pantry. "I should've stopped at Winn Dixie first—you got to be kidding me. No chips?"

"My fridge was stocked until Peter showed up on my doorstep—and

Brik eats enough for two pregnant women. This kitchen was stocked yesterday. I'm just—"

"Good, then I won't tell Evelyn you're starving yourself on purpose," Kiki said. "You're still not on that crazy diet are you? What in Elijah's holy name? Is this a jar of meat paste?"

Jon laughed. "That, my dear Kiki, is the handyman's vegemite."

She sniffed the suspicious looking stuff and gagged. "Have mercy—that's vile. You men are so pathetic without women."

Jon nodded sadly. "Kiki, you're the one who got away."

She bit into her peanut butter and pita. "Lies atop lies, you lying liar. Sweet to say, Jonny-baby, and you know I love you, but I don't date men with werewolf hair and brain cancer." She took a drink. "That's the smile I wanted to see." She squeezed his hand. "Oh, I ran into Abby Flowers. She told me about your midnight booty call. She told me she sent you some flowers as a thank you."

"No, I don't think she—"

"Hmm, maybe it was a letter or a package."

Jon closed his eyes. "Skatá—the flashlight on the fridge. Get that. I'll be on the porch."

Kiki laughed. "Why do you need a flashlight?"

"Because if she sent me a letter, then it's under the damn porch." He had neglected to give Brik the task months ago—of course, it would be THE ONE task destined to bite him in the butt.

And so, it was exactly thus.

The metal letterbox bolted to the wall outside had an opening in the bottom. The rusted-out ragged slit was wider—letters could easily slip through it. He crouched when Kiki joined him. "The gap between the house and floor. Shine it there."

She directed the beam into Jon's eyes. "It's not under the porch."

"GAH—what's not under the porch? Shine that elsewhere."

Kiki laughed. "What Abby Flowers sent you—I was just messing with you to get you to come outside. You really do have a problem though—I hope she didn't send you anything. Anyway, it's behind you. The thing I wanted you to see."

Jon turned around. It took several moments before the spots in his eyes cleared. He was relieved that he would not need to remove the lattice cover and crawl under the floor on hands and knees. Through dead leaves, spider webs, twigs, insects, bits of blood-orange paper, glass, bones. Well, not tonight—and not him either.

This was a task for Peter tomorrow.

His vision cleared. There was a picnic basket.

"What's this?" Jon asked. "Why is it here?"

Kiki calmly picked up the basket by the handles. She nodded for him to follow as she went back into the house. They went to the kitchen. On the tiny table, she set the basket on a discolored pile of old mail and opened the lid. "Be quiet—she's had a rough drive and a strong sedative."

Jon's heart pounded like a sledgehammer in triple time.

He peered inside and stifled a happy shout. "Where? How? When?" Kiki put a hand on his shoulder as he carefully lifted his sleeping—and oh, so very groggy—twice-rescued Pomeranian from the basket.

"She's warm."

That was all he said.

Jon sat down in the sleek dinette chair to carefully inspect the dog. She looked healthy. When Minnie finally recognized him, those big eyes widened and that tail started wagging.

He had a thousand questions to ask, of course, but now was not the time—besides, he was incapable of speech. Unable to stop the flood of joy, he finally let go, like another Atlas shrugging. And his relief was so great that he could not stop laughing. It welled up like lava from inside him, bursting forth until he was unable to control himself. He laughed until tears streamed down his face.

*

The El Camino sat atop the curve overlooking the concrete pier of Spring Bayou. A large floating screen sat in the water for the annual viewing of *Beneath the 12-Mile Reef,* a 1953 Cinema Scope film starring Robert Wagner as a young Greek sponge diver who falls in love with his dead father's rival's daughter.

It was Romeo and Juliet set in Tarpon Springs.

And so, this coming Saturday, participating townsfolk would dress up as characters from the movie and interact with it 'Rocky Horror'-style. Always a respectable crowd—not Epiphany numbers but solid.

"Looks like they're about done," Brik said. "Better call Peter."

Jon steadied the dog in his lap and rolled down the passenger-side window. He put two fingers in his mouth and whistled. From the pier, a short dark-haired young man waved enthusiastically before bounding up the steps and sprinting to the idling car.

"We're going to Clearwater now—everything ready for tonight?"

Peter drummed on the door. "Yeah, we're good. Some divers are scoping out the water for January's plunge—they accidentally fell in. Hey, if I had a chance to get the cross, then I'd fall in too."

Brik honked the horn. "You got a chance, brah. Your size is your asset. And so is your tiny barrel chest. You'll be fine. I promise—*Hck*—chin up, chin up, chin up."

Peter scratched Minnie's head. "Sure you don't want to watch the movie tonight? I mean, if they don't drain too much spinal fluid. I could clean your old wheelchair and put cold packs in the seat."

Jon shook his head. "How about you focus on cleaning Aunt Evelyn's house. The cottage house garage. And get started cleaning mine." He patted the young man's hand. "Kiki said she'll stop by with some food for you—so be on the lookout for her Jeep Wrangler."

Peter mumbled and waved as he went back to the concrete pier.

Brik put the car in gear. Jon rolled up the window. No sooner were they going south on Pinellas Avenue than Jon doubled was over in pain. The headache that had smacked him from inside his skull was back again—the handyman's strongest weed barely touched the pain. A wave of nausea followed. And then a burst of alien music in his ears.

Breathing exercises, long slow breaths until the ache subsided. Jon kept stroking his dog as he continued inhaling and exhaling in a steady rhythm—*talk about something else.*

"Think she'll want to be with me, Brik? Abby Flowers?"

"She's postponing the inevitable."

"Her job at the pet hospital is done—she doesn't need to stay in Tarpon anymore," Jon said, sucking his teeth, trying to focus. "She wants to see me. Wants to talk to me."

"When, brah? You didn't tell me that—*Hck*—boom, boom, boom."

"I should tell her to get the hell out of town before it's too late."

Brik laughed. "I think she's way past that."

"I think I am too—damn."

"Yeah, the love of your life really sucks," the handyman joked. "Poor Jon."

"You hush your mouth." Jon opened his eyes. "Brik?"

"What's wrong?"

"Oh, nothing—I just can't see out of my right eye."

The car swerved. "What do you mean you can't see?"

Minnie began to whimper.

"I mean I can't see out of my right eye," Jon replied, holding his head at the temples. "This pressure must be goosing the optic nerve. Nothing like a spinal tap before telling the woman you love that you want to spend the rest of your life with her. I'll be fine."

Jon petted the dog to soothe her—she finally settled into his lap. "Let's just get to Clearwater before my brain explodes."

"*Hck*—not funny, brah. When did Patel say he's coming back? Halloween? Day before?"

"Slow your roll, catfish—you just ran a red light. Half blind, and even I saw that violation. How about we not die in a car crash before my spinal tap? I've been looking forward to it. Sing to me."

Brik snorted. "Hell no, I'm not singing."

"Fine—if I go blind, I'll blame you."

"*Hck*—blame me all you want," Brik said, singing, "or blame it on the rain—yeah-yeah."

"Alright, I hope your golden pecker falls off—singing Milli Vanilli at me."

The handyman laughed. "What are best friends for?"

"Golden—Hannah said that word," Jon said, rubbing his eyes. "Said that it would lead me to—oh, my God." The vision in his eye began to clear. "I'm such an idiot! Why didn't I see it before?"

"What's wrong now? Are you blind in both eyes?"

Jon waved and settled into the seat. "Just got excited—the women in my life keep telling me I have trouble seeing the forest for the trees." He fished his phone out of his pocket. "I never would've gotten it without the hint. Basic math, really. And so effing obvious."

"I can't verify it for you, brah—*Hck*—talk to Han—"

"I know you're not allowed to say anything. I'm texting Hannah now," Jon said, thumbing his message. "And now, all we need to do is wait for—buzz, ping! Let's see if I'm right."

Jon smiled. He was not a great detective, even regarding his own family tree, whose branches were bare because of his lack of clever intuition as much as anything else. But Hannah's mother was no longer a mystery to him—indeed, he had never been so happy about being right.

Adam Disston was right after all.

*

Halloween morning had arrived.

It was a big day—well, for Jon it was a huge day. He supposed that Abby saw it much the same way that he did. No doubt that Peter did too, as he wanted nothing but happiness for the people around him. As Jon waited for Abby Flowers to arrive, he rocked himself on the front porch swing. Minnie was curled up in a sleeping lump beside him.

Creak...croak.

Peter had been a tremendous help. It was Peter who had been taking care of Minnie since last week's spinal tap. Peter who helped Jon shower, dress, and feed himself every day. Peter shrugged off the heaps of praise dumped on him. He had to do the same for his father in the last months of his life—he simply said that was what family was for.

Jon knew what that meant. It was all the depressing work that needed doing when someone you loved was very sick or slowly dying. It was the cleaning of fluids, changing of clothes and sheets, the cleaning all over again—the managing of tubes and beeping machines. The handholding and counseling. The night watches and day watches. The constant vigilance—the unending parade of doctors and nurses and visitors. The despair and anger. The isolation and terror and vulnerability.

Yes, Peter had been forged in those fires.

"Mr. Christakos?"

Jon looked up at the same time Minnie lifted her fuzzy head. "Dr. Flowers—I didn't hear you," he said, his heart suddenly pounding in his chest. "Um, did you walk?"

"Yes, it was too beautiful a day not to walk."

"We get so few days with no humidity—if I weren't so sore, I'd be walking up and down the Pinellas Trail myself. Why don't you come have a seat next to Minnie?"

"Did Kiki tell you that I was on call when they brought her to me?" she asked, sitting carefully in the slippery bench. "That's a brave girl."

"I figured the picnic basket had to be your idea."

Abby laughed, which made Jon's heart bump itself off the track and into the ditch of his chest cavity. There it continued to spin its wheels, thumping madly until it was secured back in place. "The reason I asked to see you is because I've been offered a new logistical nightmare to fix up in Lakeland," she said, gently stroking the dog. "I haven't accepted the job. I wanted to talk to you."

Jon cleared his throat. "Why?"

"I've not been good at saying goodbye. Not you—I'm the coward here."

"No, you're not."

"Yes, I am—please don't patronize me, Jon."

"Sorry, I was just—"

"I know what you were just trying to do—please stop doing it," she said, getting to her feet. The swing barely moved. She began to pace, from one end of the porch to the other—a good 30 or so feet across. "If I lived in Lakeland, that's only an hour away. I could come see you after you get better."

"What if I don't get better? What if this is all the time we have?"

Abby looked stunned. "Why would you even say that?"

"What do you want me to say? Want me to wish you well, but ask you to stay the night? A cuddle on the couch under a sweet haze of smooth jazz as we toss candy to the costume-clad panhandlers for a few hours before we go upstairs? I've left you alone for months, just as you wanted. You're right—you've got the coward problem. But I've got the goodbye problem. I don't want to effing say it."

"I know, and it's grossly unfair of me—I keep giving you mixed signals," she said, pacing faster to and fro, even as her voice quickened. "Do you know how hard it is to love someone you only just met?"

"Yes, I do."

"In the first moment your eyes meet?"

"Yes, I do."

"And you feel your carefully prepared life vanish," she said, "all because your gaze locks and your heart clicks into place?"

"Yes, I know this thing."

She turned on her heels. "Well, I didn't want to know this thing."

"So you've told me."

"Tell me what I'm supposed to do with it then."

"I can't tell you that."

"Stop it, Jon!"

Minnie whined and tried to duck away.

Abby immediately dropped to her knees and apologized into her fur until that pink tongue licked her hands, telling the good doctor that it was okay now. Jon touched Abby's hair. She did not flinch, which was a surprise. "Tell me what you want. I'm useless as a mind reader. I couldn't figure out an obvious hint about Alicia Safford—and well, my point is that I'm not a thinking man—I'm not clever."

Abby sat up and wiped her eyes. "Tell me about Bentley Safford—is it true that he tormented your family over this house? I'm just curious. I just want to hear your voice, and you saying that name made me wonder. No agenda question."

And so, Jon did his best to tell the story.

Here were the facts. Bentley Safford had a lot of money. He was obsessed with reclaiming property George Cheyney had purchased in the 1930s. Bentley hated the fact that the old Safford manor was moved back from the bayou to make room for Cheyney's two new houses—again, now owned by Jon and Evelyn. Bentley Safford started a war over ownership. He used Tarpon's Historic Homeowner's Society to bully Jon's aunt and uncle into selling it. First, he bombarded them with warning letters and complaints to the HHS—he enlisted others to do the same. Aunt Bessie went into a fugue state if the man walked by. Bentley Safford sent forth his daughter Alicia to divide the two teenage boys living in either house. Jon fell for her, but she left him to be with Panos. That nearly handed Bentley Safford the keys to the house. Had it not been for the Epiphany festival two years later, he would have succeeded.

"Why the Epiphany festival?" Abby asked.

"It's the most important day of the year for Tarpon," Jon replied. "I'm not active in the church anymore, but the day still affects me—it's hard to explain unless you grew up here."

"Maundy Thursday still affects me. What's the celebration like?"

"Thousands crowd around the bayou to watch a ritual that's been around here for over a hundred years. Dozens of Greek teenage divers, in naught but shorts and T-shirts, jump into the murky waters to claim a white wooden cross the Archbishop throws. The one who finds the cross is blessed with good luck for the year. He gets fame and money. There's a parade on the shoulders of his friends back to the church. *Glendi* is the celebration that lasts late into night. Epiphany is a special time, even more so than Thanksgiving or Christmas."

"You never got a chance to dive for the cross?"

Jon shook his head. "I was too sick. When Panos and I were boys, we'd fantasize about that cross. Kiki coached us. Swimming, diving, holding our breath. God bless her. Brik is doing the same thing for Peter—I think they're out in the Anclote River right now."

Abby sat down on the bench and took Jon's hand.

"Anyway, we'd sit around and picture how we'd do it," he explained. "How Panos would get it one year. How I'd get it the next. And how Kiki would get 10% of the money we collected—you wouldn't believe how much these Epiphany divers can rake in after they get that cross. This community takes care of them. Panos couldn't stand that I had cancer. He was horrible to me for well over a year. I wanted to watch him dive. We were going to move to Tampa so that I could recover. Miracle of miracles, Panos broke the surface with the cross above his head. He came back to me. He came back to us. Bentley Safford lost his war. Tarpon Springs saw him as the monster he was."

"What happened after that?"

"Bentley blew his brains all over the walls of Alicia's bedroom—that's what he did."

"Dear God—why on earth would he do that?"

Jon shrugged. "I doubt the reason was of the earth, whatever it was. Alicia hired a small staff to keep the house in her absence. She finished school up in New York. I saw her again in Atlanta one winter, when I was performing at one of the theaters downtown. I didn't see her again until June of this year. Alicia came back to Tarpon with a daughter no one knew she had. Not even her father."

Abby squeezed his hand. "Because it was under your nose, Mr. Christakos," she said, gently. "You're not very good at noticing the things under your nose."

"So I've been told—and by you more than once."

She laughed. "I already know about Hannah, so stop worrying."

"Who's worried?"

Abby sighed. "I was worried when I showed up here—now, not so much."

"Who told you then?"

Abby smiled. "Hannah told me about Hannah—she told me before she went back to school, and suggested that I keep my distance from you if I had plans to break your heart." Her eyes filled with tears. "All my life I've been smart about my decisions. I'm intuitive and perceptive, not easily fooled. But when I'm with you, it all goes out the window." She kissed his hand. "I wish you wouldn't look at me like I don't know what I'm signing up for. I know what it is you're facing."

"Then please don't take that job—stay here with me."

"I will if you make your peace with Alicia Safford." She got to her feet. With a smile full of calm joy, Abby said, "I'd rather not help you with the panhandlers, so how about I come back later tonight. Around nine o'clock? That should give you enough time to have a chat with her."

*

Jon sat on the front stoop next to a pair of broken jack o' lanterns. He was there to make peace with the woman he once loved. The woman he once despised. The woman he did not know was the mother of a daughter he just met this summer—it was so obvious to him now, the connection. He would have climbed the steps to ring the doorbell, but he was too tired after trudging across the arc of the bayou to get here.

He was sore and dizzy—and nervous.

Jon decided to wait for Alicia to find him there. He had time before Abby met him at his house. He was content to toss pennies at older trick-or-treaters out late to cause trouble.

In his peripheral vision, he spied a flyer advertising the movie last week. Brik and Peter had said it was a blast. He reached with a groan to pluck the paper from the grass. He looked it over and shook his head. The flyer was designed like a cheesy movie poster with copy describing the event and basic plot of the film. It read like a pulp paperback novel:

BENEATH THE 12-MILE REEF. Mike and Tony Petrakis, father-son Greek-American spongers, compete for territory in the fertile waters off the Florida coast with the Rhys family, who'll do anything to protect their livelihood. When the families discover the love affair between Tony and Gwyneth Rhys, will it be wedding bells? It's Romeo & Juliet set in Tarpon Springs! Come to the Spring Bayou pier Oct 29 - 8:30 p.m. FREE admission, soda, and popcorn. Dress as your favorite character!

Jon balled up the flyer and tossed it into the bushes. For a quarter of an hour, he stared at his hands, trying to understand what he knew he simply could not. He could no longer pretend to despise Alicia anymore—especially now. He trusted Adam Disston, yes, but it was Abby Flowers who convinced him to take this first step. In his heart, he knew it was long overdue, asking Alicia for her forgiveness.

"Hello, Jon."

Jon turned around.

"Hello, Alicia."

"Are you going to sit there all night?" she asked with a laugh. "No, stay put. I'll come down there." She sat beside him and sighed. "Quiet night—oh, maybe not as quiet as I thought. Poor pumpkins."

Laughter echoed loudly across the water.

The streetlamps and dock lights, the moonlight, the spooky orange and purple displays—all made for an eerie glow. His house and Evelyn's house looked like two ghosts floating above the ground. Just beyond was the dimly lit outline of the Safford House Museum. Faint, but visible.

"I'm ten years old and going door-to-door selling boxes of chocolate or raffle tickets—I can't remember what for," he said. "Panos was working the other side of the bayou. I was working this side. I was heading to the Cheyney house next door. A scream stopped my heart. My hands shook as I followed the sound to your backyard fence. I opened the gate, and when I saw what I saw, I peed my pants and ran. It was the fastest I ever ran. I don't know if it was luck, fate, or coincidence, but a police car was coming toward me. I told the officer about the situation. I felt so helpless and weak as I watched him do what I wanted to do—save you from getting hurt by your brother and his friends. I sat down on the curb and stared into my box of collected money. The only recurring dream I have is hearing you scream as I sit on the curb frozen in fear. I was weak."

Alicia needed a moment to consider his words, the weight of them. "You were only a boy, Jon. My brother would've beaten you to a pulp had you done anything."

Jon nodded. "I remembered something I'd forgotten. I'm remembering lots of things—memories suddenly hitting me like splashes of ice cold water in the face."

"What is it you remembered about me?"

"That I'd already forgiven you years ago," he said quietly. "Years ago, after Atlanta—I honestly don't know why I reverted back to the way I felt when I was a teenage kid. Anyway, I'm here because I wanted to apologize to you and ask for your forgiveness. And not just because you're the mother of my only daughter either."

Alicia smoothed her lap. "I was seven when my father raped me the first time. I'll never forget the pain. I was nine when he did it again. It was disconcerting how my parents pretended to be royal-born, the magnificent Saffords. I was the mistake, of course. Until my older brother proved to be a total psychopath like my father—they put him away before people could talk. My mother taught me how to go about my day, pretending to be normal and better than everyone else. I believed it in order to survive, Jon. Even now, it's hard to think otherwise. My parents broke me like a horse. It was easy to do what they wanted after that, easy to play their games. I played it to perfection with Panos. My father wanted me to tear your families apart. Panos saw the truth. That eventually liberated me. But you had to forgive first, Jon—you have always had that burden. Otherwise, Panos would've crawled back to me and my father would've seized your aunt and uncle's property. It was never Panos, Jon—it was your strength, your faith. Without you, people would be the weak insignificant things they are. It was your face that I saw, Jon—your smiling face that changed the course of my life. And our daughter's life. Who would've imagined that I'd get stuck in Atlanta during its coldest winter in years— the same time you were there. It was fate, destiny—a miracle for me."

Jon smiled. "Those four days of snow weren't so bad."

Alicia looked at him sideways. "I'm glad we're on the same page," she said. "Finally. I really need to send Abigail Flowers a bouquet and a bottle of wine. I'm happy you have her."

"That miracle has yet to happen."

"Well, that shouldn't be too hard for a wonderworker like yourself. Anyway, I wanted to tell you about Hannah since I first came back to Tarpon. Hannah made me promise to keep my mouth shut because she wanted—oh, no." Alicia jumped to her feet and pointed.

"Jon, your house is on fire."

*

CHAPTER 15

Transmigration of Souls

"God creates out of nothing. Still more wonderful:
He makes saints out of sinners."
~ *Søren Kierkegaard*

They had been sitting on the curb watching smoke rise from the ruins for hours. What a strange fire it had been too. It engulfed only the side facing east. It hardly touched the western side facing Evelyn's house. The structure of Jon's abode appeared to be mostly intact, if not entirely stable. It looked like the dollhouse of a giant's pyromaniac child.

If that was not a sign from God, then Jon did not know what a sign was. One half of the house stood quietly—one half was nothing but charcoal shambles.

"Father, Son, Holy Ghost—that's so effing cool, brah."

"*Kyrie Eleison*, brah!" Peter shouted.

During the course of last night's events, Jon counted no less than 25 of the handyman's turns of phrase coming from his young cousin's innocent lips. And then there were the stories. Enough to turn Peter into a hobo disciple—*kid's gotta learn about the real world at some point.*

Alphabetically listed backward, Brik's adventures took place in any (or none) of the following: well, warehouse, undersea cave, truck stop, sunken ship, street party, river dock, pavilion, meat locker, haunted lighthouse, garden, funeral, edge of waterfall, covered wagon, coliseum, cloister, canyon, boxing match, bell tower, bathhouse, antique wine-cellar, and abandoned asylum.

Jon cracked his knuckles. "You and Brik need some time apart."

"Bite me, homeless," Peter countered. "Speaking of which, what happens now?"

Brik laughed. "*Hck*—Jon gets the cottage house," he said, turning to Peter. "You are gonna help me move my stuff into Evelyn's house." He draped an arm around the younger man's shoulder and pulled him to the side, whispering something in his ear. Peter immediately bolted to do whatever it was that needed to be done. Brik sat on the curb with Jon. "If it wasn't six o' clock in the morning, I'd say that we all needed a drink. Sorry about your house."

"It's just a house—I was expecting it, sooner or later. I'm just glad that Peter had taken Minnie out for trick or treating. There's a blessing."

Abby shot him a look. "You were expecting this to happen?"

Jon shrugged. "Let's just say I had a warning and leave it at that," he said, pointing to the side of the house still intact. "Brik, you think you could get something from under my bed without dying?"

Brik brushed his hands. "*Hck*—It'll hold long enough."

"I can see my entire bedroom," Jon mumbled. "I'm so glad I made the bed."

"Lots of photographs are still on the walls—and mermaid paintings," Abby said sadly. "At least the one on the second floor landing looks like it could be saved."

Brik spat. "It's a crime scene. They took pictures of everything, but I don't—"

"Just the fireproof lockbox under my bed—and the storage container if it hasn't melted. In truth, I'm relieved—Minnie was nowhere near the blaze. None of us were near the blaze."

Abby nodded. "It was kind of Alicia to take Minnie to her place."

Jon smiled. "I think so—Brik can fetch her later too. Hannah should be here by then."

"*Hck*—in all likelihood."

Jon staggered to his feet and retched until he dry-heaved.

Again.

His equilibrium would not reset fast enough. With Abby's hands on the back of his neck, a blanket of calm settled over his body. The nausea passed, and she helped him back to the curb.

Peter returned with a wet towel and cold seltzer for Jon, who tried to blow things off with excuses about the smoke and exhaustion. "Peter, would you mind going to my store and getting—" He stopped himself, closing his eyes in embarrassment. "I don't have a store—sorry."

"You need rest, brah—that's all," Brik said, looking at Abby. "I have some extra clothes that I'll bring over to the cottage house in a bit. How about you get him settled in? I'll take care of your things too, ma'am—just take him and get him cleaned and in bed."

Abby steered Jon toward the gate on the other side of Evelyn's house. He stopped and turned to Brik. "The butterfly diorama Eric gave me—maybe it survived."

"Sure, sure, sure—*Hck*—get some rest. Rest means sleep!"

The handyman turned to Peter, who was talking at length with Neal Peruski a few yards from the property line. They were waving frantically at him to hurry over there. From the looks on their faces, the news was not good. In fact, what happened to Jon's house was the good news.

*

Abby lifted the washcloth and squeezed, letting the water drip down Jon's shoulders. "I can't believe you let me shave your back," she said, squeezing more warm water over his pink flesh. "I'm glad I didn't get into the tub with you until you refilled it—my God, Jon. Why are you so damn hairy?"

Jon leaned back and smiled when he felt bare breasts. "Kiki thinks I look like an Ewok."

"She does know her animals, Jon. She speaks true." She kissed his cheek and smoothed his forehead. "How are you feeling now?"

"I'll feel better when 'rest' really means sleep. And when I eat something. I'm suddenly ravenous. Might be the pot, might be the sweet lovin'—maybe I'm just happy about the house."

"You're getting all pruned, Jon."

"Tell me something I don't know," he said playfully. "It's a good idea—tell me."

Abby thought for a moment. She traced his clavicle with a wet finger. "You first."

Jon did not hesitate. "I love you, Dr. Flowers."

"I already knew that, Mr. Christakos," she said, her voice nearly breaking.

Jon hummed. "Your turn. Tell me a story."

"Um, okay—it's three in the morning. No moon. I can't sleep, so I go downstairs and drink some water. I go outside. The street lamp is flickering. A wind blows as I sit on the curb and look at your house. You walk outside your front door and I can't breathe. My brain buzzes as I walk up to you and try to take you back inside and tuck you in bed. I don't understand why I love you—it's the first night we spend together, and I feel this pull toward you. I know you're sick. I know you have cancer—I don't know what kind, of course. I just start to feel like I'm a girl again. And I don't know what comes over me, but I tell myself that I can't stay. I need to make up a reason for it—I just don't know what it'll be yet. And then I tell you I want space to think about my feelings after you open up to me. I saw in you at that moment all I'd ever wanted, and I was terrified that I'd lose you. I was—"

Abby smiled when she heard snoring.

She held Jon close until the water was too cold. She got him standing and dried. She led him to the master bedroom. He fell onto the bed, both arms outstretched into a 'T' and his head just off the edge. She managed to swing him around lengthwise. She put her hair up in a haphazard sopping twist and wrapped a towel around her waist.

The late morning sun poured through the window. It shone upon his naked body. His was a weary body waging a secret war for survival even as it struggled to find rest. Knowing that truth was the thing that informed her thoughts about seeing it now. A sublime vision—that was this man's body.

Abby marveled at the imperfections. She counted the ribs on his sides, hoping he would not flinch as she tapped them. In the sunlight, she could see more of him.

At first the idea of trimming his growth seemed silly—she realized now that it was his gift to her. It was his way of daring her to deny what he was going through. She counted the tiny freckles on his arms. He was so pale, so emaciated. His veins were blue streaks of lightning under the surface of his flesh—his forearms bruised from countless piercing needles. She brushed her fingertips over the tiny punctures, a grotesquery of little angry red mouths.

She was surprised that Jon had opened himself so freely.

He had every right not to, and she had no reason to expect it. And yet, here he was, all of him laid bare for her—that he had no clothes to wear was a fact not lost on her either.

She took off her towel and curled up beside him. The terrible cost of forsaking him was denying herself the joys of being with him at his strongest—not that she believed he would not grow strong again.

The burden he had carried alone was partly hers to carry now.

Knock-knock-knock.

Abby tucked a comforter around Jon and left to answer the door, grabbing a robe on the way. She was tying the flaps when Brik came inside with Minnie, who danced about their legs.

"Well, good morning to you too, happy girl—has she eaten?"

The handyman put several bags into the small living room. "Alicia said that she fed her around seven—*Hck*—excuse me," Brik said. "This suitcase has enough clothes to get Jon through the next few days. I do have his lockbox at Evelyn's. Half the diorama." Making himself at home—and that meant raiding the refrigerator—he opened a bottle of beer and sat on the floor. "Is Jon asleep?"

"Out like a light—he needed sleep badly."

"Good," Brik said, drinking the beer in one gulp. "I've got some bad news—*Hck*—really horrible news actually. When it's time to wake him, I suggest you put the dog on the bed and let him hold her for a few minutes before you tell him what I'm about to tell you."

*

Afterward, when Brik was through, and Abby stopped shaking her head in disbelief, she looked at the handyman with red-rimmed eyes.

"God help him—I don't believe this."

Brik looked at her with his own reddened eyes. "The plane went down at the same time the house was burning," he said, his voice breaking. "A month ago, Jon would've said something about how it never rains but pours—*Hck*—or some other lame adage." The handyman shook his head. "I saved a few photographs and one painting—I might be able to save some more with Neal's help. He and some firemen buddies of his are gonna help me grab things that have nothing to do with the crime area. The bin he wanted was nothing but a twisted wreath of burned plastic. I hope nothing important was inside."

"The heat from those flames—think you can salvage more?"

Brik shrugged.

After a long moment of silence, he got another beer and drank that one in a single gulp.

"Abby, he was counting on Raj Patel. Counting on the surgery and treatment to start. For five months he's been symptom-free. Maybe he's got another month or longer. I don't know. Dr. Faklis says that she needs time to study Patel's notes. She'll perform the surgery herself in December."

"But I thought she—"

"Patel went to India to learn this radical new technique," Brik said. "Without the surgery, the targeted chemo treatments won't be as effective, if at all. Faklis said as much several times. When Evelyn gets here, she'll want to talk to us before she speaks to Jon. I'll know more later tonight."

Abby grabbed one of the sofa pillows and screamed into it. After she composed herself, she said, "What would you have me do?"

Brik leveled his gaze at her. "Keep him occupied." He got to his feet. "I need to pick up Evelyn at the airport," he said. "Peter's flying up to stay with his mother for a week—Jon needs his mother with him. Kiki has volunteered to fly back and forth to help all of us remain calm. And feed us too—God knows, I couldn't make toast right now."

Abby narrowed her eyes. "I'm here too, you know."

"Look at me. Forget this recent reconciliation with Jon. Forget whatever happened this morning when you two got here. After you tell him the news about Raj Patel, he will ask you to leave him."

"I refuse to believe that. I won't do it if he asks."

"Then he will tell you to leave him," Brik replied. "I've spent the past five months taking care of this man, and I know him well enough to warn you. Be prepared to leave him."

"Why should I?"

"Because he's a stubborn ass, Abby, but if you're set on being with this man, then you're going to do exactly what he wants you to do," Brik said. "He waited for you to get yourself together. You owe him the same thing—if you love him, you will."

"And then what?"

The handyman smiled.

"And then, when it's time for you to come back into his life, you'll come back into his life for good." He looked at his watch. "I've got to go—be strong." He kissed her cheek. "You need to be the strong one now. You need to be his rock, with or without him."

And then Brik Buckman left.

Abby sat on the sofa absently petting the dog. She did not know what to do. She went ahead and packed her bags and put them at the front door—just in case. She gave the dog a bath.

It was a good way to keep busy and plan her words.

The thought of telling Jon the news about Raj Patel's plane crash made Abby sick to her stomach.

It tore a hole in her heart—*God, hasn't he suffered enough?*

Grace was Jon's tender, his currency. He freely meted it out to those in need of saving.

His unconscious charity aroused a desire to talk to him.

To be with him. To touch his arm or shake his hand.

He prized connection above all things.

Connection was all that mattered to him. It was the source of his joy and gratitude. It was the key that opened portals and gave him the courage to let go and let God.

Even now, Abby could picture his face.

The otherworldly glow in his eyes as he spoke of this profound notion he had discovered—that his life depended on his connection to others.

His epiphany about life, how it had poured from him after she asked him, "When you were sick, were you afraid of dying?"

"Brik Buckman," Abby said to herself. "You are wrong. He needs me." She drew in a sharp breath that cut her lungs.

It was time to tell Jon the news that Raj Patel's plane went down in the Indian Ocean. That his lifelong friend was one of 256 people who perished in the crash. That the very doctor who had left the United States to find a way to save him was now gone from the world.

How would Jon react to that?

If he no longer felt connected to that one hope, would it not be reasonable for him to rail against his fate? Would it not be reasonable for him to kill the messenger?

Perhaps Brik was right.

Jon was a man, nothing more. Simply accepting this new tragedy as a messiah or a stoic required a strength beyond that of a mortal.

God, give me the serenity to accept the thing I cannot change...

Abby decided to wake him now.

She had prepared for the worst—she had yet to start hoping for the best. She did not know what that was, not exactly.

What if the best possible outcome for Jon was for her to leave?

If he demanded it, would she be able to do it?

She had fought so hard to get to this place in her heart and soul—did she have the strength to let that go? Wasn't that what Brik tried to explain to her? Abby scooped up Minnie and headed to the bedroom where Jon was still soundly sleeping.

*

CHAPTER 16

Pattern of the Prodigal

"Even the son who had fallen could still be saved."
~ Søren Kierkegaard

Jon sat alone on the bench waiting for the next Jolley Trolley to take him to Tarpon Springs. Dr. Faklis had always been honest about the chances that he would remain symptomless and be able to move about with relative freedom. That he was sitting at the bus stop without a chaperone was a blessing. It was a solid indication that his strength remained. Of course, he was losing everything else that mattered, but at least he had enough strength to watch his life fall apart.

He and his house had something in common now. They were both ruins. Over the past two weeks, mourning the loss of another friend robbed him of hope. That Raj Patel was gone from the world filled him with an anger he had not felt since he lost Panos. Unfortunately, he set fire to the world around him—Abby Flowers was one of the casualties.

He had been cruel to her.

All she did was tell him the news about Raj.

At least she did not put up a fight when he told her to go. When he told her to take the job in Lake-land. Told her that he did not want to be with a woman who could not make up her mind—the single spot in time that left him without hope for a future with her.

Or for himself.

And yet, there were blessings.

Were there not blessings to count?

That Minnie was safe from harm was a blessing. That he still had the support of his friends and family was a blessing. That he was willing to let Dr. Faklis attempt the operation was a step forward, if not a testament to something deeper—there would be no more epiphanies for him.

No more revelations of the spirit.

Hell, he could barely keep up with the passing days. Time and memory were his worst enemies now. And grief—Jon had never been a weeper. It was all he did anymore.

The tears Jon wept for Raj Patel and Sita were as constant as they were exhausting.

And everything was exhausting.

The number of meetings he and Evelyn had to have since the news broke was exhausting. Trying to hold steadfast to a shaking faith doing everything in its power to uproot him from the ground was ex-hausting. Keeping his effing chin up when he walked down the street—which was nigh impossible ever since the night of the fire and news of Raj reached the population of Tarpon Springs—was exhausting.

Most of all, Adam Disston was exhausting.

A man he had known most of his life somehow managed to become a zealous weirdo within the span of a workweek—five business days was all it took to put this genius over the edge. Thankfully, Weirdo Adam left Abby alone. He was apoplectic when he learned that she had left him.

That she did exactly what Jon told her to do.

The recent LIBERTINE article was more than enough to make hiss head spin. That it was the most popular post this year only made things worse. He supposed there were worse things than having Adam Disston on his side. That was a blessing too—a really annoying one. It was bet-ter than not having him in his life at all—*Raj, I'm so sorry.*

Tears fell into his lap—again. "Please, forgive me."

Please, God—take this cup from me.

*

GULF COAST LIBERTINE
ADAM DISSTON

Saint Jon

Gather round, kids. I have a confession to make. I've rendered for you, my rabid readers, a decent man in the worst possible colors with the sole purpose of keeping his name on your wagging tongues. Jon Christakos was born a good man always on the verge of becoming a great one. My plan was to reveal that truth about him slowly, over time. But time has run out.

Today's article is one of three entries that will, I hope, remedy my many trespasses against him.

Jon is not perfect. He's kind of a grump. He's sweet natured and rather stubborn. Talented. A humility that runs too deep for anyone to see. A horrible temper. A champion for the weak and downtrodden. A hero when he's called upon to be. He was there to see a car careening around one of the sharp turns of Anclote Road. Without thinking, he leapt into the marsh to save lives. He managed to save two passengers in that car—the driver died on impact. But I was one of those passengers.

Jon altered the trajectory of my life when he saved it. A couple of years before he stooped to save me from my own bad choices, he fought and won a battle with cancer. Fast forward to this past summer. Jon was given six months to live because the same brain cancer had returned.

His team of doctors made plans for a radical surgery and treatment that were to have begun today.

The man who was to perform this procedure recently died. An Air India Express Flight overshot the runway and dropped over a cliff on October 31. The ensuing explosion killed all 256 on board, including Raj Patel and his beloved wife Sita—both friends of ours.

As Jon is fighting to survive, I am challenging you, as I am challenging myself, to use his time as if it were your time. You've been given one month to live—what will you do with it?

Over the next month, I'm going to be the journalist Aunt Beverly thinks I am. With the assistance of others braver than I will ever be, I've laid a foundation for a bold story that will benefit my hometown—it is set to come out in three weeks.

To all the corrupt officials I'm about to expose—you know who you are—prepare to eat thy just desserts. To the Greek community, I'm sorry for not doing what I should have done years ago. That I have done this is a testament to Jon Christakos, a man who will inspire me for the rest of my life.

If you come to Tarpon Springs, he might inspire you too. Come to the Sponge Docks. Visit any one of the businesses on Dodecanese Boulevard and mention the name of my column. Get half off. Until next time—make good choices, kids.

*

Friends and family, with hearts full of gratitude and joy, sharing a meal of abundant food made with love—this was Thanksgiving for Jon Christakos. For as long as he could remember, a generous touch of Greece found its way into every celebratory meal.

Roasted turkey stuffed with savory ground lamb, rice, and chestnuts—delicately seasoned with all-spice. Bowls of buttery mashed butternut squash and red potatoes topped with candied walnuts and feta. A blood orange and cranberry chutney. Bowls of olives and feta cheese. A Greek salad, with a generous helping of potato salad beneath. Baskets of warm pita and tzatziki sauce for dipping. For dessert, a cup of strong metrios coffee with Evelyn's homemade pumpkin baklava with honeyed pistachio butter.

Thanksgiving dinner at the Kouskoutis house never failed to do either one of two things: put guests into a diabetic coma or spit them out for a 24-hour walk on the Pinellas Trail.

Peter and his mother had retired to the cottage house because of the former. Hannah and Kiki escorted Seamus and Mr. Willie back to the Island Rock because of the latter.

They should be on their way home by now, Jon thought.

Evelyn and Alicia Safford were arguing inside the house. The two women had been clearing the air for over an hour now. They had opened a cornucopia of issues that had been festering for years. Alicia knew that she had it coming—she told Jon as much before she arrived at the house after dinner.

Jon shivered as he paced the gazebo.

The weather was too chilly for him to be outside without a jacket—and it was not like he had the body fat to compensate. Considering the lack of seasons in this part of Florida, cancer or not, he was going to enjoy this cool weather. He was content to be out here with Minnie, breathing deeply the aromas of the season as he nervously paced the floorboards. He envied her thick coat of fur.

Brik was in Ohio putting finishing touches on the house Adam Disston recently bought from Evelyn's sister last week. What he wanted to do with the house was a mystery—Jon suspected it had some-thing to do with Felicity Noel. He and the handyman were set to return to Tampa in a week or so.

For Jon, living a normal life was a dream now.

It was something that existed only in the past and only for brief moments. If he were to venture to the ruins of his house next door, then he would find flowers, cards, stuffed animals, and posters lining the sidewalk and empty driveway. The shrine on his dock had grown twice in size since yesterday—the number of lit candles, gifts, tokens had increased four-fold. Well-wishers from all over came by to take pictures of the burned house or pin prayer memos to the dock railings.

This outpouring of love from strangers overwhelmed him.

He often felt guilty about it. And sometimes angry.

Still, the strangely disconnected love from strangers inspired him to get out of bed. It gave him strength and rekindled some of his faith. He wondered what he had done to deserve this—in his heart, especially after what he had done to Abby Flowers, he believed he had done nothing.

Jon suspected the final round had begun.

His teeth were chattering. He wanted a blanket, but dared not go inside until the dust settled.

*

Evelyn: How dare you not tell Jon that Hannah was his daughter, Alicia Safford? I could strangle you for not telling him.

Alicia: I can't believe the hypocrisy, coming from you.

Evelyn: Hypocrisy?

Alicia: Yes, I'm not the only one who kept secrets. You knew about Hannah. You stayed up in Ohio partly to give Jon space to figure out the big mystery. Don't you dare judge me for withholding her identity.

Evelyn: Why is it that you won't stop causing trouble?

Alicia: Keeping secrets from Jon is what we're talking about here. I'm guilty of it, but so are you. I'm not afraid of you.

Evelyn: Good—then you're not the coward your father was. Are you hungry? I made you a plate earlier—you need to eat.

Alicia: You made me a plate?

Evelyn: Of course. Someone has to—now come eat it before Peter does. We have much to talk about now that we've cleared the air. I want to know everything about my granddaughter.

*

DECEMBER

CHAPTER 17

Where Angels Fear to Tread

*"It is not known precisely where angels dwell... It has not been God's
pleasure that we should be informed of their abode."*
~ Voltaire

Jon looked at the clock on the wall of his makeshift studio in the cottage
house garage—*you're late, Peter, dammit.* He went back to his painting,
refusing to think about the young man's whereabouts. Well, not for another 30 minutes. Then, there would be hell to pay—*I'm starving and getting ready to eat me a Pomeranian.* Jon looked at the little dog lounging
at his feet. "I bet you're gamey and tough."

Minnie barked in protest.

Jon perused the last two canvases of floating women. Not mermaids,
but women in white gowns floating in clear water.

Ophelias drowning.

They were studies, really, but he was fairly certain that his next crop
of paintings would be harvested from these seeds. He conceptualized the
monochromatic paintings after the news about Raj Patel put him over the
edge. For Jon, over the edge meant telling Abby Flowers that he did not
want to see her anymore. And making sure that she would never want to
see him again, whether he lived or not.

Thoughts of Abby filled Jon's head as he prepared a new batch of
paint. But then, she was always there in his mind.

He mixed acrylic paint with charred newspaper clippings, fabrics, furniture, and flooring plucked from the house fire. He vowed to utilize as much of the ruins as possible before the city demolished it.

That happened a few days ago.

Jon managed to salvage enough to suit his artistic needs.

Admittedly, it felt odd looking at the empty lot. Still, building another house on the property was not going to happen—Alicia Safford was helping facilitate a deed transfer to the city of Tarpon Springs.

If I survive the surgery, then I'll worry about finding a place to live.

Once the debris, refuse, brush, and rubble were removed, the Safford House Museum would be visible from any point on the arc of Spring Bayou. The unobstructed view inspired Brik to draft a plan for something better suited to the space—some amazing landscape design that would bridge the Golden Crescent to the important landmark.

With Alicia Safford's influence, the Historic Homeowners Society gave their resounding seal of approval. It was up to the city planning board to do the rest now.

God only knew how long that would take.

Jon positioned the final canvas onto his easel.

With a pencil, he sketched the layout of the scene with bold lines and shapes. In his heart and mind, he could not help from imagining Abby Flowers as the drowning woman—every canvas was like digging a new grave for his love for her. And his hope of ever seeing her again—he had never regretted anything as much as he regretted what he said—and how he said it—to her.

Even now, his face burned with shame.

Jon's stomach growled.

Looking at the clock and then at Minnie, he said, "You're off the hook, puppers." He scratched her head, immediately forgetting his melancholy and hunger pangs and irrita-tion—having a dog simply made life bearable. "Dammit," he shouted, throwing his brush.

And then he threw himself against the canvas.

He created an image with sweeping bands of thick gooey mixed media paint, with accents of primal screaming. He was happy to sacrifice depth for physical intention and the release of pent-up emotions. He did not know he was crying until Minnie's burst of barking broke his reverie.

He jumped when someone tapped his arm.

Chucky held up his hands in silent apology. "Hey, I just wanted to give you something."

Jon mumbled something snarky. "What's in the suitcase?"

Chucky handed him an envelope. "Open that first and we'll get to the reward."

"Please tell me you have hamburgers and fries in that case."

"Open the damn envelope, Jon."

*

GULF COAST LIBERTINE
ADAM DISSTON

The Fall of Ozymandias

Midnight. The Greek Village. Three of us—Chas, Nik, and me—headed toward a row of houses a block from the Sponge Docks. There was nothing special about the street—looked like any street in the neighborhood.

The criminals we sought were about to face justice, and no one would know un-til long after the deed was done.

I fell over a root growing in the gap of the sidewalk. Nik clung to my arm, but I went face forward into the bushes nonetheless. Busted my face, loos-ened my jaw and made me see stars—plus, I got an old flat bicycle tire in the eye.

"Almost there," Chas said. "That's the house."

Nik pulled me up and helped me navigate around the root in the darkness. Chas was our connection. Nik was our 'muscle' for just in case scenarios that needed martial arts. I was there to record the story and take our stolen property to safety.

We were not acting alone; however, as others were assist-ing us unofficially—they were at the ready in the shadows. I won't be-tray their identities or reveal their exact purpose either.

Chas looked at his watch and led us toward the house. I swal-lowed my par-anoia—I'm sure Nik did too. We took staggered breaths. Sweat soaked our shirts—there was blood on mine.

We stepped into the light of the streetlamp and crouched behind a black GMC Jimmy. The motion sensors on the house failed to bring up the spot-lights. Chas had disabled them earlier. At first, the dark house seemed empty—then there was movement.

We saw two shadows through the window. Chas put a finger over his lips. He held up two fingers, directing them at his eyes and then toward the house.

Seven minutes to go in and get out.

We entered without knocking and silently moved down the hall toward the sounds of conversation coming from the back.

Chas took the lead. The house was a strange place. It was empty, sterile, cold. No decorations on the walls. No furniture. No carpet. We passed a utility room. Nik heard panting on the other side of the door.

Chas directed us to inspect the noise and went on ahead. Nik and I slipped inside the small room.

We could not see, but we heard padded puppy paws and the click-clicking of unclipped claws. Then came the whining and excited yipping. Nik turned on his phone for a moment—here was our quarry, a stolen dog that frantically kept licking his face.

As soon as he got hold of the dog, Nik took the stolen animal outside. Chas was standing at the end of the hallway waving me over. There were two people in the room. A fat teenager and an old man. Both were talking nonsense—everything was garbled.

We decided to go into the room. The shriveled chunk of old man sat on the floor in a corner wearing what had been a Hugo Boss suit—it was tattered and filthy now.

The doughy kid was sitting in the opposite corner wearing a similar suit in the same condition. Chas opened his hands like the Scales of Justice.

"Spiros Zervos and his right-hand boy—both high as kites. Time to set the trap—Nik outside?"

I nodded and looked at the man who had terrorized the Greek Village for generations. Here was the man whose name mothers had used to keep unruly children in line.

Spiros Zervos was just an illusion, an emperor without clothes, a piece of un-man, a grizzled, unshaved gremlin. And the dough-boy rolling around in a pool of drool was equally pathetic.

I knew who he was—he had stolen the dog. He had broken into my friend's house. He very likely set fires to some buildings in the Greek Village and the Sponge Docks last summer.

Chas looked at his watch. He crouched beside the drug-addled old man and sent a message from his phone. He moved to the fat kid and shook his head. Turning around, he fixed his gaze beyond my shoulder.

There were two men standing in the doorway behind me.

"Time for you to go, Adam—we'll talk about the rest of your story later. Right now, I have business with these two."

The men escorted me to a car idling across the street. Nik and our recovered canine were inside waiting for me. The driver took us to my hotel and let us out.

We watched the vehicle disappear into the night.

*

Jon waved the envelope.

"Why hasn't this been released yet? I got Minnie back in October—it's almost two months later. What gives?"

"Adam just wanted you to have part of his first draft," Chucky said. "The entire article is set to run tomorrow morning in all the big Tampa area papers. There's more to what happened besides a dog rescue. Other scenes have played out and have yet to play out. What you have in your hands won't be in the papers—that's not the true story. It's not the whole story either."

"I'm grateful to know about the rescue, but I'm not—"

"Jon, I'm grateful to you," Chucky said. "That morning in the alley you told me something I desperately needed to hear. I hated you for it, but I knew you were right. When I refused to back Dickey's version of what happened, it sent me scrambling to find protection. The money I borrowed bought me time. It turned my sinking boat around. And I'm here to repay my debt."

"Chucky, you don't owe me anything."

The young man popped the latches of the case. "It's not hamburgers, no, but there's your leap of faith fully restored, with interest—heavy on the interest. Very heavy."

Jon closed the lid. "I can't accept this—are you insane? That's WAY too much."

"You'll just give most of it away anyway, so just take the damn money and let me be done with this." Chucky squatted to pet Minnie, who did not growl when he did. She let him rub her belly.

"Full circle," Jon said with a snort.

"Heads will start rolling soon," Chucky continued, surprised that he was still grinning. He stood up. His mood changed. "The dominoes will fall because you dared to love this city more than you love yourself. Tarpon Springs owes you." Chucky shook Jon's hand. "Kick the crap out of that cancer. The world needs you in it."

"What are you going to do now?"

Chuck Parker only smiled. Jon watched him go. He never thought his Hail Mary pass had a chance to succeed. Despite the specifics of the outcome, he was pleased that it did.

He read the article again.

And then he read it again.

The illegal actions that Adam Disston and 'Nik' Buckman committed on his behalf did not please him.

Truth be told, the fact that they willingly put themselves in danger for him made him sick to his stomach. Jon wondered who the others were—the unidentified helpers. Neal? Kiki? Or Peter, for God's sake? Were they involved with Chuck Parker's coup?

Don't ask, don't tell—that's my motto.

Minnie barked and pawed at Jon's foot.

Suddenly, his head felt as if it had been rung like a bell. There was a clanging and boom. He threw up.

A stabbing pain along his spine struck him like a tsunami. Consciousness was there, but barely.

His brain was a shoe tumbling in the dryer of his skull. A barrage of voices, smells, and visions pummeled him. His world spun wildly away from him. Too weak to call for help, he succumbed to the waves breaking against him, a ship tempest-tossed in a stormy sea.

Minnie whined.

Jon teetered over, like a tree falling. And his last thought before blacking out was the smiling face of Abby Flowers.

*

CHAPTER 18

Beneath the 12-Mile Reef

"The soul becomes dyed with the color of its thoughts."
~ Marcus Aurelius

Breaking news from Tarpon Springs. A day after the arrest of arson suspect Richard Dolley, the body of alleged Mafioso Spiros Zervos was pulled from the Anclote River early this morning. As many of our older Tampa Bay viewers know, Zervos has been accused and acquitted of several crimes over the decades. News Channel 8 is on the scene covering the unfolding story from Tarpon Springs, where interim Police Chief Kenneth Harris will issue a statement regarding the grisly discovery. Harris will also address the flurry of allegations about widespread corruption running rampant through several municipalities in Pinellas County, including the cities of Palm Harbor, Holiday, and Tarpon Springs. Looks like we're in for another long day. Stay tuned."

Jon groaned. "Felicity, will you turn that damn thing off?"

"I will do nothing of the sort," she replied with a warm smile. "After months of fashion shows and photo shoots and red carpet events, I need this local news to ground me. This is big news, Jonny—our hometown is in the spotlight. Extortion, racketeering, money laundering, and—?" Felicity shot a look behind her. "Hannah-Montana, what else was there? I was too bored to give a crap."

"Drugs and human sex trafficking," Hannah shouted from Evelyn's living room. "Neal Peruski is talking to the press like a badass on Bay News 9—Brik says he'll be lieutenant when this is all over. Just Badass—

go Neal! Go Neal! Go Neal!"

Jon blinked at the woman hovering over him. "My daughter—so classy."

Felicity blew into his face. "Hush—she IS classy when she's not being real," she said, looking at his head from every angle. "She's got no need to be anything but herself in the privacy of this house. Think Neal will stay now?"

Jon sighed. "Dunno, my darling—he and Olga were set to head up to Ohio before this mess happened," he said. "Adam won't hold them accountable for the house situation—least, I hope not."

Felicity laughed. "He won't—I offered to take it off his hands if Neal decides to stay."

"Why on earth would you want to have that tiny house—oh, never mind. Your *new* man lives in Cleveland. I forgot about your *new* man."

"Do I detect a note of jealousy?"

"Yes, my dear—always with a resounding yes," he said. "Only because I'm selfish."

"Jonny, I can't shave your head safely if you keep moving," Felicity said, poking his shoulder and blowing in his face. "I can't blame you for being jealous—I'll be in the next Sports Illustrated swimsuit issue, so you'd be a fool not to be. Keep still, dammit. And you be nice to Hannah, or I will cut you out of spite because, well, girl power. If you hadn't been such an ass to Abby Flowers, I wouldn't be stuck with this job—you need a good cut to make you bleed for a while."

He snorted. "That's a guarantee if you keep hacking at my flesh."

"You're all done, baldy—have a look."

Jon looked at his reflection in the hand mirror Felicity offered. He rubbed a hand over his scalp. "I look like an extra from CHUD. The last time I shaved my entire head for a surgery, I ended up paralyzed for a year. Looks good though—thanks for doing this."

Felicity shrugged. "Consider it payment. You convinced my father to stay in his room," she said. "Seamus and I had our first family dinner in years because of you. Here, put on the cap."

Jon frowned. "Really?"

"Yes, really—it's time to go now."

Jon nodded. Evelyn bought him a knit wool cap, which he slid over his freshly shorn head. He adjusted it into various shapes before settling on faux beret. "Perfect," Felicity said, voice trembling. "I think it's time to go to the hospital." She helped him to his feet and slipped an arm behind his back. She kissed his cheek as Hannah opened the front door. "I'll see you the next time I see you, Jonny."

Jon smiled—he would not say goodbye.

Hannah took his arm and guided him down the steps of the front stoop. He almost lost his balance, but Hannah held him steady. "I'll be there when you wake up."

"Cross your heart?" Jon asked, suddenly feeling like a boy.

Hannah traced an 'x' over her chest. "And hope to die—you'll do great, Daddy."

Evelyn took him over to the El Camino idling in her driveway. Brik eased him into the passenger seat and buckled him in. Evelyn climbed into the backseat with Hannah. The handyman got behind the wheel and backed out, trying not to hit one of the thousands gathered around the arc of the Golden Crescent to pay their respects.

"Moe, Larry, Curly—I'm just having a little brain surgery," Jon mumbled, his eyes heavy as he gazed at the people waving at him. "See? I'm not such an asshole after all, am I?"

Evelyn snorted behind him. "Little do they know."

Hannah laughed. "I take it the preemptive medications have hit."

"Indeed they have, dearest daughter—I'm quite relaxed," Jon said with a contented sigh.

"All that fear and worry is out the—look, there's Kiki up there at the corner! I should ask her how much she charges before—what's wrong with this window? It's not going down when I press it."

Brik gently reached over to pull Jon's hand from the release handle. "*Hck*—how about you just wave and smile like a good prince? Wave and smile, wave and smile, wave and smile. Good brah."

"Where's Dr. Flowers? Is she not here for my parade?" Jon asked.

Evelyn touched his shoulder. "You'll see Abby Flowers after you wake up from the surgery," she lied softly. "Just close your eyes and relax."

And that is exactly what Jonathan Christakos did.

*

Jon did not know where he was—he only knew that he was *inside.* Inside what, inside where? And why inside at all? He had no answers. His best guess was that he was inside the wide belly of a sponge diving boat—one about 60-feet in length, by his estimation.

She was out to sea in deep water too.

The waves were large and powerful, more like thick walls of stone rather than the foamy breaking rockers closer to shore. The tick-tock roiling was a careful, rhythmic side-to-side sway akin to the labored ambling motion of an obese woman climbing a flight of stairs.

Where am I going?

Somewhere on deck, up there above his head, he heard voices. Muffled voices, yes, but he couldn't make out what they were saying.

Hello?

Who's there?

I'm down here—can you hear me?

He smelled sweets baking. Cooling blackberry pies and honey drenched baklava. Fresh-from-the-oven almond cookies and warm Polish bread slathered with butter and dusted with cinnamon and vanilla and powdered sugar. Roasted pecans, freshly ground coffee beans, clove and nutmeg, allspice and gingerbread, pumpkin—all the heady aromas of Christmas and Thanksgiving at once.

Is someone cutting into my brain?

HEY! I think someone is cutting into my brain—hello?

Jon heard music, such sweet music. Strings of cello and violin, and viola, like children of the night. And the haunting, mournful weeping of oboe and bassoon. A tinkle of chimes and piano keys. The sudden acidic

banging of steel drums. A chorus now, with voices chanting in exhila-
rated tones, their echoes gliding through darkness as ghosts wailing and
keening hallelujah, with joyful holiday fear.

Why do I feel so dizzy?

Here, let me sit down and rest.

He was tired, so very tired now. All he wanted to do was sleep for a
few hours. Maybe a few days or so—a week at the most.

He went to the hammock in the corner and climbed inside it. His violent rocking quickly eased into a counterpoint rhythm against the ship's
sweeping dreamlike motion.

Is someone cutting into my brain?

Evelyn, are you cutting off the heads of those grasshoppers again?

Is it summer?

Suddenly, Jon felt as if he were a captive. That he was trapped in the
bowels of a pirate ship—*ahoy, mateys!* He was cold and wondered if this
was just a dream.

Perhaps he was dreaming.

Yes, he was, and he knew he was, but he wanted a better dream. Not
this dream within a dream skatá—not this place of dreaming outside inside dreams of dreaming.

He wanted to dream of family—his daughter Hannah.

He wanted to dream of loves past and lives lost. Of a brother who
never died. A mother and father who didn't drown. And there was the
face of a woman he loved always in the forefront of his queue of thoughts.
She loved him, yes, and he deeply loved her—he made her go away.

He couldn't remember why though.

Maybe it was because he refused to allow her to weather the storm in
such a small boat—look at this tiny thing.

Where am I?

He wondered if this place was a dream ship. Was it real?

Perhaps, but he felt rested now. He no longer wanted to sit in the
hammock and dream his life away, *merrily-merrily.*

He got to his feet and wobbled. His sea legs were missing, for certain. After righting himself from a surprisingly violent fall face forward, he staggered over to the wall and parked there. Just until he got his bearings and could move without face planting again.

Where am I?

A dimly lit cabin—*yes, this is a cabin, and it is dimly lit.*

There were photographs on the walls. A hurricane lamp hung from the ceiling and swayed back and forth like a pendulum. Its eerie warm glow revealed a dresser, a mirror, a table, two chairs—if there were stairs, he did not see them.

He sat down at the table and poured himself a glass of water. The voices he had heard before were louder now. One of them belonged to a man. Another to a woman. No, there were at least three female voices— *crikey, how many are on my boat?*

There were other voices too.

They all sounded familiar but they were too jumbled to makes sense of them. Jon began smelling those delicious smells again. And hearing the same haunting music again.

Although he couldn't remember why he was sitting at the table, he felt lighter somehow, as if he'd been given the antidote to a poison he swallowed. He was so sleepy again too—so very tired and sleepy. He closed his eyes and dropped his head onto his arm and fell into a deep sleep on the table, the glass of water still in his hand and full.

Yes, once more into the dream, dear friends, once more!

Jon did not know when it happened but the ship began to sink.

Water came rushing into his cabin. Filling up the small space with him inside it. And he began to choke and scream for help that did not come. He thrashed about doing everything to keep his face above the surface to suck the sweet air.

He did not know why he was going to die inside a sinking ship.

Nico said he belonged to fire, but here he was drowning in water.

Jon wanted to be done with water.

There was no more air, so he let himself sink. He did his best not to struggle. All he wanted to do was pass out and never wake again.

It was all darkness, black and deep, like liquid sable. An ocean of inky cold velvet. For some reason he could breathe.

A tiny little light at the surface caught his eye, so he swam toward it. The more he reached the farther away it got. And then, in a flash of neon sun, like a supernova of the mind, Jon was treading white light. Not water, not oblivion, but the brilliant light of a white room. With a window and white curtains.

His clothes were white.

He had a white cane in his hand, and he pressed it to the floor like a fancy man ambling across the white hardwood floors.

He seemed to be in a place of waiting, so he sat down and waited. People entered the room. They all wanted to talk to him.

And all this time, I thought I was alone.

Their voices were soothing.

At first he could not make out the words, they were speaking over each other, conversations stacked atop conversations, like pancakes of dysfunctional communication.

Jon did his best to listen, but it was impossible.

Still, he remained seated and waited for one of his visitors to call him over. Suddenly, he was pulled to his feet and guided up a flight of white stairs into an empty cabin on a higher floor.

The room had pale colors, still bright but dusted in coats of pastels. He found himself sitting at a table on the far wall. He heard the guests downstairs prattling on about something.

Up here was easier on the ears.

A small fuzzy dog trotted over with her tail wagging, her bright pink tongue panting with excitement—she dropped to the floor at his feet and put her head onto her paws. She warmed his heart.

"Can you hear me?"

A very handsome man was sitting in the chair across from him.

He would not stop talking.

"My buddy-brother and his family lived in Hawaii. We went hiking above the rim of an active volcano. He was leader. Wife and girls in the middle. Me in back. And we're all climbing up to the edge of the volcano. This young man was lagging behind his group. Right in front of us, he lost his footing. Slipped under the rail. His screaming—it stopped your heart. My brother lunged for the guy when he slipped. Grabbed his arm. Didn't think of the consequences.

"So, everyone's screaming now. My buddy's over the edge, keeping this stranger from falling. We had enough time to pull them both to safety. Amidst the tears of joy and relief, I kept wondering why he did that? He had a family and could've gone over. We were sharing a fifth of JD later that night, and he told me instinct took over. The choice was automatic. And why? My buddy didn't know, but I think he recognized himself in the face of that man. It triggered the primordial part of his brain, the survival part. Seeing the stranger on the brink of death was like seeing himself. Saving the stranger's life was saving his own.

"I hope you can hear me, brah. I'm taking care of Minnie—*Hck*—and I am holding your hand. Wishing you'd give me a sign or say something. Come back to us. Whenever you can."

Seal away all the lies that we made—never scream about
All the mire that we carve in our face in the Dreamout
Do we prey on the history we save—future's new route
Steal the graves when the sun's out of place in the Dreamout
I am blind—I'm wandering in my mind…

The man had a nice voice—the song was pretty. He could not finish singing it though. He was so wracked with grief that he didn't feel the touch of the woman next to him. She managed to get him up to lead him away to a place where he could be alone with his sadness.

I wonder where I am then…

A petite blonde woman took the empty seat—such a lovely smile.

"It's been two weeks, Dad—Dr. Faklis says you have a good chance to get through this. We just need you to come back to us. You're famous now. More than you ever were. I know, Peter's the one to blame, but Adam Disston's guilty too. Evelyn gave me permission to use those Super 8 films of your mother and father—as soon as I saw them I got an idea and concocted this big dramatic art installation at the Riverside Grill building. I can't wait to show you."

Jon smiled when the pretty woman left the table.

A young man sat in the chair she vacated. He was short with dark hair. And he seemed to be excited about something.

"The other day, Brik and I got matching mermaid tattoos. Jon, you gotta look at this." He rolled up his sleeve. "See them? There are two mermaids, like mirror images, and that's a starfish between them. It's a movement, Jon. I've never seen anything like it. Okay—I gotta go—Aunt Evelyn's giving me the evil stink eye."

The young man got up and waved. "See you when you wake up. Oh, and don't let these crybabies worry you."

Jon smiled when the short young man left the table. He waited a long time before the next visitor sat down. He recognized her as his mother. He sat up straight when she took his hand.

"Not to besmirch their memory, but Bessie and Dmitri were old when they adopted you. I was a brand new mother with a brand new son. It made sense that we share the responsibility of raising you as brothers. As far as I'm concerned, I gave birth to two boys. In my heart and soul, I feel that you are my flesh and blood. I can't imagine life without you, Jonny. I won't. None of us will."

The woman wiped her eyes. "The other day, Althea Faklis started swearing at this reporter from Tampa Bay Times. To hear that educated woman cursing like a Greek deckhand was the funniest thing I've heard in ages. Everything's been funny to us though. I think we started getting punchy when the tattoos became a thing. And then the gifts started piling up at the Mother Meres mural and the sidewalk in front of your empty lot. Flowers and letters, cards and stuffed animals, marriage proposals, pictures of naked women—Brik's keeping those. Let's see.

"People in town are wearing agates now. Bracelets, necklaces, ear-rings, belt buckles—pick an accessory. They all love you and want you to come back. The Epiphany festival will be huge. The Tarpon Chamber of Commerce expanded the event for all of Spring Bayou, not just the Crescent. Thousands are coming to see you—they're all hoping to see you.

"Damn, I thought that would've made the machines beep."

*

WINTER

Life seems so black and white
When you're looking from the outside in.
Sometimes the stumbling steps we take
Are always washed in our own sin.
I know I ransack my photographic brain—
Drown all my memories in mnemonic rain.
So, baby, how could you ever know
It's you I'm trying to win?
Try to remember, baby, you
You clicked on my maintained high
I'm tripping a bit on this Mobius Strip—
Why to twisted why.
Baby, I know that lump in your throat
Is a stranded butterfly.
If you can, whenever I fall, don't walk away.
Don't pick me up—I'll rise when I can stand.
I may howl to the moon that I am not whole,
But if ever I say that I hate you—
It means I love you to the point of passion
That unhinges my soul.

—Brik Buckman, *Song of the Wonderworker*

CHAPTER 19

Song of the Wonderworker

"Someone filled a sponge with wine vinegar, put it on a staff,
and offered it to Jesus to drink. 'Now leave him alone.
Let's see if Elijah comes to take him down.'"
~ *Mark 15:36*

Jon opened his eyes. The light hurt. His head hurt. His neck and shoulders hurt too. It hurt to breathe. It hurt to stretch. It hurt to move his fingers. It hurt to move his mouth, to make sure it still worked. When he tried to speak, the pain in his throat made it impossible.

He panicked.

And the machines beside his bed beeped noises and clicks that scared him. He flailed and felt the tug of a needle shoved in his arm. It was connected to an IV—the drip-drip-drip was hypnotic.

His blurry vision began to clear. Fast asleep at the end of his bed, curled up in a cow-colored ball of fur at his feet, was Minnie—*where am I?*

The room was not familiar.

It was Spartan, cold, clinical—*where am I?*

He wiped his eyes with heavy hands—his arms felt like eels overfed with buckshot and sand. Sleeping in the corner chairs were Hannah and Brik. Snoring loudly too.

A pleasantly plump and pretty nurse entered the room—presumably to check his vitals and/or play with the machines beeping around him. Her eyes widened when she saw he was alert and moving.

"It's good to see you, Jon—I'll get Dr. Faklis."

Jon rubbed his eyes. Minnie's head popped up. She yawned and stretched when she felt the bed shake. Her master was up. He tried to speak, but his voice was uncooperative. The dog barked. Brik scrambled to sit beside him. Hannah was scrambling to sit on the other side of him.

Jon patted his throat and smacked his mouth.

"*Hck*—the feeding tube," Brik said, frowning. "An orderly shoved it in too hard and your throat got infected—blame it on the rain, blame it on the rain, blame it on the rain."

Hannah slid a hand over his arm. "You're fine. It was a week ago."

Jon mouthed, "What day is it?"

"First day of winter, brah. Not that you'd know it—it's warm and humid. Supposed to cool off tonight—*Hck*—ho, ho, ho." Brik kissed Jon's forehead. "Glad you're up."

"I knew you'd wake up," Hannah said.

"*Hck*—you've been stewing in an induced coma since the operation," Brik said, gesturing. "This a special room they made for you at Patel's office. Dr. Faklis will explain—no, Jon, squeeze my hand. See? You're not paralyzed, brah. Just doped and groggy."

"Jonny—finally." The familiar voice came from the doorway.

"Evie," Jon managed to croak.

"Don't ever say my name like that again," Evelyn said, sitting on the side of the bed Brik just vacated. "You're in good hands here."

"Paws too, brah—*Hck*—three French hens, two turtle doves, and a Parti-Pomeranian tree." The handyman closed his eyes. "I'll ask Faklis to induce my coma now."

Brik put his forehead to his arm as Dr. Althea Faklis swept into the room. Her sunken eyes and nest of wild hair were a shock for Jon to see—she was usually put together without flaw. She knuckled her eyes and let out a long sigh. "I heard you croak from my office. I was planning to commit suicide or hari-kari-Krishna or something." She gave her patient a small glass of clear liquid. "Drink that slowly—it'll numb your throat so you can eat solid food. You're awake. And alive. Thank God."

Jon managed to sit up. He lifted his gown with the tips of his fingers, making a face of disgust. "Filthy. Need shower," he said, his voice less croaky. "Throat feels better."

Dr. Faklis casually checked his pulse. "It's remarkable how that ring of scar tissue shielded you from the cancer. A miracle situation—one in a hundred million. The opening in the back of your unsightly head will be—no, don't touch or I will plug you back into the Matrix. That's for the final two treatments, today's and tomorrow's. And then you're done. The aroma of the discharge back there is the most repellant thing I've smelled in all my years of medicine. Try not to touch it. Okay?"

Evelyn nodded her head violently. "Skatá—I always said you were a shit for brains."

Jon's laughter broke into a fit of coughing.

Evelyn told everyone to leave. She took Jon by the hand when they were alone, besides the beeping and clicking machines. "We're not out of the woods yet," she said quietly. "Althea was not able to perform the surgery like she and Raj had planned. She was only able to explore the area and prep you for the chemo injections. Very strong, very targeted."

"What is it, Evie?" Jon asked.

She squeezed his hand. "So, do you want me to tell you the truth? Or do you want me to tell you what you need to hear?"

"How about both?"

"These treatments are a last ditch effort, Jonny. The cyst ring started breaking an hour before they got in there—the cancer started spreading immediately," Evelyn replied, trying not to cry.

"Spreading where?"

"It's in your lymph system mostly—and throughout your brain."

"How long do I have?"

Evelyn kissed his hand. "That's where I come in," she said. "Because what I believe is more important than the medical truth. What I believe goes beyond charts and statistics. A mother knows these things—and a Greek mother, who is the Oracle reincarnated, knows more about the mysteries of life and death than even the well educated."

Jon wiped a tear as he laughed. "And what's that?"

"That I know with every fiber of my being that you'll beat this thing, Jonny. I have faith that you will live a long life once the miracle comes. And it's coming soon."

Yes, it was exactly what Jon needed to hear.

*

Christmas Eve.

Jon's favorite day of the year had arrived. He did not feel terribly merry and bright about it. He struggled with gaps in his memory, short and long term. The holiday he had always seen as special now exacerbated his anxiety. The whole day, from morning to sunset, used to be one filled with magic anticipation, a day filled with the possibility of miracles—a day of pure joy and sincerest love.

Since coming home, Jon's sense of time was off.

Every hour was akimbo. Every moment was askew and off kilter.

Between heartbeats, time either stretched like taffy or accelerated beyond light speed. He had trouble keeping new thoughts from spilling out of his head, or out of his mouth—his words were unfiltered and untamed, and just this side of offensive if he was overtired.

It seemed that he was asking about Abby Flowers every other minute. It seemed that his heart broke every time he learned why. The ache he felt for her was beyond anything he recalled ever feeling before.

Last night, he cried himself to sleep from missing her—it was the medication, of course. And knowing he would soon shuffle off this mortal coil seemed to put him in a foul mood that he could not shake—go figure.

His stomach growled.

He was sitting up in bed reading from one of his 'therapy' books. They were actual books rescued from the ruins of his house before it was demolished. He liked to call them 'therapy' books because he did not read them for pleasure—he read them aloud to sound out words and phrases, and to recite passages he had memorized.

Doctor's orders, my hairy rump.

Physically, Jon felt fine.

Even so, his daily routine and exercises exhausted him. Leaving the bed to relieve himself was enough to bring on a panic attack. His non-diseased tissue needed time to heal. As if that really mattered. Or that this long reboot was not already extended for too long. Now that he was at home—which meant a room in Evelyn's house—he felt scrutinized, as if he were under a microscope.

Well, he was more or less an invalid.

He could barely walk. He was moody as hell. His comfort levels with visitors varied from hour to hour, minute to minute—depending on how well his thoughts and memory were gelling.

Evelyn had purchased a few volumes of Shakespeare's popular plays—books were stacked everywhere in the room. Scattered about by design, as he had to get out of bed to make a selection to read. He hated getting out of bed to do much of anything, let alone 'fetching' a book.

Yesterday, it was *Hamlet*.

Today, since it was Christmas Eve, he wanted something cheerful— *Twelfth Night*, perhaps.

Closing his eyes, Jon passed a beanbag back and forth in his hands as he recited old monologues and soliloquies he had memorized from his performing days. His hands were moving in time to his words. He dropped the beanbag and absently started signing as he spoke, unaware that someone was watching him.

He opened his eyes.

Evelyn was standing in the doorway with a tray of food. Her cheeks were wet. "I didn't want to interrupt you," she said, floating into the room. She laid the tray across his lap and stuffed a napkin into his shirt. Wiping her face, she checked the bandages around the back of his head. She poked and prodded his neck and arms, asking if he wanted anything for pain or sleep.

"I'm fine, Evie—quit fussing."

"Don't push me today." She fidgeted with the bed sheets, trying to find a reason to linger. "You must be excited about Hannah coming over," she said, pointing to the tray. "Peter did the lamb. And that's his attempt at a Tarpon Greek salad with feta. The lamb's tough."

Jon grimaced. "Can't I have Greek chow mein?"

"Maybe Santa will put some in your stocking."

She kissed his forehead and left.

He devoured his meal. Everything tasted fine—looks were deceiving. When he rang the little bell on his nightstand, Peter leapt into the room, which startled the recovering cancer patient, who accidentally let go of the handle in his hands. The bell shot through the air directly over Peter's head. Had he been taller, it would have smacked his face.

"Peter, I'm sorry! You scared me half to death."

"My bad. My bad," he said, laughing. "A busted nose would've given me character." He picked up the tray. "It's like the whole world is sending you flowers and teddy bears, sponges with googly eyes—you're a rock star. Framed prints of your mermaid paintings are the hottest thing now. You're raising a lot of money for charity. It's what you wanted, right?"

"Is it really?" Jon asked flippantly. He picked up his empty glass and chucked it across the room. When it hit the wall, it sank into the dry wall—half of it stuck out like a badly installed porthole. Peter shook his head. "Why are you so angry? You're alive."

"Am I really? I didn't want this attention."

"Whatever, rey—you reap what you sow. Better count your blessings." Jon threw the beanbag. Peter ducked from the room laughing.

If Evelyn and I were not the only ones who knew the truth, you would be nicer to me! Angry Jon the Invalid wiped his mouth with his napkin bib and dropped it on the floor. When he heard a knock at the door, he barked in frustration. "I want no more visitors!"

"I don't care what you want," Hannah said, gliding into the room. "Still grumpy, I see."

"Maybe," Jon replied with a pout. "Don't stay too long."

"Looking forward to it," Hannah replied. "Think you'll be up to going to the bayou tonight? I think you need to get some fresh air. Your public is dying to see you again."

"What about your mother? Go with her."

"She's in New York," she said. "She got you a present though. I was going to wait and give it to you later tonight, but why wait?"

Jon smiled. "That's my motto—alright, what's the gift?"

Hannah reached into her purse. A book wrapped in bright gold leaf paper. "Mom said that you had to tell me about Atlanta before I gave this to you. That's the rule."

"Is that so?"

"Yep—so, spill it."

Unsure about where to start, Jon plunged into the story. "I'd been in Atlanta for a few months trying to forget my tragic life in Tarpon Springs. Unbeknownst to me, your mother had been traveling the world, trying to forget her own tragic life in Tarpon. That's the strange thing about it all—kismet underpinnings. The last leg of your mother's world trip put her in Costa Mesa, California—a public workshop for a new play by Richard Greenberg called, *Three Days of Rain*. Anyway, I was beginning my run of *Twelfth Night* when your mother's plane landed at Atlanta International Airport. It was a bitterly cold winter night. Ice. Snow. Freezing rain and sleet. From the Great Lakes down to Savannah. A magical layover stranded your mother, who happened to be between fiancés at the time. With nothing else to do, she took a cab to downtown, which dropped her off next to the theater where I was performing."

"Mom never told me this," Hannah said. "Are you exaggerating?"

Jon laughed. "No, not a bit. I remember she sat in the back row. It wasn't a packed house, so I could see her face when the stage was fully lit. Of all the cities her flight could've been delayed in. It was my best performance. Because she was there I was better than I should've been—showing off, like I'd done when we were teenagers. That performance was my ticket to do a week of performances at Shakespeare's Globe in London in the summer. Anyway, after the curtain closed that night, she came home with me. To my crappy little studio apartment. The next day, when we came up for air, we ventured outside for a while. Played in the snow like kids. Returned to our private world in my crappy apartment. Repeated the previous night. And the next day too. I took her to the airport on the fourth day—this was before September 11, so I walked her to her gate. She said we'd always have those four days of snow. Always. And then she disappeared. She didn't want anything to do with me."

"Well, those four days of snow sound like something private and powerful, something that you'd want to keep where it happened."

Jon took Hannah's hand. "We made you. So, I'm not bitter about it anymore." He kissed her knuckles. The thought of not seeing her again filled his veins with ice water. "I'd like to take you to see the Wonderworker tonight. If that's okay with you."

Hannah looked askance. "Wonderworker?"

"The Icon of Saint Nicholas," Jon explained. "A framed picture just inside the entrance to St. Nicholas Cathedral. Kiki's brother is one of the sextons—he promised to let us look at it once the last service is over and the church is empty. If I decided to stop by." He winced as he shifted his weight. "A little before nine o' clock tonight, we'll head over to the church. May I open my gift now?"

"Oh, yeah—it's a book."

"You think?" Jon said, adding (with a wink), "brat." He slowly peeled away the pretty paper. Indeed, it was a hardcover book about half an inch thick. "Huh—it's a copy of *Twelfth Night* signed by Dame Judith Olivia Dench." He turned it over in his hands.

His eyes brimmed as he read the inscription on the following page. 'Four days of snow, Jon. Eternally grateful—Alicia Soledad Safford.'

Oh, the memories triggered by those words. Sighs tinged with sharp edged sadness evaporated when gratitude filled his heart. "What's this?" Taped to the inside back cover was a key. "Hannah?"

"Oh, that's the key to your new house," she said. "Mom's house, actually—she's been working the deal with Evelyn ever since you emerged from your butterfly cocoon. If you protested, Evelyn said to tell you that 'power of attorney's a bitch, and so am I'." Hannah laughed. "You okay, Dad? We all thought you'd see the poetic irony in this."

"Alicia Safford," Jon whispered. "Unpredictable as always. And then there's Evelyn, who defies and defines predictability."

Hannah nodded. "You were the love of her life, you know. She admitted that much to me before she handed me your present."

Jon swallowed a thick lump.

He placed the book on the nightstand. "Will you sit with me until I fall asleep?" he asked. "Please?"

Hannah took his hand. "Of course, Daddy."

Jon smiled lazily. "Thank you—I just have this strange rushing sensation flooding my body," he said, offering her a glimpse of his arm. "Look at the goosebumps. I feel like I'm soaring through the air like a bird. Or maybe a butterfly. Hannah, if I forget you, don't give up on me."

"Why would I ever give up on you?"

"Promise me that you'll no forget me, honey. Okay?"

"Yes, of course." She looked worried. "I don't understand—"

"Last night I dreamed that I died today," Jon said. "It happened suddenly, like lightning out of a clear sky. I'm not afraid of dying. I'm just afraid of not being me anymore. Promise me. Right now. If I die, you won't forget me. And if I get lost, you'll help me get back."

"Okay, okay—I promise to help you find your way back."

"No matter what it takes?"

"No matter what it takes."

"Thank you, Hannah—thank you very much."

She stroked his hand. "You know, the weather service says it's going to be colder tonight than any Christmas Eve in memory. A few people are talking snow."

"Here? In Tarpon Springs? Never."

"Why not?"

"That would a be a miracle."

Jon drifted to that jumping off place. The twilight waiting room of lucid thoughts and fever dreams, where falling and flying were interchangeable. Where people he knew and loved were there to greet him before takeoff. And then he dove into a manatee filled Spring Bayou awash in a constellation of flickering candlelight and falling snow.

＊

GULF  .TINE

December 24

St. Nicholas Cathedral is a stunning piece of Neo-Byzantine architecture. Modeled after the Hagia Sophia, with 23 stained glass windows illustrating Jesus Christ and the lives of myriad other holy folk. Glorious chandeliers from Czechoslovakia. Murals of breathtaking beauty. The bishop's chair, the altar, the choir stalls—imported white marble from Greece.

A feast for the eyes that, when coupled with the smells and sounds of incense and chanting, you cannot help but feel transported. I'm an atheist, but I don't deny the power of this place. Still, it's not where I thought I'd end up on Christmas Eve.

I love the candlelit walk along Spring Bayou. I never miss the lambathas on December 24. Thousands of candles lit inside small white sand-filled paper bags around a large salty pond— from sunset to nightfall.

It was the coldest Christmas Eve ever recorded. I was alone, as

per usual for these types of things. Bumping into Jon Christakos
and his daughter Hannah was not intentional. They asked me to
accompany them to the cathedral. And so, I did.

As we neared the steps to the church, I asked Jon why he wanted to see the Icon. He simply said that he had to see it tonight.
That he had a feeling it was important.

Kiki Kontodiakos met us at the bottom of the church steps. Her
brother the sexton told us to move quickly. Jon got out of the
wheelchair unassisted and walked up the steps to those beautiful
doors. Hannah, Kiki, and I followed, but we gave him space.

Jon crossed himself and headed over to the framed image of
Tarpon's patron saint—again, unassisted. I would've sold my
soul right then just to get a glimpse into that head of his. He
stumbled, but steadied himself and continued with his mission.

He looked like a toddler as he took those last steps closer to the
Icon. He pressed closer to kiss the glass and frame. The moment
he did, he straightened, as if he'd been poked with hot stick. He
didn't move—but then he slowly turned to face us.

He laughed and took a step forward. And then he stopped, looking each one of us in the eye. I'd never seen that look on a face
up close. Definitely not the face of someone I knew personally.

I've seen photos. I've seen it on paintings and sculptures—the
crazed holy light of divine ecstasy. With that look in his eyes, Jon
reached out for Hannah and Kiki. I stood at the door, uncertain
as to what I was to do or say—hell, I was this close to running.

"He's weeping again," Jon said, his hands shaking with excitement. "The Icon is weeping—I feel the light burning me clean."

Had I not seen him do and say this, then I would not have believed it—he wept with trembling joy. His tears were crimson. When Jon Christakos laughed, his red tears went clear.

He insisted upon climbing down the steps to his wheelchair alone, which he did smoothly, confidently.

Not once did he slip or wobble or stumble. Then, at the bottom of the stairs, he went rigid as a plank. His whole body locked before he collapsed into the chair.

Jon stopped breathing.

Hannah rounded up coats from passers-by and threw them down away from the lamplight. Next to the statue of the boy holding the cross in the church plaza. We pushed him over there and stretched him atop the wraps and jackets.

There was a crowd now.

Kiki and I took turns giving him breath and massaging his chest until the EMTs arrived. They took over—but there was no response. That was 8:57 p.m.

The moment I saw him touch the Icon I knew he had changed. I knew he had been altered from within—an alchemy of spirit I was honored to have seen. But why wasn't he breathing now?

Another sexton kept people from crowding the area beside the bronze statue of the Epiphany boy. As if the boy holding the cross might look out for Jon, watch over his soul as it hummed and vibrated.

Three minutes passed.

People were whispering about the Icon weeping again, for the first time since December 1973. They were speaking of a miracle. Upon the utterance of that word, Jon took a breath.

He continued to breathe and cough until he was stable enough to hoist into the back of the ambulance and take you to the hospital. And that's when the snow started falling.

No one realized it was happening. Folks gathered there were too busy praying or spreading news about your death and resurrection—that there was a Christmas miracle unfolding at St. Nicholas. It was as precious and significant a moment in my life as there ever has been or will be.

For the first time in decades snow fell upon our coastal town. Big fat flurries coated the entire area, from Dunedin to Weeki Wachee Springs.

Thanks to Jon Christakos, the Tarpon Springs Wonderworker.

December 31

In the week since the Icon started weeping, since Jon Christakos bore the brunt of a miracle that inspired others, I've been humbled. In the life that I've lived since Jon first returned it to me, I often wondered whether I was living the one I was meant to live.

I had an epiphany. I know—atheist Adam Disston had an epiphany. Call Richard Dawkins—tell him to revoke my membership.

I could've been another dead teenager lost to the world after another accident due to youthful recklessness. The life I was meant to live was always this one—it was a miracle I couldn't understand until I watched the life of my friend pause.

Before the ambulance took Jon away, before they loaded him into the truck, I felt that I had been blessed.

News about the Icon began spreading—indeed, the news metastasized quickly. As if the Christ child was about to be born in Tarpon Springs, the night exploded with the joy of the season. It continued every night afterward.

And here we are, New Year's Eve.

My final words for this column. Fitting that they should be about St. Nicholas Cathedral, where I witnessed a real wonder. For this atheist, bastard playboy, it was a privilege. Whether or not miracles occurred that night is up to you. I know what I saw.

As for Jon Christakos, who had slipped into a coma that night, he woke early this morning with no memory of what had transpired Christmas Eve.

He has little to no memory of what's happened since either, with one exception: the cancer is gone.

Hand to God, kids—Jon's cancer is gone.

Tonight, Brik Buckman will be performing music from his upcoming album, *Song of the Wonderworker.* Cap'n Jack's. Starts at 9 p.m. All proceeds will benefit Lemon Street Housing Ministries and St. Nicholas Greek Orthodox Cathedral.

Come spend the night with us sinners to raise money on behalf of our Saint Jon. Felicity Noel will be there with her new Hunky Hollywood Hottie—the same brilliant actor collecting all those accolades at the moment—so, yeah, THAT kind of famous.

I'd rather Jon Christakos not know about his divinity. Or my temporary religious conversion. I will, however, speak of his unbelievable talent—about that I'll be happy to preach. As for this column, in a few more keystrokes the LIBERTINE shall be no more. Blessings and joy to you and yours, kids. Make good choices—amen.

*

CHAPTER 20

A Confederacy of Giving

"The heavens were opened, and the Spirit of God descended like a dove
saying, 'This is my beloved Son, in whom I am well pleased.'"
~ Matthew 3: 16-17

The pealing bells of St. Nicholas echoed in joyous celebration. It was a clear, sunny day, one to make you believe in miracles. That such divine events occurred in Tarpon Springs was no longer contested—well, not since the weeping Icon of Saint Nicholas started weeping again. And the fact that Jon Christakos was alive and well, and cancer-free. His was not a life easily measured by secular humanity's rules—his was measured only by metaphysical rules. The seeds of miracles had taken root, around the world it seemed.

Indeed, it was to this sleepy sponge diving community that tens of thousands from every faith and culture had made a pilgrimage.

To Tarpon Springs the masses came.

They gathered around the banks of Spring Bayou, the largest crowds ever assembled for an Epiphany celebration. All were clasping hands and holding breaths as they watched and waited for the promise offered by this day. Blessings bestowed upon the Anclote River and Gulf of Mexico. Blessings upon the boats and divers traversing dangerous waters. Blessings upon of the souls of this community, Epiphany City. And so, with one voice lifted in prayer, a collective expression of gratitude for the past and new year—for bounty, for renewed hope and faith, for a deeper abiding love of family and friends—they praised God.

From the cathedral, a colorful procession of clergy, altar servers, dignitaries, band and choir members, children in traditional attire, the dove bearer, and others made its way to Spring Bayou.

The assembly congregated on the pier. Roped in the water just beyond was a ring of anchored ceremonial boats. In them were the dozens of soaking wet teenage boys clad in shorts and T-shirts. All were at the ready, waiting for the white wooden cross to be thrown.

The Archbishop said a prayer, a blessing for the bayou, boats, and young men about to dive. The dove bearer released the dove into the air. His Eminence threw the white crucifix into the cold murky bayou. And Fifty-four teenagers leaped from the boats into the water.

Peter was the smallest—he was also the last to dive. For a minute or more, the heads of boys broke the surface for air and then disappeared. After two minutes, the clusters dissipated into smaller pockets of divers—all of them large and athletic, none of them successful.

A murmur bubbled up and passed through the assemblage.

Clergy gathered on the platform exchanged curious glances. None were as worried as the faces of the dignitaries—one of them in particular.

Peter, come up soon, Jon thought—*God, watch over that boy.* He looked up at the woman standing beside him. Evelyn was Jon's escort. She patted his shoulder, nodding encouragement. He thought it amusing that he was considered to be a dignitary, sharing the stage with the mayor-elect and Archbishop. Evelyn actually belonged there. As did Neal Peruski, who stood at the far side of the pier—his face was full of worry too.

Brik and Hannah were on their private dock with Peter's mother Fotini and Kiki, whose brother retrieved the cross a few years ago. Generations of the Kontodiakos clan had managed the same feat. One of her young cousins was currently splashing about in the bayou right now.

Evelyn gasped and pointed.

A small head popped up near the sea wall by the ladder. He was far from the splashing groups of larger divers searching the bayou, bobbing on the frothing surface of the water. The boy looked hurt.

It was Peter.

Another murmur of sympathy rose from the crowd when the sexton draped a towel around the small diver's wet shoulders. Peter violently shook as he crept toward the Archbishop. Even as the other divers were still searching for the cross, Peter was reaching behind him. And from the belt beneath his wet shirt, he pulled out the white wooden crucifix.

Something in the air changed.

A strange energy coupled with a strong breeze.

The palm trees dotting the banks of the bayou swayed. The clouds rolled into thin wispy strings that vanished into the dazzling blue. And the dove, released only minutes before, reappeared. It circled high above the crowd, hanging in the air before it descended to the pier in a steep dive. Suddenly, the bird swept upward in a magnificent glide toward the spire of the cathedral, disappearing into the trees beyond the dome.

A collective cry of joy erupted from the crowd—*Axios!*

Jon managed some applause, although it took some effort—*Peter is indeed worthy.* Another chorus of cheering rippled in waves of shared joy as Peter knelt before the Archbishop and kissed the cross as he presented it. The other divers climbing from the water soon joined their little brother as the primate offered a final blessing.

Again, the crowds cheered—*Axios!*

Some of the larger boys grabbed Peter and hoisted him onto their shoulders. They presented him once again before carrying him toward St. Nicholas, its bell ringing in celebration. The traditional parade to the cathedral, for which many spectators had begun to line up, would have to wait. The official ceremony had ended, but an impromptu pageant had yet to conclude.

Gripping the cross as he floated on a sea of muscled arms and hands, Peter tapped the ones carrying him. They lowered him to the ground and cleared a path. He ran back to the pier where Jon was watching and wondering—*what is this boy up to?*

Clutching the cross to his chest, Peter reached the wheelchair.

No one moved. No one breathed. A new blessing was unfolding—indeed, one of those miracle seeds that had been planted long before today.

No one wanted to miss this moment. With chest heaving and arms trembling, Peter gingerly placed the cross into Jon's lap.

"You need this more than I do."

Jon Christakos lifted the crucifix. Rolling his eyes (to keep from crying more than anything), he patted his lap. Peter hopped into it and shook his mane of dark hair.

There was no applause, no cheering.

There was only the ringing church bell, its sound as ethereal and delicate as a wind chime.

Jon hugged the wet young man—his love for Peter filled the emptiness he so keenly felt. The reprieve, however brief, was a blessing. Emptiness affected him more than the hiccups of his recovering mind. The gaps in time, the taffy pull of thoughts, the forgetting and remembering of places and faces—all irritating and embarrassing quirks of recovery that were slowly driving him nuts.

Emptiness haunted him—Jon did not pretend like he did not know why. After all, he had told Abigail Flowers to leave him. Sensing his emotional distress, Evelyn squeezed his shoulder.

Peter climbed down.

By then, the other divers had returned to the platform. With outstretched arms, hands, and hearts, they circled Tarpon's famous son, the man responsible for giving to everyone but himself. The band of Greek brothers touching Peter's head slowly formed the spokes of a wheel that radiated outward.

The circle grew.

More people, including clergy and dignitaries, also touched the shoulders and heads of those around them.

The circle grew outward.

More people joined it. Hundreds of outstretched arms became thousands, and thousands more, and many thousands of hands and fingers seeking and finding, grasping and holding—only connecting.

And the circle grew.

It expanded until it became a great wheel of connected people. All was silent until the still small voice of Peter floated above them in song:

"Kyrie eleison. Christe eleison. Kyrie eleison."

They were irrevocably joined in a singular moment of spontaneous grace. An arrested moment of sacred time. The Holy Spirit had descended upon them, as it had done when John the Baptist ordained the Son of God in the River Jordan—*Amen.*

*

It was a cool beautiful late afternoon on the Anclote River.

Evelyn wheeled Jon along the dockside walkway. With the number of people this year, it was bound to be a late night. After His Eminence honored the divers and Peter, she took Jon outside and pushed him toward the Sponge Docks.

"Wish I'd forget everything for good," he mumbled.

Evelyn shook the wheelchair and spun it around. "Do you know what today is? What it means to this town? Our family?" She had tears in her eyes. "You're stronger than this." He tried to look away. She would not allow it. "Quit whining and be grateful. Maybe God isn't finished healing you yet. You are worthy of a miracle, Jon Christakos."

"Sorry, Evie. Where are we going?"

"Crazy, that's where we're going—keep quiet for a while."

They passed the Riverside Grille building.

A group of men and women dressed in out-for-cocktails clothes were gathered at the main entrance and entered when the glass double doors opened. From three large vans in the loading dock, men were moving square crates into the open bay door.

"Evie, what's going on?"

Evelyn did not answer his question. She simply started whistling as she steered the chair past the harbormaster's office. Past the maritime museum, Shrimp Wrecked, and Sponge-O-Rama. The owner of Dimitri's on the Water saw them approaching. He led them to the back of his mostly empty restaurant. Handing an envelope to Evelyn, he said, "A gift for Peter from us. Behind those curtains—they're expecting you."

Waiting in the private dining room were Draco Bilirakis, Luke Dukakis, and Vasile Faklis. The moment they spied Evelyn they shouted praises and smothered her with affection. They really could have been mistaken for brothers.

Everyone knew these men essentially represented the collective voice of the people who made their living on the Sponge Docks. Everyone trusted them to put the community first when they conducted business behind closed doors—in places like this, privately, respectfully, and efficiently.

But why are we here?

Vasile Faklis patted Jon's shoulder. "We have much to talk about."

Soon, the dining room echoed with laughter and reeked of cigar smoke. Jon had known these men all his life. Still, he struggled remembering his connections to them. Not surprising, as he struggled remembering his connections to everyone else. It was like having to watch the same home movies on repeat until his memory returned unaided.

Draco was part of a well-known political family. "We were all content to live out our twilight years competing with each other." He patted the empty chair next to his. "But then Nico Cocoris left for Greece. His premonitions about fire and water made him crazy."

"Crazy came true," Vasile shouted, slapping the table.

"It did for me too," Jon muttered.

Evelyn shook the chair. "Keep your mouth shut."

Luke snapped his fingers. A server approached the table with a bottle of ouzo and several small glasses.

After they toasted, Hannah entered the room and strode toward the table. She lit a cigar and stood behind the empty chair that was Nico's seat when the Greek Triage was a Quartet.

"Glad to see you, Pops."

"Pops, really?"

Hannah laughed. "I always called you that."

"No, you didn't—you called me Dad," Jon replied, narrowing his eyes. "Brat."

Hannah kissed his cheek. "The survivor's guilt shtick is getting old. The Icon of St. Nicholas weeps. Your mind gets buggered in a flash St. Teresa-styled ecstasy. Your cancer is gone. We all know what you've been through, so stop being a whiny martyr." She looked at her watch. "Gentlemen! We have to go." She lowered her gaze. "You boys have your tasks."

Vasile nodded. "We meet Adam Disston in an hour."

"The paperwork will be signed by then," Draco said.

"I'll stop by your office as soon as it's done," Luke added.

Jon had no idea what had transpired—apparently, they were closing a deal. After they shook hands and kissed cheeks, the three men mysteriously departed in a cloud of smoke and chatter. Hannah smiled knowingly at Evelyn and said, "Alright, follow me."

They headed back to the Riverside building. The vans had gone. Moving trucks were parked there and were in the process of being unloaded. They went to the main entrance and walked through the two enormous glass doors. The decor was the same garish interior since the restaurant closed years ago—Jon remembered that much.

There was music—familiar music, faint and floating from afar. They passed a large fountain that sprayed no water. At the top of the ramp they made their way to the back of the empty dining hall. There, the music was coming from back there.

Hannah passively gestured as she spoke. "My office is back there. The main gallery is over there and will be partitioned into satellite galleries beyond that wall. The multi-function formal hall is behind those curtains. The mermaid-themed bistro bar will occupy the veranda deck overlooking the river. The second floor will have studio and workshop areas. Tarpon's first artist-in-residence will have the freedom to create, teach, explore by the end of March, first week of April."

Jon shifted in his chair. "Who's the artist?"

"Every city worth its salt has an artist-in-residence," Hannah explained, speaking directly to Evelyn. "Tarpon Springs needs Jon Christakos to be the first. Our investors insisted on it."

Jon harrumphed—this confederacy of giving bothered him.

Evelyn shook the chair. "Just because I breastfed you doesn't mean I won't dump your butt onto the floor—your job is to keep your mouth shut and shake hands. After we schmooze and make small talk, I'll wheel you outside. A surprise will be waiting for you at Nico's statue if you behave."

Jon looked at the archway. "Sounds like a cocktail party in there. And I know that's Brik Buckman singing and playing guitar too." He glanced up at Hannah. "Is that his new album?"

Hannah did not reply. She and Evelyn gave him a curt nod before they entered the room arm in arm without him.

Snorting in frustration, Jon left the safety of the wheelchair. He moved toward the entrance, taking small steps as he crossed the threshold into a narrow hall that led to an adjoining room of exposed red brick. His hand on the wall, he kept moving until he rounded the corner.

In the center of the room were dozens of men and women chattering and laughing. Making small talk and moving about the space, refilling drinks at a tiny cash bar or plates of food at the hors d'oeuvre station next to it. Above was an open ceiling with a fly space and track lighting.

His artwork was on display—each wall had a large mermaid painting. Playing in faded bouncy color atop each of the paintings were home movies—reels of Super 8 films in a constant loop. The projector perched in the ceiling spat out four separate moving images as music poured from speakers mounted in the corners—Brik Buckman's music.

Something stirred deep inside Jon's brain, something he thought was lost. On that wall was a beautiful mermaid a-swimming—sight and sound were triggering him.

I have lived a thousand years searching
For my soul to find that I have cried a thousand tears
But can you read my mind, my mind...

On that wall, a well-dressed man with a charming smile was jumping around a maze of two-top tables in a small lounge. The blue curtains behind him opened, revealing a woman in Lycra fins swimming in a sea of bubbles—his mother and his father.

I have touched a thousand lives hoping to feel for you
And I've been cut to pieces with the knives
Of empty love inside, inside...

On that wall, a little girl with platinum blonde hair was spinning wildly—she seemed so familiar, as if she were the only star of his most lucid dreams. Hers was a face that haunted him all his life. He would have sworn on a stack of bibles that he knew her—and did not know her. Either way, he was telling the whole truth—*so help me, God.*

For I have sailed an ocean of time
To find you again like we've done so many times before
Remember, when we have to go
Love, it lasts forever and finds another door.

Jon felt a tap-tap on his shoulder.

It was Hannah, whose face matched the face of the little girl projected behind her. His heart bounced.

Alicia Safford, stunning in her little black dress, sidled up with Beverly Disston Pink, looking regal in a flapper-style dress and pearls. After she greeted Jon and Hannah, Alicia excused herself to go speak to a quartet of women gathered along the far wall.

Beverly embraced Jon with a genuine sincerity that nearly made his knees buckle—he remembered that morning she came into his store looking like a haggard old bag lady. "I should've barged into your store five years ago—I regret not making that decision. Nonetheless, that you're alive makes this old bird happy."

Jon's heart pounded harder—it made him dizzy.

Something was happening, inside his head, inside his body.

He seemed to be floating, as if he were playing in and out of a daydream. His sense of time was askew. And he was staring at a blank part of one of the walls.

"What is this place?" he asked no one in particular.

"The Rebecca Mathis Gallery," Hannah said. "As the city's first artist-in-residence, I thought it would be appropriate for you to meet the donors and investors here. I also thought it would be good for your soul, seeing these images. You need to let go of this guilt, Dad."

Jon could not speak. His eyes darted. His pounding heart left him breathless AND dizzy—*haven't I heard this song twice already?* He pulled Hannah to him. "How long have we been here? Ten minutes?"

"An hour," she replied. "Everyone's heading to the Jolley Trolley."

"Oh, that's disturbing. Why the bus?"

Hannah motioned for Evelyn, who was wrapping up a conversation with Alicia. "We're all going for a ride. Well, you're staying put." She was guiding him down the hallway. "You don't remember shaking hands with everyone? Thanking them for supporting the arts?"

Jon laughed. "Vaguely—I just need to sit down," he said, pointing. "My wheelchair. Don't let me fall before I get to it."

"I won't let you fall."

There was truth in Hannah's words. After all, hers was the face he had been painting for years—hers was the face that belonged to his mother. Jon staggered under the weight of that sudden realization. It was not enough to completely shatter the wall surrounding his mind—but there were plenty of cracks now.

This dam was about to break. Providence was paying him back in full, with interest—heavy on the interest.

Evelyn was there to push him now.

As they left the building, Evelyn began to tell Jon about the changes happening to Tarpon Springs. How he had inspired the townspeople to be brave, to count their blessings, and to have faith until a collective spiritual connection reached critical mass on Christmas Eve, when the Icon of St. Nicholas started to weep again. "There were lots of miracles."

"I spoke to Roman and Bret Grelik last week," Hannah said. "Babcia had a massive stroke on Christmas Eve. The doctors couldn't explain why, but she was fine the next day. Clean bill of health."

Evelyn picked up the baton. "A woman had stillborn twins earlier that night, but she refused to let anyone take them from her chest—she wanted to hold them until Christmas morning. Those babies started to breathe the exact moment the Icon started weeping."

"Both babies are healthy," Hannah said. "The male nurse on call that night sat with the mother. He would not leave her side—they were married yesterday. What is it, Dad? Are you okay?"

That was the moment it happened—Jon began remembering everything that he had blocked from his mind. Memories came slowly at first, but they were all lined up and ready to greet him like old friends. Details were still fuzzy, but the memories were there.

Memories of this morning were especially lucid—when Peter retrieved the cross, when the dove descended, when thousands of strangers touched. Memory of that mass connection filled him with the same electricity that had stopped and started his heart Christmas Eve.

A tide of explosive, little epiphanies of the soul swept over him.

The waves rendered him mute, filled his head with hope and relief. Jon looked up into the bronze face of Nico Cocoris—*when did we come outside?* The statue was the first stop on Leon Rain's Hallelujah Line, but where were Hannah and Evelyn?

People were boarding the Jolley Trolley.

Donors, friends, acquaintances, former rivals, strangers—all were shaking his hand before climbing into the bus idling at the curb.

The sun had just dipped below the horizon—the sky was awash in streaks of orange and purple. A chill had returned to the air—but he was not cold. The Sponge Docks was buzzing with activity now that the revels from the community center had spilled into the rest of the city.

Jon shook his last hand—it was Peter's.

"When did you get here?"

Peter hoisted his backpack onto a shoulder. "Just now."

"How much money did you rake in tonight?"

"Enough for a used car. A semester at St. Pete College. A summer in Greece. With just enough left over for an investment opportunity." He grinned. "I wouldn't mind backing Brik Buckman if he ever decides to leave Tarpon Springs. He could be a huge star."

"Where is he?"

Peter pointed. "The back of the bus with Evelyn and Hannah," he said. "You heard his album? It's dedicated to you—you're in the title."

"No, I'm not."

"*Song of the Wonderworker*—that's you, rey."

"I'm not the damn Wonderworker."

"Okay, Grumpy-pa. Whatever you say."

Jon's mind no longer reeled.

He almost felt normal again—well, despite the gushing memories flooding his skull. He did not like being accused of working wonders.

Ding-Ding!

The sound of guitar and voice wafted from the back of the bus. Brik Buckman played until everyone knew the melody and lyrics well enough to join in. The crowd made the song an anthem that lifted the spirit.

> *Leon Rain vowed*
> *He would never fall in love again*
> *About a million miles ago*
> *A woman broke his heart*
> *And he's never been back, yeah*
> *But then a steam train*
> *From out of his dream came*
> *To take him for a ride*
> *On the Hallelujah Line*
> *And when a fallen angel appeared*
> *Leon lost his mind—*
> *I said, Leon lost his mind.*

Jon fished two keys from his pocket and put them into Peter's hand. "The big key goes to the El Camino. It's yours now that I'm not a dead man walking. I don't need a car. The small key goes to a suitcase in the cottage house garage," he said, smiling as he recalled what Chucky had told him about giving it away. "What's inside is all yours."

Fire in his heart
As he screamed in the dark
For Elijah, Elijah
Please send your manna down
Shelter me from harm
I can't see—
I can't hear a sound
Protect me
Keep me warm.

Peter dropped an envelope at Jon's feet and boarded the bus. At the top step, he turned around and pointed at the envelope. Jon had been too busy folding his wheelchair to notice.

"Hey, gimme a hand."

"Sorry, but that's not the plan, Jon. You stay here."

"What? C'mon, Peter."

"You're staying," he said, heading to the back of the bus. "And you need to read that letter."

Ding-Ding!

Leon Rain tipped his hat.

"Have a good night, Epiphany Man. Alright, ladies and gentlemen, welcome aboard your Chariot of Fire."

Closing the doors, Leon finished making his announcement to the passengers, who acted as if Jon no longer existed. They only listened to the musician and the driver, who put the bus into gear. The fat wheels lurched and rolled toward the end of the marina.

And then the Chariot of Fire disappeared into the night.

Jon snatched the envelope. He laid the wheelchair on the sidewalk and sat on the bench behind him. At first, he thought to rip it up and pout until he got cold enough to roll his butt back to Spring Bayou.

The image made him laugh.

Besides, Evelyn was the Oracle of Delphi reincarnated and would kill him if he ripped one of her letters. Good or bad, her epistles were sacred.

He would not have saved them in a fireproof lockbox if they were not.

*

January 6

Jonny,

I wanted to tell you that you've done something to me that can't be undone. From the moment I nursed you, my heart opened so wide that I couldn't imagine it being any different.

I clearly saw the beautiful colors of your sweet soul, and in a flash of light, I knew you were important.

But a mother with two infants has little time to entertain deep thoughts—that spark of recognition went away as quickly as it hit me. I only recalled it years later.

After you lost your aunt and uncle and I lost my husband and son. After you went to Atlanta for two years. I never told you this, but I needed that time too.

I tried to seal my heart when you left.

It didn't take me long to figure out how stupid I was to try. You were my son—period. All the pain vanished the moment I remembered that flash of light.

Loving you has been an incredible privilege.

It has inspired me to find my courage and strength. It has matured me, both as a mother and a woman. I'm changed because Heaven saw fit to send your sweet soul down here to grace my life with yours. I'm not the only one who thinks so.

~ Evelyn

*

Jon folded the letter and placed it back into the sleeve.

Despite his efforts to the contrary, it was time to navigate the troubled waters of his recovering mind with less attitude and more humble resolve. The realization that he had been acting like the Greek Village idiot made him laugh harder than the image of him rolling his pouting butt home did. He deserved a slow roll back home.

Alone and in shame.

The truth was that he was not facing a dark night of the soul. Had he been a weaker man, Jon might have traded tonight's epiphanies with December's days of dreamless lotus sleep.

But he took too much delight in discovery.

Having been born into the world with less than most, he was grateful for the lessons to be mined from mistakes.

With some exceptions, he often succeeded—even if it took time. He had Raj Patel, God bless his soul, to thank for his spiritual education—that the cores of mistakes were little Buddhist gifts. As a shudder went through Jon, he closed his eyes with a contented smile.

Breezes heavy with the scents of a rising tide and breaking water swept the boulevard. Above the street lamps and rustling palms, the fragrant air swirled. Waves lapped the creaking hulls of sponge-laden boats docked nearby. The god of the sea had finally eased the thunder inside his restless mind—*it's time to roll my butt home.*

And then a familiar voice spoke to him.

"I've been standing behind you for 15 minutes waiting for you to turn around and look at me," she said. "I'm this close to pushing you off the dock, Mr. Christakos."

Jon's heart exploded in his chest. "My God—Abby!" He very nearly tripped on the wheels of his chair when he got up to turn around.

Dr. Flowers was there to keep him from falling.

*

SPRING

Where was the sun
When it rained yesterday?
Why did the moon hide
From the night?
How did you break all the waves
Crashing in my head?
What did you see when you gazed at me,
My head in your hands?
Did you want to be the moon,
Deep inside, when you saw me bend?
I'd never dare imagine
You'd ever want to be my friend.
But I could swear I heard you breathe,
And I could swear you said a prayer.
I could feel your hands on me—
You were there.
You were there.

—Brik Buckman, *Song of the Wonderworker*

Epiphany Man

"Living in the present can pass like seconds or years—
the choice is yours."
~ *Rajeev Patel, MD*

The first day of spring, an hour after sunrise, and Jonathan Nikolas Christakos is wide-awake. He stares at the ceiling with a contented smile and sighs of fire and water. The lump under the covers next to him moves and moans—*there is a miracle in such warmth,* he thinks. There are other miracles too, and just as intimate—of third chances, of forgiveness and salvation, of love and unconditional fidelity. All prodigal sons, in remission or otherwise, would do well to surround themselves with the workers of such miracles.

Jon quietly extracts himself from the paradise of his Egyptian cotton tomb and goes downstairs to make coffee. No longer in the mood to wait patiently for breakfast, Minnie is nipping at his heels. The Muppet-faced dog lifts a paw to scratch his ankle.

"I didn't catch that," he says, waiting for her to paw again. "You sure you want more food? You just ate last night."

Minnie spins and sits, her fuzzy face full of anticipation—she loves this game. She lets him know with a fruity bird-tweet bark. "If you insist," Jon says, lowering her bowl. "This morning's selection is organic chicken breast, ground flax seeds, feta crumbles, and carrots. Bon appétit."

He pours himself a cup of java (sans booze) and goes outside (with effort this morning). Waiting with expectation and anxiety, he sips his coffee and paces to loosen his stiff joints. He absently pats his head. His hair is growing back now—it itches around the scab of his Matrix hole. As he scratches his scalp, he takes in the view of the bayou—*quite a different view from the one I grew up with.*

With a shudder, he wraps his robe tighter and sits in a rocking chair. He misses being Evelyn's next-door neighbor, and the anything-goes possibilities of each day. He rolls his eyes at his maudlin thoughts—*as if I'll never see her again.*

"Dammit, Peter—where the hell are you?"

Jon goes back inside and heads upstairs. Minnie follows close behind. When they enter the dim bedroom, the dog jumps into the bed and snuggles the warm shape stirring there. He sets a cup of hot coffee on her nightstand. He draws back the curtains on the far wall, letting light into the room. He opens the window overlooking the backyard and takes a deep breath.

March is erupting in full color. A volcano bursting forth with whites and pinks and new growing greens, a spectacular flow of liquid hues erasing the dreary browns and drab grays of winter. Budding and flowering shrubs, canopies of dogwood blooms, patches of feathery sweet grasses—and life. On the move are hummingbirds, ladybugs, honeybees, and butterflies in the crisp dawn.

Jon shudders—*what the hell is this nonsensical chill doing in Florida?*

Beneath his gaze, a frail flutter on the sill stirs his periphery. The peacock-colored butterfly creeps blindly along the white ridges of wood. It teeters on the edge of takeoff, precariously balanced between flight and stasis. Several attempts at flight fail—the breezes are too swift. Its body shakes, antennae flicking, as it paces. Its wings are moist with dew—*it needs to be patient until they dry.*

"Close the window, Jon—c-c-cold," Abby says behind him, her voice muffled beneath the comforter with a series of concurring barks. "Minnie says she's cold too."

Jon laughs, a familiar sound he often repeats throughout the day, the serenity prayer of a middle-aged clown with IBS and squeaky red shoes. Last night, when the sky was sparkling violet and bitterly cold, he and

Abby laughed on the back porch for hours. It was hardly enough to keep them warm, but that was remedied with the fire pit, a bottle of wine, a pint of Ben & Jerry's Phish Food ice cream, and a well-packed pipe of Buckman's Best Botanicals—*for my glaucoma*.

"Still c-c-cold," Abby repeats.

Spinning almost too quickly, Jon totters between vomiting and fainting. He closes his eyes to wait for the spell to pass. He shuts the window and *slowly* makes his way to the bed, tickles the two lumps there, and leaves the room with a spring in his step. He goes back downstairs and opens the front door as Peter sprints up the drive. He raises a hand in breathless apology before handing Jon a brown paper bag.

Here are the facts. In the weeks since Epiphany, Jon's fame has shifted onto Peter's sturdier young shoulders. His growing popularity might have made other boys too big for their britches. Not so for the short charismatic Greek transplant from Ohio. For him, fame continually restores his innate humility and gratitude. The glow permanently affixed to his face is a most infectious contagion, a fitting testament for one baptized by the Holy Spirit in Spring Bayou.

"Sorry, Jon. I was on the other side of town."

"Oh, yeah—doing what?"

"Nunya Damn, that's what." Peter offers a wink with his wicked little smile. "Mom and Aunt Evelyn are busy with the HHS. They've got that reception in the garden at sunset." He points across the bayou. "A crew is setting up tables and chairs now. Does it make you sad?"

"Nah—a view of the Safford Museum is a better use of the property. Is Brik over there?"

"He's on a ride-along with Neal and Kiki for some reason—Hannah's managing the crew."

Jon smiles. He knows about the handyman's recent shifts in priorities and proclivities. "Did she say anything when you picked up the bag?"

"Only that she'll see you at the opening—gotta go, rey. See you later!" And then Peter dashes off to do God knows what.

Gallery opening—skatá. I'd better do this quick.

Jon looks at the brown sandwich bag and goes back inside the house. His skull is pounding again. Despite the throb between his ears, he feels better than ever. Just winded and sore, as per usual. He climbs the stairs and heads to the bedroom, where the sounds of warm woman and canine snoring rattle the crown molding and wainscoting. With a goofy grin, he hops over bands of sunlight on the floor as he moves toward the bed.

Minnie's fuzzy head pops up with a yip.

Abby stirs beneath the covers, speaking in tongues as she turns onto her side. The top of the comforter comes down, revealing a wild nest of hair. Clearing strands from her face, she peers at him with sleepy eyes. "Stuffy—open the window."

"Yes, ma'am," Jon says, walking crabways with the bag clipped to his dark side. He opens the window—half-mast this time. The butterfly is still there on the sill. He notes her odd struggle for flight from his periphery—*Brik would be all up in those wings taking pictures by now*. After leaving the bag on the floor, he takes a seat on the edge of the bed and tucks a strand of hair behind her ear. He kisses her brow and eyelids. Jealous Minnie skedaddles down the hall to pout in the guest bedroom.

Abby pats his face. "I'd like a shower now. I feel disgusting."

"You look rather gross," Jon says, adding a flurry of apologies after she pelts him with decorative pillows. "No, a sweaty night gown sticking to your body is sexy. And the way your hair's all matted and bunched and tangled. And how your skin looks like a chupacabra's belly."

Abby removes the gown and sashays into the bathroom. Jon watches her go, admiring her backside until she disappears around a corner. The phone on his nightstand buzzes—a message from Hannah.

> H: what's the word bird ;) you ask her yet?
>   J: had 2 hide box – getting now
> H: hurry up we're dying over here
> H: evelyn says get on yer knees
> H: adam says something vulgar – won't repeat
>   J: this my private moment – butt out
> H: blah-blah-blah-blah—go get/ask

J: i'll never ask for help again

H: you're so lame and old

H: love you, daddy

Jon tries not to tear up—a difficult task to manage lately. The ancient words of magic wielded by daughters since the dawn of history— *brat knows she just destroyed my heart with those three words.*

He dons a robe and wends his way from room to room, opening curtains and doors along the way. Sunlight begins to fill the house, inviting life and spirit inside it. Head spinning like a merry-go-round, he sits down to catch his breath—*not too much, Jonny-baby.* He grins at the image of Bentley Safford's corpse spinning in his unvisited grave.

To be living in that man's former home amuses him to no end.

Jon likes having his small mermaid paintings on display here. His large mermaid canvases—those currently not touring—will be housed in the new Christakos Gallery on permanent exhibition. Today is the grand opening. For weeks, Hannah and Adam have been ball-busters about managing their artist-in-residence and the flow of his work. Right now, there is a moratorium on painting new mermaids, which is a daily challenge. The work is enjoyable, of course, but his heart has yet to find rest inside those new whorls of color and technique.

Jon gets to his feet. He opens more windows to capture a cleansing cross breeze. He goes back up-stairs (much slower this time), sweating from the exertion. The sound of a revving hair dryer tells him to move his ass—*God, don't let me do a face plant on the floor.*

He takes a blue box with white ribbon out of the brown bag. He places it on Abby's nightstand. Strategically, and just in time—she is coming this way. He limps back to his spot at the window.

The butterfly is still there. Wings open and close in silence. He offers an open palm. It climbs into it and curiously crawls around his fingers. Legs like tiny suckers as it ambles in nervous steps.

Behind him, the sounds of Abby moving on the bed, babbling about feeling clean and ready to start the day. He smiles when her questions of 'what's this box' and 'what did you do' precede a joyful shriek that concludes with a sweet sigh.

Her voice trembles as she asks, "Is this real?"

Jon turns around. Abby is sitting on his side of the bed, the open Tiffany box beside her thigh. "You're not kidding?"

"It's Hannah's fault if you don't like it."

Abby screams as she hurls herself at him. She wraps trembling arms around his neck. She pours salty wet kisses over his cheeks. She leads him over to the bed and sits while he looks at his feet. She bumps him playfully. After a dramatic sigh, she puts the ring back in the blue box and turns away.

"What are you doing, Dr. Flowers?"

"On your knees, Mr. Christakos," she says. "Ask me properly, or I will tell Evelyn that you didn't officially put a ring on it. Kneel and ask, you vassal."

"Did you really just say, 'put a ring on it'?"

"Verily, I did."

Trying not to wince, Jon chuckles in bemused pain as he drops to his knee. Pain is an ever-present reminder of his bumpy road to health—*who knows what this phase of his recovery is called?*

He clears his throat. "I'm no wonderworker. I'm Polish by blood, Greek by baptism and the un-yielding love of Evelyn Maria Kouskoutis. I may or may not have a long life. But I've been yours since the day you ordered me to love a dog or burn in hell. If you'll have me, and I hope you will, then I want the world to know it."

"I will have you—right now."

Abby remembers the effort it took him to achieve bended knee. She joins him on the floor, making it easier to kiss and be kissed. Of course, kissing inspires them to pull the bed on top of them. And that eventually leaves them in a heap of satisfied disarray an hour later.

Over pillows and under rumpled sheets, a landscape of well traveled dunes on the carpet, she coos in their afterglow. "Look what I found." Reaching under the bed, she pulls out a phone and taps the keys. Her eyes are glassy. She tosses it onto the bed as Brik Buckman's music pours from tiny speakers. She pulls the comforter and snuggles into his chest.

Let's pretend we're children
Running swiftly, joyfully
We're playing in the garden of our dreams
Let's pretend were laughing,
Drowning in our ecstasy
Let's forget we're ripping at the seams
We're holding hands and smiling
Forget about the tears
We're holding onto
Memories and years
Let's pretend we're lovers
From Greek mythology
We're watching stars and basking in their light
Let's pretend I'm Orpheus
And you, Eurydice
I'll sing to you and chase away the night
I'll be there to hold you
And save you from the fire
I'll guide you through the darkness with my lyre

After a protracted moment of silence, Jon kisses her eyes. "We should get ready soon."

Abby shakes her head. "They can wait as long as it takes."

A breeze from the garden wafts into the room. Abby shudders. "Why is it so c-c-cold today? What's that on the windowsill?" She gets to her feet and wraps a blanket around her shoulders. "Jon, come here. She's gorgeous. You gotta see this."

He crawls over to bump her backside with his head. He uses the wall to stand up. A cool wind carries the hint of winter, an unseasonably (and unbelievably) chilly peppermint kiss—*why is it so cold?* He looks out over the garden, listening to the trill of birdsong and the babble of the fountain. She brings him into the blanket and points to the sill.

"Butterfly," she whispers. "Look."

Jon lures the winged creature into his palm again. "It's been here for a while now."

"Not an IT, a SHE, if you please—look at her colors."

"I should set HER down then."

Abby pulls the blanket tighter.

"Here, hold your hand like this. Toss her into the next breeze when it comes." She looks into his eyes and finds herself, only herself exactly as she is now. Seen through his eyes, she lives a lifetime in these moments with him. With a firm grip on his wrist and his elbow, she waves his forearm. "Wait for the breeze—no, silly, give me the weight. Wait for the breeze." She softly repeats the phrase, herding the insect to the tips of his fingers. "One more second—and whoosh."

A burst of air swirls about them.

Suddenly liberated, the butterfly spirals downward, falling without grace until another flow sweeps her up to a stable pocket. High above the dogwoods, with each flap of her wings, she splashes heliotrope and indigo, and other moody hues over the hoary blossoms.

"Nicely done, Mr. Christakos."

"Thank you, Dr. Flowers."

Abby scoops up the dog when she yips to be held. Jon presses closer, blissfully at peace.

Here are the facts. The garden is alive with the activity of flower-hopping, leaf-eating insects. No one is there to threaten them with silver sewing shears. There is only the peace of spring and the promise of new beginnings. Tethered to zephyr above this dance of life is a soaring butterfly, the last in a chain of perfectly timed miracle moments—not that the insect is aware of such things.

She flies because of the man and woman standing at the open window of a house that, miraculously enough, would not belong to them had the dog not run away on the first day of last summer.

As it is with the fall of every sparrow, so it must be with the flight of every butterfly—Providence is there.

Not that Jon and Abby are aware of such things.

For them, past and future only give way to the present.

And right now, that means keeping each other warm, breathing fresh air, and watching a butterfly soar until the sun blocks her from view—there in that blinding center where it hurts to look.

THE END

ACKNOWLEDGMENTS

And now, I'd like to thank the following **REAL** people for their generous time, support, guidance, patience, and love. George and Maria—thanks for your company, food, and conversation. Tim and Maddie-Blue—thanks for helping me open my heart again. Cousin Kate—thanks for taking the time to talk about the miracle work you do. Dee and Kelly—thanks to you both for reigniting a fire I thought to be long dead and gone. Milesy—thanks for keeping me sane and making me laugh. KiKi—you are a fountain of youth to my aging heart, and I so appreciate you letting me borrow your name and personality. Pamela—as always, you are a goddess and deserve to have your own Sacred Feminine festival; you've been the keeper of my honor and guardian of my creative soul since I've known you, and I will never be able to thank you enough for all you do. And Tina—I'd be living in a cave and drawing on walls with spit had you not claimed me.

ABOUT THE AUTHOR

Author D. B. Patterson writes contemporary inspirational fiction for adults, as well as fantasy adventure fiction for teens and kids. Short works have been published in Elephants & Other Gods, Ramble Underground, Larks Fiction Magazine, and Cerulean Rain. Novels include *Perdido River Bastard* and *Epiphany Man*. Books for young and early readers include *The Christmas Witchling* and four illustrated Lamby Lambpants storybook adventures. Aside from writing, Patterson is a vocal and artistic mechanic, a classically trained actor (Shakespeare's Globe Theater, for one), a graphic designer, an illustrator, and 1995 1st Runner-up National Karaoke Champion (don't tell anyone). He is married and lives in Tarpon Springs, Florida, with his wife and daughter.

OTHER WORKS

EPIPHANY MAN, *a Novel*

ISBN-13: 978-0692640463

DBP Press | Post Office Box 399
Tarpon Springs, FL 34688

Facebook.com/dbpatterson.author

lambpants@me.com

www.ingramcontent.com/pod-product-compliance
Lightning Source LLC
Chambersburg PA
CBHW020726210626
46807CB00016B/276